ANATOMY OF A SOLDIER

Anatomy of a Soldier

HARRY PARKER

FABER & FABER

First published in the UK in 2016
by Faber & Faber Limited,
Bloomsbury House,
74–77 Great Russell Street,
London WC1B 3DA

Typeset by Reality Premedia Services Pvt. Ltd.
Printed and bound in the UK by CPI Group (UK) Ltd, Croydon CR0 4YY

The right of Harry Parker to be identified as author of this work has been asserted in accordance
with Section 77 of the Copyright, Designs and Patents Act 1988

This book is loosely based on a true story.
All events, places, characters and names have been fictionalised.
Any military, medical or cultural inaccuracies are the fault of the author.

A CIP record for this book
is available from the British Library

ISBN 978–0–571–32581–8

2 4 6 8 10 9 7 5 3

For my mother, father and brother

I

My serial number is 6545-01-522. I was unpacked from a plastic case, pulled open, checked and reassembled. A black marker wrote *BA5799 O POS* on me and I was placed in the left thigh pocket of BA5799's combat trousers. I stayed there; the pocket was rarely unfastened.

I spent eight weeks, two days and four hours in the pocket. I wasn't needed yet. I slid against BA5799's thigh, back and forth, back and forth, mostly slowly but sometimes quickly, bouncing around. And there was noise: bangs and cracks, high-pitched whines, shouts of excitement and anger.

One day I was submerged in stagnant water for an hour.

I went in vehicles, tracked and wheeled, winged and rotored. I was soaked in soapy water then hung out to dry on a clothesline and did nothing for a day.

At 0618 on 15 August, when I was sliding alongside BA5799's thigh, I was lifted into the sky and turned over. And suddenly I was in the light. There was dust and confusion and shouting. I was on the ground beside him. He was face down; he was incomplete. I was beside him as rocks and mud fell around us.

I was in the dust as a dark red liquid zigzagged towards me over the cracked mud. I was there when no one came and he was alone and couldn't move. I was still there as fear and pathetic hopelessness gripped BA5799, as he was turned over and two fingers reached into his mouth, as his chest was pumped up and down and they forced air into his lungs.

I was picked up by a slippery hand, fumbled back to the ground, then picked up again. I was pulled open by panicked fingers and covered in the thick liquid. I was placed on BA5799. I was turned. I tightened. I closed around his leg until his pulse pushed up against me. And he grimaced and whimpered through gritted teeth. I was wound tighter, gripping his thigh; stopping him bleed out into the dust.

I clung to him while he was lifted onto a stretcher and he bit deeply into the arm of a man who carried him, when he no longer made any noise. I clung to him as we boarded the helicopter. I was wound again then, and gripped him harder.

I clung to him as we flew low across the fields and glinting irrigation ditches and the wind rushed around the helicopter, when he pleaded with God to save him and metal pads were placed on his chest and his body jolted. And I clung to him when the machine read no output, when there was no pulse against me.

I was there when they ran across to the helicopter and took us into the cool of the hospital.

I was there when the doctors looked worried. I clung to him when he came back, when he had output and his faltering heart pulsed again. I was still there when they hung the bag of blood above BA5799 and they cut the remains of his leg away.

And then I was unwound and loosened and I was no longer there; BA5799 no longer needed me.

My serial number is 6545-01-522. I was at the bottom of a surgical bin and then I was burnt.

2

I was placed on a broken pallet with three other identical bags of fertiliser outside a shop in the village of Howshal Nalay.

I had been on the pallet for two weeks when Faridun came on his green bicycle. He greeted the shopkeeper and they started to haggle. Then Faridun handed him money and the shopkeeper lifted me onto the bike's pannier. I sagged over its metal bars that pushed into my plastic skin and he fastened me down with orange twine from the shop. Faridun shared a joke with the man, then swung his leg over the crossbar and we rode away.

Faridun cycled us out of the village on the exposed road; a raised, sand-coloured backbone running through dusty green fields. The bike's buckled rear wheel squeaked below me as we weaved past potholes left by the winter rains.

He sighed when he saw the checkpoint through the vibrating air. He dismounted as we approached and pushed the bike along beside him. An iron bar was propped on two oil drums across the road, and a red-tanked motorbike leant next to it on its stand. A group of men sat in the dark shade of a compound. One of them stood and walked towards us. He beckoned Faridun over with the hand that wasn't holding the weapon.

'Peace be upon you, young man. How are you?' he said.

Faridun shielded his eyes and looked up at him. 'Peace be upon you. I am fine, praise to God.'

The man was a black silhouette against the sun.

'I am on my way home from Howshal Nalay, I have been to the market,' Faridun said quietly. 'I need to get back before dark.'

The others emerged from the shade and gathered behind the man. Faridun glanced up at them and recognised his friend Latif. Latif had also recognised Faridun; he looked uncertain and then walked forward and whispered into the man's ear.

The man's face tightened. He stepped out and kicked hard against the bicycle's crossbar. Faridun caught his ankle under the sprocket and fell into the dust. I slumped onto the road with him, twisting under the orange twine. The man held the gun with both hands now and stepped onto the bike, crushing Faridun's leg.

Faridun didn't make a sound.

The man was over him and forced the barrel down against his mouth. Faridun pursed his lips closed, shaking his head from side to side. But the man wormed the weapon back and forth until Faridun's lips were pushed apart and the barrel slid against his teeth, slipping up to peel away the gum from his incisor. Faridun opened his mouth in pain and the weapon banged through his teeth until it knocked into the back of his throat.

'Is your father Kushan Hhan?'

Faridun gagged and his tongue curled up against the metal. He nodded in shock. The man pushed down harder and Faridun convulsed and choked around the barrel again.

'Your father is working for the infidel,' the man said. 'If he continues to do this against the will of God, I will cut off your sister's head. Do you understand?' He pushed again a final time. And then the weapon was pulled clear and he stepped away.

Faridun's eyes were wet but he held the man's gaze as he got up out of his shadow and lifted the bike off the ground. The twine lost its grip and I fell off the pannier. Faridun's lip was already thickening and he looked over at Latif.

'May God be with you, Latif,' he said, before slowly wheeling the bicycle down the road, away from where I remained in the dust.

The men laughed and patted Latif on the back. One of them walked into the middle of the road, picked me up and threw me down against the compound wall.

That afternoon the men reclined in the shade and waved a group of nomads and their camels through. They took fifteen dollars in tax from a lorry driver and chatted with a group of men on their way home from the fields. Finally, as dusk sharpened the horizon, two of them left on the motorbike. The others moved the pole and oil drums into the compound, said they would meet again after prayers and drifted away.

The last man lifted me onto his shoulder. He walked down a path beside a silver strip of water until we reached a dark area of undergrowth in a maze of crumbling walls. He opened a wooden door, put me on the floor and pulled it shut behind him.

I am a bag of fertiliser. I contain NH_4NO_3 and I waited in that dark room until I was opened and used.

3

I was taken from a box and laces were threaded through my eyes. My tongue was pulled out and a man wrote *BA5799* in black permanent marker that bled into my fabric.

I was in a room with things laid out on the floor, stacks of clothes in rows: T-shirts, combat shirts, trousers, hot-weather underwear and socks rolled in balls. There was a pile of notes and maps, a book about a distant country where conflict persisted; another pile with tubes of toothpaste, toothbrushes, insect repellent and malaria tablets; a third with a GPS, a torch and a med-kit. There was also a leather diary, a helmet and a stack of magazines, oiled and shining, with a rifle-cleaning kit rolled up next to it.

A large black grip-bag and a Bergen lay open, ready to be packed. Everything was named in black, like me.

The man sat on the single bed. He put his foot into me and I was pulled tight to his ankle by the laces he wrapped around my neck three times before carefully tying a knot. I could feel his toes wiggle and then he pulled the mirror of me onto his other foot.

He walked around the room and flexed his toes again. We left the room, went downstairs and outside.

I flashed past my pair and then was stationary on the ground. It flashed past me. We were running. We went quicker as we pounded up a chalk and flint track through gates topped with razor wire. The track was lined with hedgerows and we skipped around puddles and plunged out of a tree line and up a green hill.

We settled into a rhythm and the man breathed with practised control. My tread folded and bent around rocks and grasped the mud with each stride. The puddles reflected the blue and white sky above and my cloth surface formed creases as I flexed to the movement of his foot. He increased the tempo because he knew he could and indulged being able to. He was strong and his breathing was still measured as we pounded on. The fitter he was, the harder he could fight and the longer he could survive.

He pushed himself faster, motivated by nothing but oblivion and he drove on up a steep slope. He stopped at the top and looked over the wide plains below, crossed by lanes and squared with wood blocks.

He tried to empty his head but thoughts washed over him. He was already there, focused on what it would be like and its inevitability. When he thought of the final week before he deployed it seemed unreal. He thought of saying goodbye.

We left the track and ran through grass. Blades stropped over my toe, leaving green scars. We went down a steep slope and he jarred through me as we descended. I started rubbing on his left heel and a blister formed. The creases in me deepened and the shape of each of his toes moulded my inner sole.

We dropped off a kerb and ran on along a metal road that was hard on my tread. We turned a corner to a gate where he showed his ID card to a soldier and stopped.

'I didn't know you were on guard, Rifleman Macintosh.'

'Deep joy, sir,' the soldier said.

'Not losing any leave, I hope.'

'No, I finish tomorrow morning, then I'll go straight home. You been for a run?'

'Just breaking in my new boots,' he said and looked down at me.

'Keen, boss. Carry on like that and you'll be colonel one day.'

'I'm sure it won't come to that, Mac,' he said and turned. 'See you later.'

It started to rain and the tarmac speckled dark in front of me. He sprinted hard for the final half-mile back to the building we had left.

He walked, his hands on his head, his chest heaving. He recovered quickly and we went back to the room. I was taken off and the heat of his foot dissipated. I was placed carefully among all the kit laid out on the floor.

He slept in the bed and in the morning shaved at a sink. He dressed in a green camouflaged uniform and pulled on boots, like me but black and leather. He smoothed a green beret over his head, positioning the silver bugle above his eye, and went out. When he came back he rearranged the piles and counted the socks again before adding another tick to a list.

The next day he put jeans and a T-shirt on and old trainers that had remained unused in the corner of the room since I had been there. He stuffed a few things in a bag and left, locking the door behind him.

I was alone in my spot, next to my pair among the piles ready to be packed.

He came back a week later, unshaven. He sighed and sat on the floor and began to pack the kit. Everything had a place and each item on his list was finally crossed through. Once finished he stacked the Bergen on the grip and I was placed next to a chair with a desert combat uniform draped over it and the green beret on top.

Another man peered around the door.

'You coming for some food?' he said.

'Sure, give me a sec, I've just got to call home.'

'Okay, mate, see you down there,' the man said and left.

He picked up his phone.

'Hi, Mum, it's Tom,' he said. 'Yup, fine, just finished packing – all ready to go . . .' He walked around the room and then sat on the bed. 'Just pizza and a film, probably, with the others . . . I think it's about ten tomorrow but we have to be ready for the buses at five . . . Thanks for the weekend. It was great to see you all.' He listened to the phone, twisting his fingers through the duvet cover. He stood and went over to the window. He talked and laughed and walked over to the chair to pluck at a loose thread on his combat shirt. 'I'll call in a few days,' he said, 'when I get there . . . Okay, will do . . . And you, take care . . . Bye . . . Bye.'

That night he slept fitfully and at four his alarm rang. He immediately clicked the light on. He sat up, gripped the side of the bed and yawned. It was still dark outside and he leant on the sink and shaved off his stubble. He stared at the reflection and its bloodshot eyes. It looked different from how he felt. He smiled, but his eyes were empty as he pulled the razor across his chin. It didn't matter what he looked like.

He packed the last of his kit into his Bergen, dressed in the combat uniform and then pulled me on.

At breakfast other boots like me fidgeted under the table. None of the men had slept well and they talked of little other than timings and the co-ordination of the next few hours.

Back in the room, he shouldered the Bergen and grunted as he lifted the grip up until it was stacked on top. He held a green day-sack in his right hand. Now almost twice his weight pushed down through me. He looked around the empty room, flicked the light off and left without locking the door.

We walked through the camp lit by pools of yellow streetlight. Other dark figures, hunched beneath heaped bags, moved from buildings and converged on a long row of buses. Voices became clearer and then we were among the bustle of people and activity in the darkness beside the road.

A voice called from farther along the line, 'B Company down the end. Grips on the four tonners, Bergens underneath. Stop mincing, you lot.'

We pushed past a flustered man unpacking his bag on the grass.

'Come on, Rifleman Milne, you've had your entire life to pack – what have you forgotten now?' a man said as the soldier ran off.

'Morning, sir, B Company's at the other end.' Someone pointed down the line.

'Thanks,' he said and he stepped me over a bag and walked along the pavement.

'Any more for weapons and serial number kit? CQ wants you now,' a storeman shouted from a container.

We walked to a truck. The grip was lifted from his back and stacked with the others and then he pushed the Bergen into a space below the coach. He stood in a queue of yawning men and signed for a rifle. Finally we stepped up into the bus and sat in the first row. The green butt of the rifle rested on the floor next to me.

A man slowly moved down the central aisle counting the soldiers relaxing against the windows.

'That's everyone, sir,' he said and sat down next to us. 'Just waiting for Rifleman Smith – he's helping the CQ's party with the grips.'

'Thanks, Sergeant Dee.'

The bus left the camp, an oval of light on the road in front. The trees were dark through the windows as the sky began to lighten. His foot relaxed and he slept.

When he woke he looked at the countryside flashing past until he nudged the man next to him.

'We're nearly there, Sarnt Dee,' he said.

'Cheers, boss,' the man said. He stood up and looked over the back of his seat. 'Listen in,' he said. 'Stop window-licking, Rifleman Macintosh, that's it. When we get off, the bags will go separately to the plane. No one is to get creative. Check in as a platoon.'

After queuing and showing his documents he sat in a lounge and crossed me on his other ankle. Men slept bent over rucksacks and with earphones in. Few of them spoke. Some lay on the floor with their combat jackets wrapped around their heads against the strip lights. Eventually men in blue uniforms came into the room. A man wearing a lumi-vest walked out among the rows of seats.

'Sorry for the slight delay,' he said, 'there was a problem with the airframe. We will begin boarding now.'

'Halle-fucking-lujah,' someone said as they stood up.

He walked out of the terminal in the single row that crept forward. All the men around were quiet, their uniforms new and undusted as they fed up the stairs ahead into the aircraft. He sighed and scrunched his toes up in me. There was no possible alternative, he thought, no going back.

Green trees tossed in the damp wind beside the runway. He bent down and touched the ground beside me and then I stepped up onto the metal stairs.

On the plane, the boots of other men lined up under the seats in front of me. He couldn't sleep and leant his head against the window and watched the tops of the clouds. An unwanted stream of thoughts and recollections drifted over him, only connecting as reminders of what he was being propelled away from.

After the flight, we descended aluminium steps out onto the runway. I felt the heat of it on my sole and the air vibrated and merged the black tarmac into the sky.

I am a desert combat boot. I have *BA5799* written on my tongue and he walked me across the tarmac towards a city of white tents and cream hangars, floating on that shimmering desert mirror.

4

I was made carefully on a wooden table with buckled legs that rested against a dry mud wall. I was made by two men silhouetted in moonlight from the doorway behind them and the jaundiced beam of a torch placed on a shelf cut into a wall. Their bodies arched over me and sweat glistened on their temples.

They cut open a bag and weighed fertiliser on old mechanical scales. They soaked cloth in petrol. Fumes slipped around the table and one of the men sneezed. They mixed the cloth with the fertiliser and then wrapped this part of me in a plastic sheet and then more tightly with black tape.

This was my beginning but I was not yet complete.

They made two others like me, scooping more fertiliser from the bag with a metal cup, weighing and wrapping it with the mix of petrol-soaked rags, until three of us were placed in a row along the side of the table – three parcels of potential energy.

The men went through the door and stood in the blue moonlight. They lit cigarettes that hovered by their sides and arced up to their lips, illuminating their faces. They called a man over and said he needn't bother to keep watch, there was no one around. He joined them and accepted a cigarette, slinging his rifle over his shoulder so he could smoke freely.

They began to argue.

'Not one of them worked. We spent three nights making them

and we watched for weeks as the infidel walked over them – nothing,' one of them said. His lips disappeared as he pulled on his cigarette. 'We used the same mix that you have here.'

'I had the training,' another said. 'Every single one I made worked. I was blowing holes in the snow all winter. And we have the new equipment from over the border. They will work, Latif. God willing, they will work.'

'Maybe it was the altitude, Aktar, or the mix you used—'

'Enough, Latif. Hassan chose me. I went to the mountains.' He dropped his cigarette and rotated his boot on it. 'Paugi, go and keep guard. We should finish,' he said and walked back inside towards me.

The men loomed over the table again. They took two strips of thin metal and attached a wire to each one, then spaced them apart between two wooden blocks, so they were parallel to each other, and wrapped it all in plastic. They did this three times.

'These are good, Aktar,' one man said. He crouched down level with where I was on the table and gently pushed down on the metal until the strips touched.

'Yes, they will work.'

'They're better than I have seen before. Firm enough to stay separate under the weight of a dog – or wet soil – but with the weight of a man—'

'Yes, it is a balance.' He took it from under the man's hand and slid it next to me and started to attach wires to the end, twisting with pliers.

This was the next part of me.

He placed a battered white polystyrene cube on the table, pulled it apart and removed one of the six metal rods that stood upright in holes.

'We'll place these in now.' He bent closer and pushed the rod into the mix of my insides. The man's tongue wrapped up over his lip as he concentrated. He left the end of the rod protruding and taped cautiously around it. He then attached the wires and crimped them on with the pliers, joining my two parts.

'We can attach the battery just before we dig them in,' he said.

I had more potential now. I was ugly and homemade, but I was complete – one part round, the other long and thin, both wrapped in plastic and tape and joined by a thin wire.

'You need to handle these carefully, Latif.' He pushed the white box with the five remaining vertical rods across the bench. 'When I was in the mountains, another student held one of these in his hand,' he said, pulling a rod out, 'and the heat of a lamp made it go off. I remember his wrist with nothing on the end – and his look of shock. Hassan was angry because the boy hadn't listened. The next day he was gone.'

'They can go off just like that?' the younger man said, looking down at the silver rod in his hand.

'He was unlucky. But yes, they are volatile.'

When the other two were also complete, the men tidied up the table and put their equipment into a rucksack. They lined us up on the floor next to the bag of fertiliser. One of them took the torch, which flickered weakly, and swept the beam across the room and under the table. Then he stepped outside and pulled the wooden door shut behind him.

I stayed there, latent. And each day a thin line of dust-flecked light seeped slowly across the room and passed over my plastic skin, warming me.

Eventually, when it was dark, the door opened. They were the same men and one of them placed a bag on the table.

'And he definitely said he was going to come?'

'Yes, he said he would be here. I spoke to him after prayers.'

'I will have to tell Hassan about this. He will be punished.'

They lifted me onto the table and checked my construction. The man's hand felt my connections, gently pulling on the wires to make sure they were still firm. He put me in a bag, and then the other two were placed on top of me.

'Take that trowel, Latif. And the water container. I will carry the bag. Have you got the batteries?'

'Yes.'

'We will do it just as we talked about. Are you okay?'

'Yes, I think so. At least there is no moon.'

'It will be a long night. One on the Nalay road, one by the bridge on the aqueduct and the last one we will try and get close to their camp. Hassan thinks this will be our best chance. We should go.' Then the bag lurched and pressed around me as it was shouldered. It swayed as the man walked.

Twice he jumped and the bag banged against his back. Then he stopped and they whispered.

'Why are we waiting?'

'Sshhh.' There was a silence and we were still. The thump of the man's heart and the rise and fall of his breathing passed into me through the sack. 'I thought I saw someone. Are you okay?'

'How much farther?'

'Not far.'

He started moving again and after a while we stopped and the bag slumped against the ground. There was the sound of scraping and the clink of metal on stones. The bag opened and a hand reached in. The first of us was taken out.

'Pass me a battery.'

After more scraping the bag lifted and we moved off.

When we stopped for the third time, the sound of running water covered the noise of the trowel. The bag was unzipped. They lifted out the second of us and then only I was left. They were framed in the opening of the bag, crouched over and digging at the pale surface of a road. They attached a battery to the second of us and then lowered it into the ground.

One man lay flat and scooped rubble over the hole. The other went down to the canal, where the water turned white as it dropped under the bridge. When he returned, he poured water over the digging and flattened the mud with the palm of his hand, smoothing it flush with the surface of the road. Then he came back to the bag and beads of sweat showed on his face as he zipped it closed. It was dark again and I was alone in the bag. We moved off.

The rhythm of the walk became slow and cautious. Soon the men were crawling and vegetation scratched against the canvas around me. We stopped again and one of them whispered. 'We are too close, Aktar,' he said. 'I can see their watchtower. Just there.'

'I know,' came the hissed reply. 'We need to get as close as we can.'

'This is too much. They can see in the dark, they have machines that can feel our heat. We need to go back.'

'Keep going. A bit farther and we will be hidden. I know this ground.'

We moved again. The sound of them snaking forward vibrated through the bag. Then we stopped.

'Here is good, Latif. Keep low.'

The zip rumbled open and I was pulled out and laid on the

ground. The sky was a dome of stars. We were in a slight hollow of dry earth with sparse grass. The men panted with the effort now. One was propped on an elbow and scooped dirt away to create the space for me. The other shuffled up onto a rise and stared into the gloom. They were both tense.

'There is no movement,' the man murmured as he pushed himself back down from the edge. 'Be careful, Latif. We cannot rush. It is not worth making a mistake.'

As he dug my hole, he recited under his breath, 'God is greatest. God is greatest. God is greatest.' The mantra focused his attention away from the danger and onto my grave.

'You must control yourself, Latif.' The other man reached out and held the hand he was digging with. Their eyes met. 'Control your fear. You've gone deep enough already. Give me the battery.'

He fumbled around in his pocket and handed a square battery to the other man, who pushed it into my connector. Electricity tingled in my wires but I was not yet a circuit. He rolled over, awkwardly pulled tape from his pocket and wrapped it around my battery. Then he slid towards the hole and carefully lifted me in. He arranged my components. He put the round part of me, the part with the potential, at the bottom, and then placed the long thin metal strips, my trigger, on top, nearest the surface.

His sweat dripped onto me as he worked. He replaced the dirt, each new handful reducing the starlight until finally the ink-blue aperture closed and I was in the dark. The men moved around on the surface, pushing and pulling the soil over me. Water was poured on the ground and soaked through the dust, turning it to mud that oozed around me. Soon the movements stopped and the men who made me must have crawled away.

I waited in the blackness. The mud around me dried and solidified in the heat and I was encased in earth. There was a daily rise and fall of temperature, but otherwise nothing.

Eventually I felt vibrations – the rhythm of walking – that were faint at first but then converged towards me. A weight pressed down. The dry mud above me flexed, cracked down and pushed my metal strips together. A circuit was created that filled my wires instantly.

I was alive.

The metal rod at the heart of me detonated, a controlled high-explosive force that triggered the mix in me to react.

I functioned.

5

I was taken from a drawer by a trauma nurse. He placed me on a stainless-steel trolley with other medical items. I was sterile and sealed in a plastic bag. He wheeled the trolley into an operating theatre. People cleaned surfaces and checked equipment. They were tense. In the room next door, through Perspex sheeting, men in medical gowns scrubbed their hands.

A man in desert uniform came in with a clipboard. 'Right, he's in the air now,' he said. 'PEDRO callsign has picked him up from District South. Mechanism is IED versus foot soldier. Nine-liner still stands. One Category A; zap number BA5799. Traumatic below left knee amputation, difficulty breathing and severe blood loss. They've already had to resuscitate, possible collapsed lung. ETA is eight minutes. When I get a sitrep from the helicopter I'll come back.'

'Okay, thanks, Jack,' a woman said. She wore a blue gown and had a mask around her neck. 'Let's prep for reception. Kirsty, how's plasma and bloods going?'

'Fine, Colonel, O POS prepped,' a nurse said as she walked across the room with bags of yellow plasma. 'But I'll test when he's in. More in the fridge if needed.'

'Good. Tim, get that equipment closer.'

The trolley I was on moved towards a bed.

'Sounds like we'll have to CAT scan when he's stable. Is

Dr Richmond up yet?'

'On his way, Colonel.'

The man with the clipboard came back. 'PEDRO has had to defib him three times; currently no output. Will let you know any update. Not looking good, I'm afraid.'

The tension left the room. One of the men peeled rubber gloves from his hands and threw them in a bin. 'Not another one.'

'Stay with it, everyone,' the woman said and looked at the clock.

There was silence. The bed, covered in green plastic, lay empty. One of the nurses pushed buttons on a machine that hung from the ceiling. Another leant against a cabinet and doodled with a biro.

The man with the clipboard looked through the door again. 'PEDRO still saying no output,' he said, 'though they had him back for a while – ETA two minutes.'

'Let's hope he can pull through. Normal drills. Output or not, let's see what we can do for him. Tim, you'd better get out there with the reception party.'

A man entered from the scrub room stretching on rubber gloves and fastening his gown.

'Morning, Peter. You've been briefed?' the woman said.

'Just dropped in at the ops room, Jack brought me up to speed. More of the same, it looks like.'

The wait continued. The minute hand tapped around on a clock above a whiteboard, divided into black squares and filled with information. And then the distant drone of a helicopter grew in the room until the walls of the temporary building started to vibrate. The pitch changed, descended and became a constant whistle.

'Here we go,' she said.

Double doors banged open and the sound of hurrying footsteps and urgent voices came down a corridor until the stretcher with you on was carried into the room. Men and women crowded around. One held a bag of liquid above you and another had a helmet with a tinted visor and a flash with stars and stripes on.

'He's sixty over thirty,' he said, 'been shocked four times in transit. We've given him a shot of adrenaline.'

'What's his output like now?'

'I think he was conscious for a second while we were landing but he's out again now. No morphine on the ground as they suspected a collapsed lung. No time to intubate yet.'

'Okay, let's intubate – quick as you can, Tim,' the woman said.

I was picked up and the plastic peeled away from my packaging. A man fed a laryngoscope into your mouth and another lifted your head back. Your tongue was held open and I was pushed into you. Your mouth had dirt in it and a blade of grass. I slid past the laryngoscope that directed me into you. I scraped down through you, grazing your voice box, past your glottis, down through your trachea, until I reached the top of your lungs. One of them was smaller and collapsed. A nurse inflated my balloon cuff that puffed out and held me inside you.

A T-piece was firmly rocked onto where I protruded from your mouth and then connected to a mechanical ventilator. I was part of a system now. I was inside you, at the edge of your lungs. Oxygen-rich air pulsed through me and I started breathing for you.

You were covered in dust; a thin coat of it ghosted the skin of your face. Your clothing was pale with dirt except where it was dark with blood or had shredded away. You were bare below the waist and the white skin of your thighs had smears and red fingerprints.

'Now let's get him on the table. Full examination ASAP.'

They wheeled the stretcher alongside the empty bed and in unison pulled you across, leaving viscous pools on the stretcher. A bag of plasma was hooked up.

Your left foot was missing and splinters of bone jutted out from your calf. Your right leg was open along the inside with bulging wounds that were glutinous next to your skin. Your right calf was gone. Each arm was punched with holes and bled. Your left little finger hung by a sinew. Your groin had a clean shining wound that oozed blood. A testicle hung open, deformed and alien.

The woman moved around the stretcher until she was over you. 'Okay, let's prep him as quick as we can. Kirsty, get his blood checked. How many bags of fluid has he had?'

'One administered on the ground, ma'am,' the man with the helmet said, 'and we've given him three since.'

'Okay, let's get the cannulas in.'

The woman stood back and assessed. The others worked around you. They cut away your remaining clothes and checked over your naked body. They wiped and cleaned you and taped your eyelids shut. They stuck pads to your chest and the machine above you sounded three times and then once before settling into a rhythm.

'Tachycardic. Sixty over thirty. Weak,' one of them said.

'Blood test done, he's O positive. Initial bloods show Hb of six.'

'Right, Kirsty, let's give him two more bags stat.'

The machine above you started beeping.

'Blood pressure dropping,' a nurse said.

And then another machine flashed and rang a clear flat pitch in the room and they were over you and pulling a small trolley towards you.

[23]

'Defibrillator,' the woman said and reached for the paddles.

I was inside you and I could feel you slipping away as your heart faltered. Gel was squeezed onto the paddles and she rubbed them together and placed them on your chest.

'Clear,' she said between each jolt of your body, and I felt your chest convulse around me as electricity bolted through us.

'For God's sake,' one of the nurses said.

But your heart flinched again – and then again – and blood moved through your lungs and the line of spikes came back on the display.

They continued to work on you. You still bled too much so they cut a vertical line along your stomach past your navel. They went inside you with metal clamps and stopped blood from ebbing out through your femoral arteries. They removed a tourniquet and threw it in a surgical bin. A nurse inserted a tube up your penis.

When they were convinced you were stable, they wheeled us out of that room and down the corridor. They placed you in a scanner that whirred around us. The doctors and nurses peered at monitors and surveyed the damage. Then they wheeled you on to surgery.

They worked on your left stump, cleaning away the earth and debris that had been blown into you. They bent all their concentration on you and slowly you were brought back from the edge. You were not a whole to them, just a wound to be closed or a level on a screen to monitor or a bag of blood to change.

A surgeon pulled away from you and blinked in the lights and looked around at the team. 'Okay. He's more stable. Bleeding now stemmed in both legs,' she said. 'We'll leave the left leg traumatic amputation as is for now. But I'm worried about the exposed femoral in the right thigh. I will work on that with Lisa.

Peter, are you happy with his status?'

'Yes, Gill.'

'Okay. Can you patch up the lesions on the arms? I also want to do exploratory on that left forearm wound. I think it could've caused nerve damage. If you're happy to make a start with that as well.' She looked at the next man. 'Tim, I think we're going to have to cut that finger away. And then sew it up if you don't mind. That's the least of his problems.'

'Yes, Colonel,' he said and went to rescrub his hands.

'Once that's all done I want to have another look at his groin. I think we'll probably have to do an orchiectomy and I want to get it right – he's been extremely lucky in that department.'

After a few hours they were less worried. People talked calmly as surgeons stretched their backs. Finally, the woman made notes on a clipboard and two people administered drugs.

I was still in you, still breathing for you. Your chest rose and fell as the mix of gases passed through me and down into you. Your arms and lower body were covered in white plastic bandages and protruding pipes that pulled the discharge from your wounds. Yellow iodine discoloured your skin and black ink showed below dressings where lines had been drawn. A blue sheet covered you.

You were moved to a room with other men who also had tubes, like me, that held their gormless mouths open. None of them were conscious. They were still, apart from the rise and fall of their chests dictated by machines. It was dark in the room, an air-conditioning unit rumbled in the corner and monitors flashed above each body. The bodies were disfigured, too, and did not fill the beds as they should. The green blankets were flat where limbs should have been.

Nurses moved between the beds and prepped them for transit. Once a machine beeped and flashed red and nurses came and then more people and the machine continued to sound a single note. A crash cart was called for. They were frantic, then frustrated and finally desolate. The bed was wheeled out and never came back.

They were pleased with how you were doing. They changed your drug dosage but kept you sedated and moved you to another room, ready for transit. The nurses who looked after you wrote in your logbook and felt strongly about you, even though they had never met you.

A man wearing a combat uniform came in, a green beret folded in his hand. He was shocked by the misshapen bodies in the beds lined against the wall and the stillness of them. He sat by you and said a few words but was self-conscious. He patted your hand before he left. 'Stay strong, mate,' he said quietly.

Later, a team of doctors and nurses arrived and stood behind each bed, flicking through clipboards and looking at X-rays. They moved around the room until they stood over you.

'Stable enough for transit. He should stay sedated.'

'We must get him back. The lesions on the right leg need plastics soon.'

'Let's do another set of bloods before he goes. And increase his sedation for the flight.'

'Okay, get him on the flight tonight. Air Support Team Bravo, I think. That'll give them two unconscious and three walking.'

They moved to the next bed. One remained and took readings from the machines above you. She moved a dial on the mechanical ventilator and the mix of gases that passed through me changed. She pressed a vial onto a cannula that hung from your wrist and filled it with blood. It wasn't yours but a combination from eight different people.

That night you were prepped for transit. Nurses and doctors came and talked through your injuries. They told the transit team everything they could, each item adding to your fragility and the risk of getting you home. They set about you with practised efficiency. My end was pulled from the mechanical ventilator and pushed into a portable unit. They stood over you and nurses said, 'On three: one, two, slide,' under their breaths as they carefully moved you across to a new bed.

The new team wheeled you out through a blue corridor, towards double doors. They were urgent and professional and cared only about the next ten hours: making sure they could get you to safety and hand you over to another team that could do more than just keep you alive.

We left the air-conditioned building and were wheeled to an ambulance through the desert dusk. We drove for a few minutes and the nurse next to us monitored the machines and checked your levels. When we stopped the rear doors opened and we were pulled out below the bright rectangular opening of an aircraft. Its engines whistled and lights pulsed on each wing. The air was buffeted by the warming jets and moved the fine hair on your forehead. They pushed us up the ramp into the rear of the fuselage and secured your bed to anchor points on the floor.

Other stretchers came and were strapped down. Then men on crutches, or with bandaged arms or a dressing over an eye, boarded the aircraft and were helped by medics into seats near the front. The whine of the engines was muted as the rear door lifted shut. The transit team moved between the beds checking the sedation and outputs were acceptable. The aircraft taxied and took off.

You travelled four thousand miles but didn't need to think and I was part of a system of tubes, valves, pressure gauges and screens, powered by microchips and overseen by people who supported your life.

The aircraft landed and the rear door lowered.

The tarmac was wet and streaked with vertical reflections; some flashed blue and red from a line of vehicles that waited. It was much colder. Fluorescent jackets glowed as people ran across to the rear door. The wheels of the stretcher skittered on the ground as the team jogged with us to the back of an ambulance. The falling rain was foreshortened to white rods against the stone sky. They pulled us into the ambulance and doors were closed.

Blue flashed through the window as we drove. Soon the vehicle slowed and started to turn corners, yellow streetlights now in the window. The siren changed pace and tone and we swayed from side to side and then accelerated again.

The siren was switched off and we stopped. Doors opened and banged shut. There was a shout and then we were pulled out and the stretcher's wheels dropped down below us and we were taken into a new building, through glass doors that slid apart automatically, and down cream corridors with safety notices and lists of departments. As we were pushed on the lists changed but we always headed for the intensive care unit, swinging around corners until a man tapped a code into a pad and frosted glass doors, imprinted with *ICU*, opened. We stopped alongside a bed.

The reception party was waiting there and they plugged you into a new set of pipes, wires and tubes. Machines blinked on and displayed your output and I was pressed into a new ventilator.

And then the air support team walked away from us. They

looked tired. One put his arm around another and smiled as they left through the sliding doors.

They decided to operate and we were taken into a theatre with white tiled walls. They opened the dressings and dirt and stones fell out of your wounds onto the table. They debrided your flesh, pulling away the dead and dying parts that we could not sustain. They cleaned up infected areas and sent bloods away. Plastic surgeons made assessments and worked on you.

After four hours they wheeled us back to the ICU. Nurses cleaned you again. Your skin had yellowed and your head rested at an unnatural angle.

Once the nurses were happy, the glass doors opened and a doctor brought in a man and a woman who were not wearing medical clothing. They were ushered across the ward until they stood next to our bed. The man looked down at us with determination. The woman clutched a red handbag and looked drained and shocked. The man's arm held her firmly to his side and he pressed her tighter. The doctor started to talk about you and introduced them to the team who looked after you.

They stayed for a long time – saying little – but the doctor came back and told them they should really get some sleep. We were left alone.

They returned many times and sat by you and waited. The woman would steal a chance to touch your hand when no one was looking, worried she was doing something that was wrong or might damage you. Often they would watch us being wheeled away to the operating room. They felt helpless. They were always there when we came back.

Seven days and four thousand miles after I had been inserted into you, you changed. They weren't expecting it but your eyes flickered and your tongue started to push against me as you gagged around my pipe. You tried to force me out and were afraid you were drowning. The nurses hurried over as your heart rushed in sudden panic and the machines above alarmed.

Doctors were called in to examine you. My balloon cuff was deflated and they gently pulled me out of you. You were mumbling and confused as I passed your teeth. I was left on a table and the man and woman were brought back in to be with you. She held your hand.

You recognised her and your relationship to them both.

A nurse picked me up, pushed the foot pedal of a bin and threw me into a yellow surgical waste bag.

I was no longer part of you.

6

I am an olive-green thirty-litre day-sack. BA5799 bought me from a surplus store in a garrison town while he was still in training. During my first exercise he tried to get me dirty so I no longer looked new but battered and experienced – not how he felt but how he wished he did.

He packed me countless times with radios, blank and live ammunition, warm clothes and bladders of water, with rations that he pushed down my sides. Everything had a place and was individually waterproofed. He used me as a seat on cold wet training areas. He crawled up streams and fired his rifle into trenches and men pretended to be dead.

He stuffed me with metal weights that were wrapped in towels and ran out over the hills as I slapped up and down against his back.

He wrote his number on me in black ink that faded as we waited to be deployed. Again, I was on cold wet training areas and he attacked positions on small grassy hillocks while people in red raincoats walked past with their dogs. He was killed and wounded a number of times and joked with the other men as he was carried through the casualty evacuation chain. He drank tea until exercise control told him he was alive again. Once a man in a luminous vest shouted, 'You're dead, sir.' He was annoyed to be out of the game so early and threw me down in the gorse in frustration.

We spent more time training. And then his room started to fill with new equipment and he named it all with a marker and laid it out across the floor. He redrew *BA5799* over the faded black lines on me.

One morning he put into my top pocket things that could take his mind off what was ahead: a book, his iPod, along with his documents and passport. He dropped his dog tags over his head and folded a beret, pushed it in and zipped me closed. We left the camp on a bus while it was still dark and boarded a plane.

When the plane landed we were part of a single file of men, all carrying day-sacks, that extended down the steps onto a wide apron. It was hot and his shirt soon dampened next to me. We walked through a city built on a grid with prefabricated window-less buildings and tents, refuelling dumps and blast protection walls, dog cages and fire points. Heavy vehicles rumbled past and small groups of soldiers strolled back to their accommodation, their uniforms sun-bleached and their hair long.

We were ushered into a hangar filled with bunk beds. Instructions were shouted and everyone filed down the rows to find a bed. The high ceiling hummed with the noise of three hundred people. BA5799 chose a bed and slept.

During the next few days he waited in queues to collect equipment. He sat in briefings about the place we had come to and what to expect and what not to get bitten by. He went to the cookhouse and ate from plastic plates and I was put on the ground between his legs. He sat with a small group of men, took a notebook and pen from my top pocket and listened as a man gave orders and they discussed the coming days.

Then he went back to the hangar and pushed me under his bed

and started to make adjustments to his kit.

A man on the bunk above rolled over, pulled earphones out and watched. 'You all right, sir?' he said.

'Not too bad, thanks. How's things, Rifleman Plunkett? Aren't you meant to be at the welfare briefing?'

'Snipers are doing it with A Company.'

'How did your ranges go today?'

'All good. Just want to get out there now. Apparently the lot we're taking over from are having a pretty rough time,' the man said.

'I'm actually off tonight,' BA5799 told him. 'I'm going forward to do the company handover with a few of the command team.'

'Do you know when the rest of us are coming forward?'

'Nothing confirmed yet. It looks like the relief in place will start in five or six days. The plan is for half the company to go out by heli and the rest by road move. It depends on the amount of lift available,' BA5799 said.

'Hope I go by heli. Road convoy would be a rubbish way to start the tour.'

'I've heard it can take over twenty hours.'

He continued to repack his gear and taped around the rim of his helmet. Then he pulled open a black tourniquet from a plastic bag. He checked it and wrote *BA5799 O POS* on it before slipping it into his left thigh pocket.

Next he took six small cardboard boxes and split them open. Copper-coloured cylinders clinked onto the plastic-covered mattress and he lined them up in rows of ten and then thirty. Some were tipped with red phosphorus and he added these one in every five. He pulled six magazines from his grip and started to fill them. He pushed the rounds through the jaws of the magazine with his thumb; he rolled each one to make sure it was seated correctly, depressing the spring until the magazine was full.

A voice shouted across the hangar.

'Listen in, everybody. The advance party is leaving now. Chopper's early and the colonel wants you out there. Quick as you can. We need you at the heliport in five minutes.' The man was walking along the rows of bunk beds. 'That means you, boss. Does anyone know where Sergeant Collins is?'

'No idea,' BA5799 said and swore under his breath, then he started to fumble with his kit. He put the loose bullets in his beret and rolled it before stuffing it into my top pocket. He was agitated, his ritual interrupted. He pulled on his body armour and swore again as he dropped a magazine that clattered on the floor.

The man slid down from the bunk above to help him. He was topless and his arms were tattooed with a regimental cap badge. They closed zips, stuffed his sleeping bag under the lid of his Bergen and clipped it shut before the man lifted it onto BA5799's back.

'Thanks, Rifleman Plunkett,' he said.

'I'll make sure the CQ gets your grip and it comes forward, boss.'

'I don't even know if I've got everything I need,' BA5799 said and patted his side pouches.

'You'll be all right, sir – this is all you'll need for now,' he said, grinning and passing him the rifle. 'Good luck.'

'Damn, where are my goggles? I'll need them for the heli.'

'Here, take mine. I'll just go diffy a pair,' he said and reached into the side of his own Bergen.

'Cheers, Plunks. See you on the other side.'

BA5799 walked out of the hangar and stepped into a Land

Rover, holding his rifle in one hand and me in the other. The engine ticked over until two other men joined us. Once they were both in and their kit was piled on top of me, the door slammed shut and we drove back towards the airport.

We entered the heliport, dismounted and walked to a Portakabin that was surrounded by T-walls of concrete and covered by a dome of mortar protection. Men stood around a bin smoking. BA5799 placed his Bergen with the others.

'Where to?' a man with a clipboard asked.

'Three for Patrol Base 43 – Barnes, Webb and Dale,' BA5799 said.

'Collins not with you? Says here there are four for PB43.'

'Sergeant Collins is on his way – we weren't expecting the chopper to be leaving so soon. We've only just been told.'

'Well the airframe's been delayed. He might be lucky if he gets here soon,' the man said and made a note on his clipboard.

They waited on benches. It was hot and several men slept. Others arrived and the line of Bergens lengthened. A man appeared, flustered, and said he'd been on the phone with his wife and had no idea. They told him the heli had been delayed and it was just another hurry-up-and-wait. I was between BA5799's legs and he took the beret from my pocket and continued to fill his magazines with the rounds. Helicopters churned the air and hot engines distorted the ground crews as they pulled out refuelling pipes. They huddled away when the aircraft lifted again into the steel sky.

The man with the clipboard stepped out of the cabin. 'Right, we've got an airframe in ten minutes. PB43 first and then District Centre – I need the bags and pax for PB43 on last. Are you Sergeant Collins?' he said to the man next to BA5799. 'You made it then. You four at the back and get off as quick as you can – nobody likes waiting around at PB43, it's one of our hottest HLSes at the moment. Pilots are a bit twitchy about it.'

BA5799 extended my straps, pulled me over his body armour and put his helmet on. Men prepared their kit, stubbed out cigarettes and readjusted their Bergens.

The helicopter floated down onto the concrete and its two rotors flattened. A row of soldiers disembarked from the rear, carrying their bags towards the reception area. Two attack helicopters landed beyond and were refuelled.

A man at the rear of the helicopter beckoned and we walked out across the apron. I was on BA5799's back; he was last in the single file of men. The wind swirled around us and he pulled his goggles down off his helmet. We shuffled forward under the blades and through the exhaust fumes as men walked up the ramp past the mounted rear machine gun. They heaped their Bergens and cases down the centre aisle and then filled the seats and helped each other strap into the four-way belts. BA5799 threw his Bergen onto the pile and assisted the crewman pulling a ratchet-strap over the bags. He was thanked with a thumbs up, then sat in the final seat and placed me between his legs next to his rifle.

The sound of the helicopter escalated and the disc of shadow lightened on the concrete behind. The aircraft twitched as it left the ground. Its shadow shrank and jumped over blast walls, protective walkways, hangars and tents as we banked out towards the desert. Through the open rear door, the two hunched forms of the attack helicopter escort lifted and followed us across the sprawling camp.

BA5799 and the others, rifles upright between their legs, sat on either side of the fuselage, unable to talk over the noise as they were projected low over the empty desert.

Soon the faded scars of habitation lined the sand below. The crewman sat down behind the gun on the rear ramp, pulled a lever that sprang forward and rotated the weapon over the increasingly dense patchwork of villages and the grids of irrigation channels that flashed in the sun. He looked back and held his hand open and shouted, 'Five minutes.'

BA5799 lifted a hand to acknowledge him before passing the message to the man next to him. Thumbs ups and nods rippled up the aircraft. The helicopter started to manoeuvre, rocking violently below the rotors as it slewed across the landscape. I slipped and BA5799 grabbed hold to keep me between his legs. Sky and then ground filled the rear opening. An attack helicopter rushed past and the green and ochre ground swept below: a road with a man pulling a handcart, a donkey tied up in a field, a tree line stretching out to a square enclosure.

The engine sound changed and the thud of passing rotors deepened as the aircraft flared into its final approach. We decelerated over the wall of a camp and its watchtower, where a soldier shielded his eyes against the debris. A green tent was blown free and tumbled away across the courtyard until it caught in a vehicle's bar armour.

Dust kicked up by the downdraught engulfed the helicopter as it lurched in the blindness. Feeling suddenly weightless, the men tensed. The aircraft bounced on its suspension, skidded sideways and then the engines howled and we were airborne again, lifting away through the churning cloud. I pressed into the floor and BA5799 braced his legs against me and closed his eyes in helplessness, his stomach lurching.

The crewman spoke urgently into his microphone and scanned the tree lines around the patrol base, his thumbs ready to depress the triggers as we banked out of the pyre of dust.

We were over the desert again, pitching from side to side, and then we slowed and passed over the same perimeter wall and watchtower. We bounced once and stopped, rocking on the suspension.

The crewman stood up from his gun, lowered the rear door and released the strap holding the Bergens. BA5799 pushed the cylinder to release the belt and slid me up onto his back. He dragged his Bergen free and pulled it down the ramp onto the HLS, out from under the rotors.

The four men crouched together as the helicopter lifted away. Wind stripped dirt and sand from the ground and blasted it against me. The aircraft disappeared over a wall and soon after the attack helicopter high in overwatch drifted away in pursuit and it was quiet.

A man in a T-shirt and flip-flops came out from behind a wall.

'Welcome to Patrol Base 43,' he said. 'I'm the second in command. That looked like a bit of a roller coaster. Maybe the pilot couldn't handle the brownout; can't be easy though. We once had three attempts.' He grinned. 'We weren't expecting you until tomorrow. Not that we ever get much warning anyway.' He looked down at me and the other bags. 'Any post with you? No? Bugger. Post's about the only thing that makes up for having the camp destroyed every time they come in. Here, let me take that, I'll show you where you'll be based and we'll need to sign you in at the ops room.'

BA5799 picked me up and adjusted my shoulder straps and we followed the man across the HLS into a courtyard of thick mud walls rounded by weather. A few men hammered tent pegs back in, another collected strewn washing.

The man pointed BA5799 to a narrow opening in a wall that led into a dark room with two Z-beds. 'That's where officers stay, and I'll just show the others to the NCOs' lines. I'll come back and give you a tour of the camp in a bit.'

BA5799 ducked through the doorway, sat on a camp bed and leant his rifle against me. He unclipped his helmet and ruffled his flattened hair, then he stretched, opened my top pocket and put his goggles away.

The man came back and stood silhouetted in the doorway.

'You okay? I'm Dave,' he said and held out a hand.

'Tom. Yes, fine, thanks – good to be here.' They shook hands.

There was a sharp clap outside and then another. They both flinched. And then two distant thumps.

'Ah, the teatime contact,' the man said and looked out of the doorway. 'The heli must've got them all excited. Grab your helmet and rifle, Tom. No better way to show you the camp.'

BA5799 zipped my pocket back up, fastened his helmet strap, clipped a magazine onto his weapon and followed the man out into the light as the air started to clap an uneven rhythm.

I was covered in foreign dust and he left me beside a camp bed in the small room dug into a compound wall. A camel spider crawled across the ground and felt with its hairy legs up and over me.

7

I was normally placed on the lime-green tablecloth in the kitchen. That day I was next to the dog lead on the coffee-stained newspaper. The doorbell rang. The dog barked. The dark outline of two figures showed through the glass panels. She came in from the sitting room and shut the dog out behind her. She craned her neck to see. She wasn't expecting anyone.

It was a man and a woman. He was wearing a regimental tie. They said her name. She nodded. They asked if they could come in. She gripped the door and didn't open it any wider and asked what had happened. She didn't want them to come in. She had imagined the horror of this moment, but she was numb. She was aware of the potential for grief. It curled around her throat and fluttered in her stomach.

She remembered her son's smile and the last time he'd walked out of the gate and said that he would be fine and she remembered wishing he wouldn't tempt fate like that. She remembered when he was eight and had cried on the way to school. She remembered when he finished training and how proud she had been.

She remembered she'd felt the same dread every time the doorbell had rung since he had been away. She remembered not wanting to go downstairs and the relief when it had been door-to-door salesmen, and how much nicer she had been to them. And now she wished she hadn't come downstairs.

Maybe she could just take the dog for a walk and they wouldn't be here when she came back. She didn't want to face this on her own.

They asked again if they could come in. She let them in but wanted them to go away and never return – to have never existed. She put the kettle on and told them they would want a cup of tea. It wasn't real until they said it.

They told her it was fine and she should really sit down. They sat around the table and the man asked a number of questions confirming who she was. She just wanted to know now, to just be told so the horror could start. She knew she was about to be damaged; it would change everything. He asked if she was his mother – of course she was.

The woman stood up. She looked grave and hadn't said anything since they had come in – she probably hated doing this. 'Let me make you a cup,' she said and went over to the kettle. She took a mug from the cupboard, but when she saw it had *Mummy's Little Soldier* written on it she put it back and chose another.

And then the man told her what had happened. Her son had been very seriously injured and was being operated on, it was the best front-line medical facility in the world. He said they didn't know many details yet but he was very seriously hurt, had lost a lot of blood and his left leg – that was all they knew at the moment.

She was relieved – he wasn't dead. Her son was still alive. The man continued to talk and asked where her husband was and if she should call him. She reached over and picked me up, pulled my magnetic clasp apart and took her phone from inside me. Her voice shook as she told her husband, not knowing how to form the words. She gave as many details as she could and then her voice started to break and she handed the phone over to the man. He explained the same things he had to her and then put the phone down and told her he was on his way back.

She remembered him, three years old, running down the beach on holiday giggling. She wanted to cry but couldn't. Not in front of these people. The woman put a cup of tea in front of her. She looked at it but didn't see it.

Then she asked what very seriously injured meant and whether he would live. They gave answers she knew they were trained to give and realised that even though she wished they had never come, they hated this too and she felt sorry for them.

Suddenly she knew the relief might be unfounded, that her son might already have died on an operating table. She thought of him dying – perfectly formed – and desperately far away, without her. And then she remembered the man had said he'd lost a leg and she adjusted the image on the operating table, and her imagination went too far and added injury after injury. It deformed him and he wasn't her son any more, and it was too much and her face began to crumple and she asked them if they would just give her a moment. She grabbed me from across the table and went out of the room and stumbled upstairs, pulling herself forward with the banister.

She put me down on the white painted chair and bent over the toilet and was sick. She was sick again and concentrated on not making any sound – not wanting them to hear.

She crawled over to the door and locked it and leant back against it. She felt inside me for tissues and wiped around her mouth and then brushed the tears away from her eyes. She wasn't crying, the tears were from being sick, and she wondered why not. She focused on her breathing and waited. There were footsteps below and the woman whose name she couldn't remember was calling up the stairs. She answered impatiently that she was fine, she just needed a minute.

She replaced the pack of tissues and left her delicate hand limp in me. It trembled and her rings glinted. Then she clenched her hand until it hurt and her skin whitened and the fine veins bulged blue.

She brushed her teeth but couldn't bring herself to look in the mirror. And then she left me and went downstairs. The murmur of voices came from below and a car crunched over the gravel and the dog barked with excitement. Her husband's deep voice entered the conversation as the talking continued. It was dark when a car left.

They both came up and she sat on the white chair while he rested on the edge of the bath. She reached down and took the phone out of me and started to text and then rang instead to tell her mother what had happened. He watched her talk and, when she had finished, said there was nothing they could do until tomorrow. He asked if she was sure she didn't want anything to eat.

In the middle of the night she came in and sat on the toilet and held her head for a long time and then clicked the light off and went out.

He shaved in the morning. She stepped past him and showered. He asked if she was okay and she could tell he felt stupid asking. There was a distance between them that neither wanted to bridge with words. She dressed and took me downstairs and pulled out her address book and phoned the kennel – yes, it was an emergency. He called his office and they sat at the table looking at the toast rack. Neither knew what to do. He walked the dog and she lay on the bed.

They received a call and were suddenly urgent. She was glad of something to do and packed a case. They loaded the car and I was in the footwell below her feet. They held hands across the gear-stick and she looked at the rivulets of rain that streamed along the window and blurred the casket-brown motorway embankment beyond.

Her throat was tight and a sickness pulled down in her stomach. The tightness remained even when she wasn't thinking about it, a constant physical reminder knotted inside her. She sighed deeply and the knot fluttered, loosened and then pulled taut again.

The car stopped and he put a small piece of paper on the dashboard. He opened her door and smiled at her. She picked me up and we walked into a building through sliding doors and down cream-coloured corridors.

He asked for directions at the desk. Her arm that held me was trembling. She wanted to brace herself but couldn't – the blow was coming. The woman behind the desk smiled at them and pointed down the corridor and she stared at her until he gently tugged her elbow and asked again if she was okay.

I was next to her in a room and she reached into me and turned the phone to silent. Its glow illuminated the pens and the address book, the opened tissues and the phone charger until it dimmed to black.

There were other people in the room; a woman whose young daughter pushed coloured blocks along a spiralling wire and glanced at her mother, another who clutched her phone and a man whose face was blank but who cried silently. They sat in silence, each of them separated by a few seats.

A nurse came in and they all looked up and she asked the man and the second woman through. They stood and shuffled out. They came back later and sat closer to each other and he rested a hand on her arm. Both of them stared at the same spot on the floor.

I was on her lap, held between her hands, when a man opened the door and asked if they would like to follow him. Her husband stood and ushered her out protectively and we walked down a corridor to another room where the man said Dr Morris would join them soon.

A man wearing a grey suit entered and asked them if they would like to have a seat. He introduced himself and explained that he was the doctor in charge of the intensive care unit. He said their son had been flown back and arrived in the hospital three hours ago. His team had assessed their son and decided to take him straight into surgery.

He listed wounds and turned his professional knowledge into words they could understand. They held hands and her husband asked questions for them that the man answered. Their son was now stable but very seriously injured – her hand clenched on my strap – and they were also worried about an exposed femoral artery.

The doctor told them they would be able to see him soon and her pulse quickened. He warned them that their son was heavily sedated – they needed to keep him that way – and there was currently no plan to bring him round.

Her heartbeat thumped in her head. They could see him. He was back from that place, she thought, and would never have to go there again. The relief flooded through her – nervous excitement wrapping around the knot in her throat. She smiled at her husband and squeezed his hand.

The doctor led them in. I hung by her side and her husband

had his arm around her and supported her across the ward, past the beds and dividing curtains, the flickering machines and the attending nurses, towards the bed her son was in. When she saw him she faltered and her husband held her closer.

She hugged me as she sat in the chair next to his bed. She looked at his face that was on its side and covered by a breathing mask – like a fighter pilot, she thought – and through the plastic she could see the thick tube that made his chest rise and fall.

There were other tubes entering her son but she wasn't sure what they all did. She wanted to hold him and hugged me even tighter on her lap. Please be okay, she thought. Please don't be brain-damaged; they hadn't ruled that out. He had lost a lot of blood but his reflexes were good – that was encouraging.

They had shown her the legs below a sheet tent but she couldn't register it. They were grossly swollen, covered in plastic dressings and pipes that drained the wounds. The bottom of one was missing – this didn't matter, it wasn't him, he was in there. She reached out and stroked his forehead. Please be you. She remembered his smile. Please be able to smile again. His hair was fairer than normal and she thought of the heat and sun where he'd been and it all seemed so far away.

We were in the transit accommodation. She couldn't recall how we had got here, only that they'd left him and now were in a room with a print of a lighthouse on the wall, where only people who worried ever stayed.

She rummaged around inside me, peered in and pushed things aside to see my contents. And then she turned me upside down on top of a chest of drawers and everything from inside me spilt across its hard surface. She looked again but couldn't find what she wanted and threw me across the room, then caught her reflection in a mirror and started to cry. She swept the address book and tissue and pens away and they scattered on the carpet as her body heaved. He came in from the toilet and held her and moved her across to the bed away from where I lay on the floor. Through sobs she told him she'd lost her phone – it was in me but had disappeared. He went over to the hook by the door and took her phone from her coat pocket and placed it in her hands and sat down beside her. He put his arm round her and she cried onto his shoulder while looking at the phone. He undressed her gently and pulled the blue duvet over her.

He picked me up and carefully replaced everything and left me beside her on the floor. She slept but in the morning her son was her first thought, there was no moment of respite.

And then we were back with him. She placed me on a trolley-table and sat down. His chest still rose and fell, though she wondered if he was yellower or there was more strain on his face. She hoped the doctors knew, but what if they didn't? What if there was something else they hadn't noticed? One of the machines above him beeped and she looked over at a nurse who walked by unconcerned. She didn't know what the digital numbers meant but she wished it wouldn't sound like an alarm.

They came and took him away again and it was worse when he was gone. They needed to reopen and re-clean his wounds and she spent the time hoping nothing would go wrong. They'd signed consent forms and listened to the doctors' explanations. She tried to understand their conversations but bent all her concentration on him – everything she had, to help him get better – and now she felt the helplessness of not being able to do anything.

She carried me through the corridors to the canteen even

though she didn't like being away. She threw her half-finished coffee in the bin and went back to wait for the doctors to update them.

We were back in the room with the lighthouse and the television was on and then her husband turned the lights off. I was on the bedside table and her eyes were open all night staring at me from the pillow. In the morning she dressed, picked me up and went back to him.

And then he woke up. He forced himself from sedation earlier than expected and they came and said he was conscious and took us to him.

I was on the trolley-table as they both stood over him and he looked back up at them.

'I'm sorry, Mum,' he said.

8

I was made in China, a genuine copy. The man who sold me didn't want a place in the market so he sat in a backstreet, away from the crowds – his customers knew where to come. He didn't sell very much: a few mobile phones; T-shirts, one with an American musician holding up two fingers above strange western script; a selection of batteries, loose in a box; and, hidden away, a pile of illegal magazines. The air was humid in the alleyway. A pool of stagnant water along the gutter attracted flies and thirsty dogs.

I was in a cardboard box beside the blue plastic crate he sat on.

Latif knew where to find the stallkeeper; his new friends had told him. He was nervous. He hadn't handled this much money before and he fumbled the dollars awkwardly as he glanced over his shoulder at the people who passed in the bright district-centre bazaar. The stallkeeper inspected each note and nodded before he presented my box to Latif.

I was too big for Latif but the man only had me. Latif pulled my laces tight until my eyes met and the fabric creased up over his toes. He didn't know how to tie my laces, so he knotted them and pushed the excess down beside his ankle. He removed my twin from the box and slid it onto his other foot. I was bright white and my reflective patches glinted in the alleyway.

He'd only ever worn sandals and I made his foot feel fire-hot as he walked back to the throng of people who pressed around the market. He was embarrassed by how strangely I flashed below his traditional trousers.

I was cotton and laminated plastic, rubber with foam, chunky and gleaming with black ticks on each flank. I was alien among a sea of worn leather sandals that shuffled between the stalls.

We walked out through the streets and jumped into the back of a truck. Men sat on benches down both sides with goods from the market; one had a goat that wriggled between his legs. We drove into the fields. The other men glanced down at me and then up at Latif's young face. He shifted and looked away over the fields.

I was a badge, a uniform. I set Latif apart: a symbol of his choice.

At a crossroads the truck stopped and we jumped down. Latif paid the driver, then headed towards a village. My sole was soft and Latif grinned as he floated over the ground. And he started running and realised why his new friends had told him to spend his first earnings on me.

Latif stopped and scuffed me against the hard mud of the side of a ditch, trying to get me dirty so I looked battered and experienced – not how he felt but how he wished he did.

We walked into the village and down a track between high walls. Latif pushed at a red gate and we entered a compound. Chickens nodded around sacks of grain under a lean-to and a boy swept ash back into a fire pit.

A girl, sitting back on her ankles, spotted Latif and ran to greet him. She called him brother and grinned as she held his hand. He told her about the market and said he would take her one day soon when Father allowed it. He took a fig from his pocket and she smiled and bit into it then inspected me with surprise. She said with a full mouth how white we were and how strange we looked – how big on the end of his legs. She placed a grubby foot on top of me, and the other on my twin, and he walked straight-legged with her on us and they both laughed. He told her how comfortable I was and she laughed again and went back to a goat's skin she was scraping dry.

He ducked through a doorway. He couldn't untie his rushed knots so he levered me off and left me at the end of a row of burnished sandals.

Latif walked a few steps into the dark room. A man and woman stood at the back looking into a recess stacked with sacks and pots. She was explaining how many bags of rice and flour they had and how much more they would need. The man's hand was on her shoulder and he nodded. He said he would ask his cousin if they could have some food but she looked at him and said how worried she was about adding to their debts this year. He muttered it would be fine and Latif would continue to help.

Then he turned and saw him and asked how the market was and if he had managed to sell the seeds. Latif greeted his father and poured tea from a pot in the centre of the room. He asked his mother if she needed more money for food. She smiled and said they were fine at the moment.

Latif sat cross-legged on a rug and drank the tea. His father walked over to step into his sandals and saw me. He picked me up and turned me over, running his dirt-lined fingers through the deep grooves of my tread and gel shock absorber. Latif watched him. His father placed me back on the floor and then looked at Latif before walking out into the compound. His mother had seen all this and looked away sadly.

That night, after his cousins and uncle had returned from the fields and his grandparents had walked the twenty yards across the compound from their room, they sat in a loose circle and dipped bread in soup.

They had all noticed me. I was too white for them not to. Latif felt defensive; the buying of me had created a distance from the family around him, and the comfortable silence that usually accompanied their meals was filled with judgement. Latif didn't think he had changed but there was something about me, and his pride in me, that made him question it and he felt ashamed.

His cousin broke the silence and asked what would happen if Latif met the soldiers at work, adding that at least he'd be able to run away now. His mother was angry and sent them out. His smirking cousin and confused sister left.

His mother cried and asked why he wasted his money on infidel shoes, why he needed to do what he was doing. It was not their problem, they could ignore it. This was their world, this compound and their fields; they were happy and the soldiers hardly ever came here – why did he need to be part of it?

His father stilled her and said it was for the best and Latif was doing what he could for them – and making good money with the insurgents.

Latif felt upset and alone; maybe he was different now. He tried to pull me on but the knots he had tied made it difficult. His mother asked where he was going and told him he couldn't, it was too late, but he ignored her and continued to struggle with my laces.

She came over and knelt in front of him and picked me up. She undid the knots and her tears fell onto me. Latif waited as she gently slipped me on his foot and tied my laces in a bow, slowly so he could see. She did the same on his other foot and then pleaded with him to stay. But we left the compound and walked out over the dark fields.

They were where he thought they might be, around a fire, and they shuffled to make room and said how great his shoes looked. We were in a ring of men illuminated by the yellow heat. Each one had shoes like me, poking from under their crossed legs.

We stayed with these men. We ran errands for them. We helped dig holes in roads that they carefully placed bombs in. Latif was the youngest but he started to feel more confident. He watched them make explosives and helped where he could. He was sent to market to buy more supplies. He spent hours standing guard while the other men did things he wanted to be part of.

Sometimes he would shake with fear and we would run as fast as he could and I would grip around corners as we tore through a maze of paths to get away. Sometimes there would be a motorbike waiting and Latif would leap onto the back and grab hold of the rider. The rear wheel would kick out and we would drive off with a trail of dust behind us as the engine vibrated in a hot blur beside me.

It rained and the dust turned to mud. I was sodden and my cloth stained the brown of the earth. It was cold and wet for weeks and we all stayed in a compound and Latif was bored. Some of the men left for the mountains and he wished he could go with them.

We went back to his family and his sister ran over in excitement. Latif handed more money to his mother and his father was pleased with him. He helped with the harvest and watched the helicopters hammer over the fields and knew, when the harvest was in, he would try and destroy them again. His mother pleaded with him to stay but we left and went back to the men.

They lived as a group and moved most days; sometimes a family would take them in and they laughed and danced long into the night. Often Latif slept under the stars and was roused when the fire only glowed. He would take a weapon and watch over the men who slept. He shivered in the chill and stamped me down between yawns to keep himself awake.

When he took me off, Latif was careful not to loosen the bows his mother had tied for him. The men knelt together and prayed. Other times I was taken off and Latif would jump into the blue water of a river and wash and all the men splashed one another.

One night, they were agitated and a pickup truck came and took one of them away. The remaining men talked breathlessly. Latif learnt of the network of influence and power that spread through the fields around them, the connections that flowed across mountains and deserts from distant countries and cities that he'd never heard of. He marvelled at the complexity and secrecy of it, at the mythic names he'd only ever heard uttered. He couldn't believe he was now part of it all.

Before dawn, while Latif stood guard, he heard a vehicle bouncing along the track and raised his weapon in readiness. It was the truck from the night before and he relaxed. The man had returned but another came with him.

He walked over to Latif. He had black leather boots with deep treads and a green vest filled with equipment hanging loosely from his shoulders. He wore a black turban. He did not smile and said he was Aktar. His accent was foreign.

Aktar told the men they would go north for the summer and they followed him. They carried the sacks of equipment that

[54]

Aktar had brought and walked single file over fields that I had never trodden before.

They had to be careful; the enemy was moving into the area. They hid weapons and equipment in empty compounds and between tree roots. Aktar told Latif to memorise their locations but never speak of them.

They dug in bombs on roads at night and whenever storms whipped up the sand. They shielded their faces with turbans but sand still collected in their noses and ears and down in me, between Latif's toes.

The men were nervous around Aktar. He said little and made them work hard. We often travelled at night and Latif slept without taking me off. There were times when Aktar's radio crackled and we left with little warning and waited in the dark and nothing happened. We moved on through villages and spoke to the elders. Aktar told them what he wanted and looked them in the eyes and threatened them.

They blocked roads for whole days and stopped the passing traffic.

They prayed more often, and Latif took me off before kneeling next to Aktar and mouthing the words in unison with him.

Sometimes Aktar sent us off alone. We would stand near the soldiers' base that had watchtowers at each corner and the flag that fluttered among tall antennas. When a line of men with weapons and helmets that shadowed their eyes filed out of the gate, or huge armoured vehicles swung up onto the road, we wandered away and Latif would send a text about a party on the mobile phone that Aktar had given him.

One day, when I was crossed over my twin, and the men sat in the shade with their backs against the wall of a compound, Aktar told Latif how well he was doing and Latif was pleased.

They were by a road they had blocked with an iron bar resting on oil drums. They had stopped a truck full of melons and talked to the driver. One of them knew the man and told him which route was safe and which to avoid and the truck moved off. They talked of women until Aktar told them to stop and they waited for the next traffic in silence.

Aktar stood first. Latif followed him and I was up on the raised road. A lone figure, a young man on a bike, wobbled through the mirages. He dismounted and pushed the bike towards us. Latif's foot suddenly tensed in me when he saw it was his childhood friend, Faridun. He didn't want to be recognised, to be reminded of his childhood or the compound with his mother.

Aktar stopped him with a wave of his hand. 'Peace be upon you, young man,' he said. 'How are you?'

'Peace be upon you. I am fine, praise to God,' Faridun said, keeping his eyes low. 'I am on my way home from Howshal Nalay, I have been to the market. I need to get back before dark,' he said. He glanced up and saw Latif.

Latif's toes curled down in me; he felt afraid for his friend. And he thought of the web of connections and honour that ran through the land around them. But he was scared of not telling Aktar – that was his duty now. We walked forward and I was on tiptoes as Latif whispered in his ear. 'I know this man. His father is Kushan Hhan. He used to be an associate of my father. He is said to help the infidel and is working to reopen the school in the village—'

Aktar burst forward and pushed Faridun. He tangled with his bike and fell onto the road level with me. Aktar forced his

[56]

weapon down against his lips. Faridun flinched in pain and then the barrel plunged into his mouth.

'Is your father Kushan Hhan?'

Tears streamed from Faridun's eyes and he retched around the weapon. He nodded. Latif watched his defiance, despite the barrel pressed impossibly deep inside him, and he was confused and ashamed.

'Your father is working for the infidel. If he continues to do this against the will of God, I will cut off your sister's head. Do you understand?' Aktar said and jabbed down once more with a grunt and then stood away.

Faridun got up out of the dust and the sack he carried fell from his bicycle. Blood ran from a gash on his ankle. He looked from Aktar to Latif.

'May God be with you, Latif,' he said.

Latif felt sudden anger and stepped me forward, but Faridun calmly turned away and left us standing on the road.

The other men laughed at Faridun and thumped Latif on the back. Aktar stood to one side. 'You were right to tell me, Latif. All must know their place. It is the will of God.'

After what he had done to Faridun, Latif couldn't go home and I followed the black leather boots of Aktar more closely. We crossed the countryside and Latif felt tied to this man who was ruthless and fearless.

9

I lived in the soil. My spores existed everywhere in the decomposing vegetable matter of the baked earth.

Something happened that meant I was suddenly inside you: meant I travelled with the soil up and through your skin, breaching the physical barrier that was designed to keep the outside out. It was an instant that compromised you completely.

I was inside your leg, deep among flesh that was torn and churned. I lived there for a week and wanted to take root, but it wasn't easy. Some of my spores were washed away with the dirt from your wounds, others were cut out with necrotic tissue, and some were destroyed by a barrage of your white blood cells.

I struggled to survive.

Except they missed a small haematoma that had formed around a collection of mud in your calf. It was an anaerobic environment I could flourish in and I started to take hold. Your blood was mixed with eight others', so your immune response was weakened and couldn't counter me; there were repeated assaults on your body as anaesthetic knocked you again and again.

The balance changed. You degraded and I thrived. You became my host.

I spread out into the hypoxic and devitalised tissue of your leg. I made you feverish and feasted unseen on your insides, defeating you. I made you wish you'd never survived.

A sample of me was taken out and grown in a controlled environment. They identified me as a zygote fungus.

I was going to survive and you were not.

I was making you die, and when that happened I would die too. But I had no option, only oblivion. I had to persist and would consume you to do it.

10

My aperture was filled with stars. I changed the frequency of the photons that entered my vacuum tube so their signature was amplified as a noisy green image.

BA5799 shifted from one knee to the other. As he moved I wobbled on the mount that attached me to his helmet and the stars blurred as I failed to maintain resolution. He lifted a hand and slotted me into position. My green light reflected off the glassy bulge of his retina and his eyelashes flicked across the surface of my lens as he blinked.

The stars were replaced by a dark horizon and the ridges of a ploughed field. He scanned across it. The grey-green shapes of kneeling figures snaked forward into the distance, disappearing into a dark thicket.

Each figure held his weapon rested on a knee or in the crook of a shoulder and peered into the gloom, each one turned in the opposite direction to protect the single file. Their eyes glowed against pale skin.

Ahead there was the sound of coughing.

We waited. BA5799 looked out at the jumble of houses and brick walls flat in the middle distance. There was no movement. His knee ached and the straps of his day-sack pressed down through his body armour that encased him in damp heat. He was hot, but now that we had stopped he shivered.

Ahead the line moved, lifting away and extending until the man in front of us levered up and walked off. When there was a gap BA5799 stood up, turned and walked backwards holding out a thumb, and the figure behind followed.

We went onto a track covered with foliage and I struggled to enhance any light in the dark. A droplet of sweat collected off BA5799's eyebrow, swung around my rubber cuff and dripped onto his cheek. We edged across a plank bridge above inky water and headed out over another field.

In front a figure stumbled with a stifled curse and the weight of his equipment pulled him down into a ditch. Two others helped him up. We walked on towards it, the man ahead swept his arm out to indicate the hazard and BA5799 did the same for the man behind.

We stopped regularly and the line concertinaed together and then stretched away as they moved on to each pre-decided feature. We waited near a motionless village and a dog barked and another echoed in the distance.

BA5799 adjusted a dial on my side and I increased the contrast of my output. He focused me on deep patches of shadow and then moved on to the next, looking for a silhouette or sudden flash. He knew they must be there, watching the single file of soldiers laden with weapons cross the open fields, alerted by the dogs and the shuffle of their clothes and buzz of radios that seemed so loud.

We stayed in the same place for a long time and he was frustrated by not knowing what was happening ahead. He lifted me up so I pointed at the stars again, swept his sleeve across his eyes and dropped me back into position. He yawned: his adrenaline was spent.

Finally, the man in front whispered that they were at the ren-
dezvous. BA5799 understood from the plan that they would now
move between two buildings and form a defensive triangle so
the others could find them. He signalled the message to the man
behind him and it murmured down the rest of the line.

A soldier who knelt beside the track counted us through. We
passed the legs of those who were in position, lying flat behind
their weapons, and dropped down. We were in a ragged triangle,
all facing out. A dog started to bark again.

BA5799 was uncomfortable: a stone pushed into his ribs and
my weight pulled his helmet forward so he had to arch his back
painfully to see. He shifted and drank some water from a pipe
protruding from the top of his day-sack.

He knew from the plan that they would appear from the direction he faced. And after his back had numbed, an infrared light
emerged that he could see only through me. It bobbed up and
down as a soldier walked out across the field, followed by another
single file of dark figures. BA5799 lifted me and could see little
through the murk without my enhancement, then dropped me
back down so the line of men reappeared.

They stopped alongside an earth mound that divided two
fields. A soldier left our position and went out to greet the lead
figure.

The man next to us slid over and hissed in BA5799's ear. 'Looks
like this is me then, boss,' he said. 'Let Lieutenant Baker know I'll
be warming his bed.'

'Mark'll be chuffed, I'm sure,' BA5799 breathed back. 'Good
luck, Sarnt Collins.'

Men lifted themselves off the ground, overcoming the weight

of their kit, and moved out of the triangle to join the others. Once men had arrived to replace them and the line of soldiers had disappeared, there was a soft double pat on BA5799's day-sack and we stood and followed off between the two buildings.

We took a different route back and the pace quickened as we neared safety. A band of light was seeping from the horizon when we stopped for the final time a few hundred yards from a squat, silhouetted watchtower. BA5799 pushed fingers up to itch below his helmet and then adjusted me against his eye.

We entered the camp and a guard at the gate counted us in. Men broke off to different tents and buildings, the smell of cigarette smoke trailing them. BA5799 unloaded his weapon and ducked under a camouflage net into a building with aerials and a generator that rumbled outside.

A man leant against the doorframe. 'How was that, Tom?' he asked.

BA5799 unclipped his helmet and I swung wildly down to his side. My sensor was overloaded by light from the room in front of us. 'Morning, Dave. Seemed to go smoothly,' BA5799 said.

'I just heard on the ops room radio they got to the checkpoint fine, by the way. Not a peep all night. The insurgents never seem to like the dark. But I'm sure they must know we're moving about.'

BA5799 put his helmet on a bench and I pointed up at him, bright green in the light of the door. 'It was pretty eerie,' he said. 'Good to get out in the dark for the first time though.' He slid his day-sack off and removed his armour, ripping the Velcro at the sides. He pinched his wet combat shirt away from his skin.

'That's your third time out, isn't it?' the man said. He held a mug that waved as he spoke. 'We've got a framework patrol tomorrow. You can join in if you want. It'll probably be a short one to check some empty compounds to the east.'

'Fourth, if you include the one last night.' BA5799 picked me up and unscrewed me from the helmet mount. 'Any news on when the relief in place is due to start?'

'We talked to HQ earlier – it's still planned for two days' time, largely by road but a few helicopter loads too. Most of your lot should be in by midweek,' the man said. 'I'll be in the last packet out, leaving on Thursday.' He drank from the mug. 'We still need a couple more sessions in the ops room to complete the handover. Fancy a brew now?' He pointed the mug at BA5799.

'No thanks,' BA5799 said and flicked my off switch. I was blind. He placed me in a small pouch. 'I'm going to hit the sack. What time's the next patrol?'

'Be prepared from ten hundred.'

'I'll get a few hours then. See you later, Dave.'

'Catch you in a bit.'

11

I'm attached to the wall by a wire. My serial number is 245-81-BS. I am a small white box with a red button labelled CALL. I've operated on Ward L4 since I was installed three years ago. Recently, the patients that use me have changed. Now they are young, fit men, often sun-tanned and sometimes with body parts missing. They can be angry but mostly they joke and go outside to smoke. The hospital has improved the food for them.

Two nurses wheeled you in late one night when the ward was quiet and the lights had been dimmed. They pushed your bed up against the wall and moved a table next to you. Your mother was there and she thanked them. They smiled at you and said the team would collect you for surgery in the morning.

Your mother sat next to you for a while and looked around the ward and at the shadows of other beds under the closed curtains. She told you this was an improvement. You felt sicker than you had since regaining consciousness but didn't want to tell her that. You said you'd be fine now, that she should go and rest.

She was worried about you. She knew the colour of your skin and the gleam of perspiration on your forehead was wrong. She asked if you were sure you were okay.

You told her she needed some sleep; she said she'd be back in the morning before you went in. The pain you felt made it sound like you were exasperated with her, but you weren't. And once she'd gone you wished you hadn't sent her away, that she'd come back and stay with you. You were lonely and the shadows that walked up and down the corridor seemed very far away. You looked over at me resting on the table next to you and my wire running into the wall.

The room closed in. You knew there were others, like you, in the beds nearby, but they were silent; it was late. And then the anxiety started to build. And the pain wrapped itself around the anxiety and you were scared. Someone walked past in the corridor and you called out to them, but your voice was still too weak and damaged from the bomb and the tubes the doctors had pushed down it. Nobody could hear you.

Adrift in the nausea, you pleaded again but they kept disappearing, even though you called to them as loudly as you could.

Something was happening in your right leg that you didn't know about, nor did the doctors. The leg was badly damaged and dragging you down. You sensed something wasn't right. But you were a soldier and trained to endure and you didn't want to bother anyone. So you endured and the pain grew where you knew an artery was weak and exposed – they'd told you about that.

And the pain pushed hard into your leg until a huge weight crushed against your bone. You remembered you were meant to be brave and withstand the pain, a rite of passage, but you cried silently and were ashamed.

You tried to shut it away but you were worried for yourself and it throbbed as part of a fear that was overwhelming. All you could experience was yourself. No past, no future, only loneliness. You thought you were a coward and the pain grew. The agony was everything and you wished you hadn't been saved. It was the most despairing thing you'd ever thought. You wished they were with you.

'Please come back,' you said.

You were sweating and thirsty. There was a plastic cup of water next to me. You tried to reach for it but couldn't bend your arm. And you were too weak to shuffle across the bed. You lay still and panted and looked at the water you desperately needed. And then you tried again and you arched your back and pain seared through your damaged elbows.

You knocked the cup over and it fell onto the floor and rolled around. You were angry and called for them again but your throat was now so dry no sound came out. Frustration distorted the agony.

You could hear them joking by the nurses' station – were they laughing at you? You reached for me and managed to grab hold. You let the pain win and pressed my button; you no longer cared about losing. You waited, panting and relieved that help was coming.

Nothing happened. You longed to press me again but you didn't want to cause a fuss. I was in your limp hand by the leg that hurt you so much, grotesquely swollen under the covers you'd soaked through.

Still no one came. So you pressed me again and again and you worried that I was unconnected or broken, so you pressed my button down hard with your shaking thumb and held it there. You closed your eyes.

You were still. At the nurses' station a few feet away, one of them said he'd handle it and the curtain around our bed was pulled back. He asked if you were okay, and when you didn't reply he came closer.

'Hello, are you all right? We were just doing our shift hand-over. I'm Paul,' he said. 'You must be our newest resident.'

'Hello . . . help—' You were feverish but didn't want to show any weakness so you mastered it. 'Help me, please. I'm in a bit of pain.'

'Sorry, come again?'

'I'm in a bit of pain,' you shouted silently through chalky lips. 'I'm very thirsty.'

'I'm afraid you're on nil by mouth. You've got surgery planned early tomorrow.'

'Please, just a sip.'

'I'm afraid I can't give you much. Oh, you knocked the cup off. You shouldn't have had that anyway.'

He wiped up the water and left, then a foot-pedal bin clattered in the corridor. You could hear them at the nurses' station still laughing and you were desperate.

Then he came back. 'Here you go,' he said, holding in plastic tweezers a small piece of blue foam that he placed on your tongue. 'Try sucking on this.'

The water was wonderful in your mouth, just too little. 'Please,' you croaked, 'can I have a bit more?'

'Just a little then.' He removed the foam from your mouth and dunked it in a full cup.

You sucked it dry, trying to get some of the liquid down inside you. 'Can I please have a proper sip?'

'Say again.' He leant closer.

'Please, a proper sip?' you said, exaggerating your words.

'I'm really sorry, your notes say nil by mouth.'

'I'm in a bit of pain.'

'Have you been prescribed any pain relief?'

'I don't know . . . Please.'

'I'll just go and check something.'

He was gone for what felt like an eternity and you were as scared as you'd been in the helicopter. You wished it had never happened, wished it would end. You cried for yourself in the dark.

When he came back he was with a young woman in a white coat. You were unconscious as they spoke about you.

'He said he was in a bit of pain, poor chap,' the nurse said. 'But he's not been prescribed any extra pain relief yet, just what he's getting on IV. He only came up from the ICU this evening.'

'Okay, he's sleeping now anyway. He does look hot, mind,' the doctor said. 'Did you take his temperature?'

'No.'

'Well, he's in theatre in the morning. He'll be fine, just keep an eye on him and give me a buzz if he wakes.'

You still held me in your hand as you sweated and mumbled through the rest of the night. The nurse and his colleagues looked around the curtain a few times, and finally he walked over, lifted me out of your loose grip and put me back on the table.

She was there in the morning with the red handbag by her chair. She could tell something was wrong.

'Are you okay, darling?' she said.

You smiled and felt better for seeing her as you woke and wondered at how different the room looked in the daylight. But your leg still hurt and you found it hard to concentrate. Her face was creased and you didn't want to upset her.

'Yes, I'm fine, Mum. It was a slightly rough night. I'm in a bit of pain.'

You fell asleep again, or what seemed like sleep. Your mother was angry with the nurses and said you were suffering and that they should give you something. Then other nurses came, and a doctor who talked to her. She said you were going down for surgery now and that Dr Morris would explain it to her. But this would be a routine cleaning of the wounds, she added. Then they wheeled you away and your mother watched you go.

You did come back, but many days later. You were in a bed on the other side of the room from me. You looked different.

12

My first purpose was to hold my head down against the ground as I brushed sand out of a small, dirty room. It was an endless battle against the hot wind that curled around the doorframe. In time, my head loosened and the nail that held it on pulled free. Someone tried to push it back on, but my head swung round and fell off. I was discarded.

That would have been the end of me – and my head was burnt with the rubbish – but I was reinvented and became useful again.

He held me in both hands and leant on me at the edge of the flat piece of ground I was so used to. The speckled shadow of the camouflage net moved in the wind.

'Where are they?' he said.

'Not sure, sir.'

The flat ground was a square, framed with a line of sandbags and green string pulled tight across it to form a grid. Men sat around three sides of the square on old ammunition boxes and a low bench. They were in T-shirts and some held water bottles.

'They might still be handing over guard,' one of them said.

'Corporal Davey, make sure you back-brief them,' he said, then looked at his watch.

'Will do, boss.'

He straightened and held me in one hand. 'Right, orders for tomorrow's operation,' he said. 'We're deploying most of the company for the first time and the whole platoon's out together. It'll be a standard route-security operation for the logistics convoy bringing in our supplies. There's nothing complicated about this patrol, but we'll be static for long periods and that will make us vulnerable. We have to clear all the road in our AO and then secure it so the convoy can travel safely through.' He moved his hand up my shaft and used me to point at the flat ground.

'Is everyone happy with the model?' he said.

There were a few silent nods from the watching men.

'Just to orientate you again. This is our current location.' He pointed me at a tiny block of wood near the centre of the grid that had *PB43* written on it in peeling blue paint. It was the largest of a hundred little wooden squares placed carefully across the earth and numbered in black. 'This is Route Hammer.' He moved my end along a piece of orange ribbon that was pinned into the dirt. 'And this blue ribbon represents the river that runs past Howshal Nalay.' I swept along the ribbon over a denser group of wooden blocks. 'These red markers are the IED finds in the last three months, so there's quite a few on Hammer.' I hovered over red pinheads.

'Everyone's been out a few times now,' he said, looking up at them, 'and we should all be getting familiar with the ground and heat. Those who came in by road last week will have seen the area to the northeast, along Route Hammer. The convoy will be coming down the same road tomorrow.' My end touched a piece of green string, which vibrated. 'This is the eighty-third easting,' he said, 'and will be our boundary with Six Platoon.' He ran my tip along it until I was positioned where it intersected the orange ribbon. He stepped back and rested me on the ground. 'Any questions at this stage?' Most of the men continued to look down at the model. 'Anything to add, Sarnt Dee?'

'Nothing from me.'

He started describing the plan and used me to direct their attention to different parts of the square. He said their mission was to secure the road and then provide rear protection. He told them how they would move out before first light and push along the orange ribbon, past the blocks with *L33* and *L34* written on them. I paused there as he explained how vulnerable this point was, and that one team would provide overwatch at the block marked *M13* while others cleared the road.

I was pointed at one of the men, who nodded that he understood.

He told them how they would spread out between block *L42* and the green string. Two other platoons would move through them and secure the orange ribbon farther up. Then he swept me over the zones they were most likely to be attacked from. He said the hardest part of the operation was to clear the crossroads at the area of interest named Cambridge; this was 6 Platoon's responsibility. I hovered over where the orange ribbon was crossed by white tape.

I had done it all before: secured sections of the ribbon, dominated areas of dirt, reassured little labels, ambushed red markers and attacked through clusters of wooden blocks. I had destroyed as my end was pushed down hard and twisted into the ground. I'd drawn lines in the sand that were fire-support positions and traced casualty evacuation routes through miniature fields. I was the master of the model.

After he answered a few questions and everyone around him said they understood their part in the mission, he handed me to another man. This one told them what to do if there was a casualty, what equipment they should carry and how they should stay hydrated. He pointed me at an emergency landing site and circled me around an open section near *M13*, so I left a mark in the dust.

He pointed me at a man sitting embarrassed in the corner and told him that if he acted like he had on the last patrol, he'd make him wish he had been blown up. The others chuckled but I swept across all of them and he said it applied to everyone. He told them what needed to happen in the hours before they moved down the orange ribbon, then he handed me back to the first man.

'Thanks, Sergeant Dee. Right, that should all be clear now,' he said. 'Just to add to the timings, we'll do rehearsals at eighteen hundred tonight on the HLS.'

'Sir, are you sure we need to rehearse this?' a soldier said from the far side of the square.

'Yes, until we're the most swept-up platoon this side of the capital, we'll be doing rehearsals before every platoon operation.'

The men fidgeted.

'Listen to me – every one of you,' he said, his hand gripped tight around me. The men looked up. 'I don't give a shit how straightforward this operation is, or how much of a waste of time you think rehearsals are, or whether you'd rather be tossing off in your beds, we will rehearse until every man in this platoon—' He stabbed me down into the model. 'We've only just got here. The last company had four casualties in two weeks, and this is new ground for us all, so no man in this platoon will cut corners.'

They all stared at him and he wondered if they thought he was a prick.

'See you at six,' he said.

He put me down on the model and ducked out under the netting and into the sun. The other men started to drift away. Some

collected in a small group and one of them picked me up and
pointed me at a spot of earth and talked them through how they
would move out to the small wooden block with *M13* painted on it.

13

'You heading to the pub tonight?'

'Not sure. Can you pass me the debrider?'

'It's Mandy's birthday.'

They talked above the beep of a machine and the hum of a pump.

'Mandy? Not sure I know her . . . Cheers.'

'She works down in A and E.'

'Can you hold that back while I irrigate? Use those forceps, thanks.'

They stood over the table, their heads covered with masks and bandanas so only their glasses were visible. They wore blue scrubs and worked below an array of suspended lights, bent over pink flesh that spilt from a leg. They cleaned or cut away putrid grey areas, glancing up from the wounds to a screen that showed magnified swirls of red, shiny bulges of scarlet and globules of white.

This mess slopped out of a body splayed on the table. The body's arms were held out cruciform on padded extensions and the head was obscured by a mask and pipes that fed up to machines. There were other people in the room who monitored the apparatus or handed the men equipment.

I was on a stainless-steel shelf at the side of the room with other things required for specialist operations. The body had been brought in a few hours earlier and rolled past me up to the operating table. They had plugged it into the machines, arranged it on the slab and removed the dressings from the first limb. It was shorter than it should have been. The men had worked on the limb before covering it again.

Then they'd cleaned everything and started on the second limb that still had a foot, swollen but undamaged. They had peeled away plastic sheeting, gauze and bandages to reveal the leg. They'd worked up along the inside, which was unnaturally thin where sections were missing. In some places it had no skin, only exposed flesh that flopped out, unbounded. When they moved up to the calf they started talking again.

'Not looking great, is it?' one said.

'We've done a leg in two hours – reckon we should finish before three.'

'No, I mean, look at this section here. God, it stinks,' he said and pushed at it with forceps.

'Doesn't look too bad to me,' the other said.

'There's so much marginal tissue. We should get Al's opinion on this.'

'Why?'

'Because it might need some drastic action. I think it looks like the infection's taken hold.' He pushed two rubber-gloved fingers under the skin and deep into the thigh, along a tract of rancid flesh.

'Let's just finish the debridement and cover him up as planned,' the second man said. 'We don't need to disturb Al. He was in surgery most of yesterday.'

'If we cover him and there's similar levels of necrosis when we next debride . . . well, I reckon with this infection there's a good chance . . .'

'What?'

'I don't know, I just think it could seriously compromise the patient. I'm going to call him. I want a second opinion.'

'I'm your second opinion.'

But the first man walked over to the door, removed his gloves and left the tiled room, while the other man sat on a stool and sighed.

A woman unclipped and replaced an empty blood bag that hung above the body. She moved down to the legs and loosened a tourniquet and glanced at her watch.

'A second opinion can't hurt, Ben,' she said.

The man came back into the room a minute later.

'Al's on his way,' he said. 'Let's keep cleaning the wounds. How are his levels, Sarah?'

'Fine. He's going through a surprising amount of blood, though.' She looked at a chart.

'Too much?'

'Not sure,' she said. 'I don't think so.'

They worked on the body until another man, dressed in blue scrubs, backed through the doors with his hands held in front of him. He came over to the table and they started to discuss the body.

He nodded a few times and then delved into the soft tissue. 'You were right to come and get me, Mike,' he said.

'What do you think?'

'The infection has spread much farther than I would've anticipated.' He stood back and wiped across his eyebrows with his forearm. 'Ben, can you go and get Dr Shakoor, please?'

'Calling the cavalry, are we?' He unhooked forceps from the front of his bloody scrubs.

'Yes, Ben, quick as you can, please.'

Soon the room was crowded with people peering down at the body and talking through options. Some of them wore head torches that bathed the wounds in hard light.

'The infection's too aggressive and I'm not sure it'll respond to anti-fungals,' he said. 'Have we taken swabs and samples again?'

'Already taken, Al,' a nurse said.

A female surgeon had joined them. 'So we debride aggressively along the length of the leg and hope we cut it all out?' she said.

'I'm not sure there's any point, Nadia. He'll get very little function from the leg. None of the grafts we attempted last time have taken.'

'On balance, my advice would be to try and save the limb; at least give it another few days and see if it improves,' she said. She had lifted a flap of muscle to inspect a cavity.

'I don't want to lose another to infection. I think there's a real danger this could spread quickly and there'll be very little we can do once the infection reaches his abdomen.'

'Okay, Al. It's your call.'

'Mike, can you get the team together and prep.'

'Sure.' Some of them went for new equipment, fluids and blood bags. One walked towards me and started to arrange implements on a trolley.

'Al, I'm a bit worried about blood loss,' the woman near the body's head said. 'His temperature's dropped again.'

'Okay, Sarah, show me.' He moved up to the machines. 'Bit of time pressure now, everybody. Do we know where the parents are? I'd better go and talk it through with them. Nadia, can you start an assessment please? We want as much function as possible but really need to get rid of this bloody infection. Back in a mo.'

'I'll help you track them down,' the nurse said. 'They could do with an update. We told them this would be a routine debridement so they might be a tad worried by now.'

'Wait, Al.' The female surgeon was peering into a cavity.

'What is it, Nadia?' He walked back and looked over her shoulder.

'It must've haemorrhaged as this section was cleaned.' When she moved a flap of flesh, blood gushed out from behind it over the slab and dripped onto the floor.

'Right, no time to lose. Sarah, get more bloods prepped. We're going to do it now.'

It happened faster than normal. I was picked up and rattled onto a stainless-steel trolley spread with tools that had been carefully lined up, but the knives and forceps spun and slid about as it was quickly wheeled over.

I was now at the end of the table next to the body.

'Someone go and tell the family.' He lifted the leg and inspected it, moving the puffy flesh.

'How high?' he asked. No one answered. He was over the body, still assessing it and the others looked at him and over his shoulder, waiting for his decision. He glanced at the body's head and paused.

'Al, we're a bit low on blood. Pressure has just decreased dramatically.' The woman was watching a machine.

'How can we be low, Sarah?' He looked up at her. 'Well, go get some more. And can someone please clean this off the floor? I'm slipping.'

He then spoke very little and the team around him started to move to each command he gave. A man cleaned the floor, smearing sweeps of blood by his feet, but he ignored them as more blood dripped down onto the tiles.

'Right, I'm going to do it around here.' His finger traced a line of blood over the intact skin of the thigh. 'There's no muscle in this region to do a myodesis, so I'll use what's left of the vastus lateralis and femoris to wrap over the distal limb,' he said as the flesh wobbled in his hands. 'We can use this skin to cover it and avoid too much exposed tissue. We then graft up the inner thigh. That should provide good function.'

'Al, his levels are stable, but I advise we get a move on.'

'Right, let's do it. Scalpel.'

He slashed decisively across the skin, smoothly splitting the flesh apart. The cuts of the scalpel swept down through the subcutaneous tissue and fascia, deep into the flesh and through muscle and membrane that covered the bone. He slid the blade around and through dead and dying flesh; blood paused after each cut before seeping out the ends of the vessels. He asked for the tourniquet to be tightened.

He went carefully in some areas and created a flap of muscle that hung down. He dissected the sciatic nerve proximally. Sweat showed on the bridge of his nose. He used absorbent sutures and then repositioned the grey sheaths of nerves with prods of his finger.

Then he told them he was now going to address the femoral vessels and the woman helped him transect an artery and two veins. Dark red blood pulsed out and the tubes collapsed. One slipped free and disappeared into the mess. She swore and delved in with forceps to pull it out. He asked for a stick-tie for the double ligation, which he manoeuvred with long metal tweezers before letting the sutures clamp around the rubbery tubes.

He grunted that he wanted the electrocautery forceps, and a small machine resting next to me on the trolley was handed to him. He placed it against the arteries and it sparked as it cauterised the ends of the vessels. He told them they had achieved haemostasis and the smell of burnt flesh wafted up.

He told them he was happy so far and he glanced down at me. He stretched his back and said that he was getting too old for this.

He asked for a Cobb elevator. A small metal implement was picked off the trolley and he cleaned away soft tissue from the bone until the white showed. He shaved away a thick ridge and all the periosteum he could get to.

The soft fleshy areas of the leg were now held apart by a bar of bone that was dry and hard between them. Two others helped him position retractors that pulled the flesh out of the way so the bone was clear. They had worked faster than I had experienced before.

He asked for the oscillating saw.

I was passed to him. He gripped my handle and placed a gloved finger on my metal trigger. He held me like a weapon, and down at the end of my barrel was my flat stainless-steel blade, with its sharp teeth pointing forward in overlapping rows. He pulled my trigger and my motor whirred and my blade-end blurred.

This was when I became useful.

He said he was happy to make the cut. He asked one of them to hold the limb. His masked face looked down over me and his head torch lit my matte surface. I was in the valley between two banks of flesh, pointing straight down at the exposed shaft of the femur.

He pulled my trigger again and I made my blade vibrate so that its teeth distorted together as one. He pulled harder until my blade was cycling sixteen thousand times a minute. My high-pitched buzz was new in the room and the men and women shifted uncomfortably.

He held me an inch above and then lowered me so my ninety-millimetre-wide blade touched the bone. The pitch changed as I started to cut down. My blade heated quickly and they squirted saline solution onto me and into the cutting face. It evaporated in steam that swirled around the bone and prevented me from overheating.

He let my weight descend. My blade-end cut through the bone, flashing splinters and dust from the thin trench I gouged out. The juddering of bone passed through the pelvis and into the body so that its skull trembled. The sound of my blade changed tone again as I cut deeper and into the marrow. A small pile of dust and shards grew on the table below me.

He concentrated, his hand steady around me as I cut smoothly down. And then I was nearly through and the trench started to pull open under the weight of the limb. He told them to support it firmly until he was through.

Suddenly I jerked down and was oscillating free in the air. The bone pulled apart and the leg and its foot moved away, the gap widening until it was no longer below the body but being placed on another trolley that was quickly wheeled away. The body had no feet.

He released his finger and my motor stopped. It was quiet in the room and the beep of a machine returned. I was placed back down.

'Make sure we take samples from that,' he said, nodding at the leg being pushed through the door.

I had changed the body's proportions for ever. It no longer filled the space it should. The bone stuck out of the muscle and tissue, the end flat with deep red marrow and surrounded by the sharp white where I had mutilated it.

He told them that he was pleased so far but wanted to get everything closed up before anyone took a break. He asked for the rasp to remove the sharp edges I had left. And then the woman near the body's head told him something wasn't going according to plan.

'Al, I think he's crashing.'

'What? Why now, Sarah?'

'I'm not sure.'

'Is he going into arrest?'

'Just keep going, but you need to be quick.'

'Mike, irrigate now,' he said. 'Get as much bone dust and fragments out as you can. And let's check ligation quickly, release the tourniquet.'

One of them poured water over the wound and brushed the pearly mass with a hand. Someone released the tourniquet and the vessels showed red and pulsed. 'Looks good.'

'No, that one's split.' Blood seeped and then burst out in a sudden rivulet. 'Quick, tourniquet back on.' He worked rapidly and re-clamped the vessel, holding his breath as his hand shook.

'Well done, Al. Shall we rasp the sharp edges?'

'No time, Nadia. I'm going to perform the myodesis now. Drill.'

The drill next to me on the trolley was given to him. He placed it against the femur and drilled holes through the end of the bone.

'Sutures,' he said. They were handed to him, and he threaded them through the holes and into the centre of the bone. He passed the curved needle back through the holes so six lengths of thin white cord lay out across the table.

'Nadia, get the medial hamstring ready. I'm going to do it

straight away.' She used forceps to stretch a white band out of the tissue. The needle was squashed through the tendon and the white thread followed until the band was pulled tight across the end of the bone.

'Secure?' he said.

'Looks good,' she said.

'Sarah, how's he doing?'

'The quicker the better, Al. His cardiovascular system is stressed.'

They worked as quickly as they could. The rhythm of the machine faltered and the woman updated them with numbers and the body's condition.

They cut the excess tendon away and stitched a flap of muscle to it with tugs of the white cord that made the flesh wobble. The bone was covered now.

They pulled in other pink slabs of muscle and sutured them together, drawing the slippery mass around the bone. They discussed whether there was a good balance in the stump, if he would have good function. But she interrupted them and said he wouldn't have any function at all if they lost him on the table.

They started to stitch layers of flesh, using surgical staples to pinch the mess together. The stump took shape and the skin closed around it. They talked to one another as they worked together across the opening. There wasn't enough skin left to cover the whole of the wound, and wet areas remained along the thigh. He told them they would leave the wound open for now and graft once they were sure there was no infection.

When he was satisfied, he stood back and dropped slimy forceps on the trolley next to me. 'Right. Mike and Ben, bandage him up, pack the inner thigh where it's still open and place the drain for the negative pressure dressing there,' he said, pointing at the groin.

'Sure. Thanks for that, Al.'

'No problem, I think we've been lucky. Sarah, is he stable now?'

'He's been through the mill,' she said. 'He'll need monitoring.'

'Absolutely. I want him on wide-spectrum anti-fungals. I'm going to see the family now. I'll nip up to ICU as well to brief the team that he's coming back. Is everyone happy?'

They were wrapping the stump in gauze when a nurse wheeled the trolley I was on out of the room to a sink. She started to clean the implements around me. When she got to me, she removed my battery, pulled my blade out of its slot and started washing me. All my parts were disinfected and then placed on a draining board to dry.

Later, they came in and started to wash their hands.

'I don't think you're going to make that party after all, Ben.'

'I'm knackered anyway. You were right, Mike, I'm sorry.'

'It's just not worth taking the risk,' he said. 'Another long session. Through the twelve-hour barrier again.'

'I hope he'll be okay. Those infections are vile. I can still smell it. That's what I find most difficult, the way it seems to linger.' They dropped their purple-streaked scrubs in a clothes bin. 'Do you fancy a quick beer? We might get last orders.'

'Taking the leg off was the best option. It was buggered anyway.'

'Poor sod.'

'I'm due back on in the morning so I think I'll head home. You should see if Mandy's lot are still out.'

14

Aktar placed me in Latif's hand and his clammy fingers pressed around me.

'It is time now,' Aktar said. 'We laid this one during the sandstorm, do you remember?' He was sitting on a motorbike beside the road.

'The one beyond the crossroads at Sadiq's house?' Latif looked down at me.

'Yes, and the wire stretches along the ditch across the field. You will be hidden behind the wall. Follow this path for two fields and then along the water until it passes under the wall. You will recognise it.'

'You said they've been moving farther from the roads recently. What happens if they discover me?' His hand tightened around me.

'You will be fine, Latif. You'll be out of sight and far enough away. I am staying back here to keep watch. Ensure that you connect the battery once the infidels are directly opposite the broken water pump. You will be able to see their approach through the gap in the wall.'

'And I place the wires against each end of the battery?'

'Yes, and God willing you will destroy them. They are exposed here.'

'God willing.'

'You are ready, Latif. You are doing well. God is with us in every hour of our struggle. These men have no right to be here,' Aktar said. He was resting his hands on the fuel tank. 'I will wait with the bike on the high ground.'

'And what if their helicopters come?'

'Stay down and do not run, do not show yourself. The water in the ditches is deep, so you can submerge yourself as we talked about. Now, you must go before they get to the crossroads. You have done well, Latif. Hassan will be proud.'

Latif dropped me into his pocket and I rolled around as he moved. He walked normally and then we turned a corner and he started to slow. He slid down a bank and his feet sloshed through water. He lifted his thighs as the water deepened and I was submerged. Small bubbles seeped through the cloth around me. He put his hand down to check I was still there.

He stepped out of the ditch. His trousers clung to his legs and his trainers were suddenly heavier. He sat down, pulled me out and placed me upright on a flat rock so I wouldn't roll off. We were at the end of the ditch where it disappeared into a culvert under a mud wall. The wall had crumbled into slides of sand and rock. It once enclosed a small field but had collapsed and was now overgrown.

Latif dragged himself up to a vertical crack. Beyond it was a wide field, hazed green with the first shoots of a crop. A crossroads bounded the far corner, and trees shaded a gated house. The road extended from the junction and split the field in front of us. Twenty yards from the junction, the bent water pump cast a shadow across the packed road surface.

He knew it and remembered the day, a few weeks earlier, when Aktar had said the conditions were perfect and no one would see them through the storm. They'd been in high spirits, as half blinded by sand they dug up the road. They had reeled out the wire and pushed it down into the freshly ploughed field. Aktar had instructed them to feed the wire through the crack in the wall and cover the end with a round stone.

He found the stone now at the bottom of the wall and the length of wire sprang out from beneath it. The plastic sheath had been stripped away at the end to expose the copper. He moved me up to the crack and positioned me on a rock shelf. He lay on his stomach, rested his chin on his hands and waited.

The water sucked through the culvert beside us and a bird called from the trees at the edge of the field. He felt vulnerable in his cotton shirt; all he had was me. Every ripple of water or creaking branch sounded like approaching steps and he flinched and looked around. But the field was empty and nothing moved on the road. He wondered if Aktar had been wrong about the infidels' route. He felt tired and his eyes closed. He shook his head. He hoped they wouldn't come and couldn't imagine it happening the way Aktar had described it.

He heard the truck first. He craned his neck but the gap wasn't wide enough. And then he saw shadows pass over the dark trunks along the avenue of trees, and the unmistakable silhouette of their helmets and weapons and rucksacks, bristling with antennas. Excitement surged through him. He picked me up in his sweaty palm.

More of them gathered around the junction and the high cab of the vehicle crawled forward. But they checked every inch of ground and he had to wait. The shadow around Latif contracted and he grew hot and frustrated. He yawned. How could he be tired and bored, he thought, with death so close?

He checked behind him again and jolted in shock. Two of them were walking slowly along the broken wall. He gasped, then held his mouth shut. They were twenty yards away. He clenched his fist around me and slowly lowered his head flat, holding his breath, every muscle tensed. He heard one of them speak.

'Yeah, push on, mate, to the end of the field.'

It was a strange and foreign sound to him. They kept moving, disappearing behind the higher sections of wall and then coming back into sight.

Now there were four of them; he could hear the scuff of their boots and the sound of their machines. One seemed to look straight at him but carried on along the wall and he saw them push through foliage into the open field beyond. They were gone.

Latif slowly lifted himself up and looked at how close they'd been and wondered if they'd come back, or if more would follow. He breathed deeply and tried to control himself. His heartbeat shook his whole body and throbbed around me in his palm. He sat with his back against the wall and looked up at the sky and his hand relaxed. I slipped out into the grass. He wanted to sprint back to safety, but then thought of how angry Aktar would be; he thought of his violence. He twisted to look through the gap again and saw the men inching out from the crossroads towards the water pump.

Latif felt hatred now. He remembered Aktar, lit by the fire, saying they ruin the land and our systems, they unbalance us; that they are the infidel. And he thought of how well he'd been doing, how pleased Aktar had been. He remembered his family. He blinked the tears away, reached for me and turned back to the crack. His vision blurred and he wiped his eyes with his sleeve and saw them clearly. He clenched his teeth. God is greatest, he thought, and then whispered it aloud.

Four of them were spaced out in a square across the road, sweeping their detectors over the surface as if they were sowing seeds, searching for bombs. They looked like machines, encased in equipment and armour, with devices that let them see farther and weapons that could kill like magic. He thought of Aktar saying they did not fight fairly, that they were dishonorable, that they were not human.

The men moved forward and then one of them raised his hand and they all lowered themselves down until they were flat against the road. Latif watched as one of them started to dig down with his hands. He heard them calling to one another.

'Go firm there, Rifleman Plunkett. Anything, Mac?'

'Looks okay.'

Their foreign voices made them less real and Latif even angrier. 'God is greatest,' he said and pulled the wire towards me.

They hadn't found anything and they slowly stood up. The weight of their equipment made them clumsy. They approached the broken water pump and Latif felt a new rush and shivered. Aktar had said that if it was God's will, they wouldn't find the bomb. Their large vehicle pulled out from the crossroads to follow them. Latif saw the heavy machine gun on top rotate and was afraid; its barrel pointed straight at him and then swept on.

'God is greatest.'

They slowed. One of them approached the pump, stepped across the ditch to check around it and then knelt as the others continued down the road. Latif held his breath. They didn't stop. They kept moving past the water pump.

'God is greatest.'

And then they all knelt and the truck stopped only several paces short of the pump. He wanted it to be by the pump. Aktar had said we would damage them most if we destroyed the vehicle.

Another foreign soldier walked out from the truck and moved up to the four men. Their voices mixed with the rumble of the engine.

'Get up front, Rifleman Davies, and guide us through.'

'Will do,' a man called back.

The truck crept forward and the man stood in front, directing it down the road past the water pump with waves of his hands. It edged along with squeals of its brakes.

'God is greatest.' Latif's teeth were clenched as he pushed one of the copper wires against my cathode and held it there with his thumb.

'God is greatest,' he said again, concentrating only on the correct moment: when the large wheels of the truck rolled next to the pump.

The water still sucked through the culvert but Latif didn't hear it. He positioned the other wire above my anode.

'God is greatest.'

The vehicle jerked forward as the man beckoned it through where the road narrowed. And then it was over the pump and Latif said his prayer again, louder than he meant to, before pressing the wire down against my anode. I instantly created a circuit that ran through the wire under the field to the device, which erupted on the road.

In a silent flash, the truck was instantly replaced by a brown vertical smudge. A moment later the noise slapped through Latif's chest and he ducked. Sand and rocks slipped from the wall.

'God is greatest.'

He was breathing faster now and dropped me. The explosion was much louder than he expected and still reverberated across the countryside. He was shocked by its violence.

It took him a moment to realise there were other noises: the infidels shouting to one another through the confusion.

'Cover your arcs.'

'Plunkett? Davies, Davies? Rifleman Davies, are you okay?'

'Medic, medic. Get a fucking medic up here!'

Latif raised his head to look through the gap. A solid fog of dust drifted across the road and transparent shapes staggered through it. Bits of debris still fell on the field in front of him. As the cloud thinned, he could see the outline of the truck. One wheel was gone, he couldn't see where, and its front had been splayed upwards in shredded metal. It lay on its side, half in the ditch, crushing the water pump. The road was now a crater. Men ran up from the junction.

'God is greatest.'

Latif picked me up and slid back from the crack but paused when he noticed the body lying in the field. It must have been the soldier who'd been directing the vehicle. Latif looked closely. The explosion had thrown him towards us. His helmet had disappeared and it was hard to work out which parts were human and which machine. Then Latif glanced down and understood that a part of the man was even closer, resting on the soil right in front of him. Latif looked at it and was afraid for himself. He knew he had killed.

He dropped me into his pocket and ran.

Latif was breathing hard when he heard the sound of a motorbike and stopped. It was Aktar.

'Well done, Latif,' he said. 'Listen, one of their helicopters is coming. That means we have really hurt them.' There was the thump of distant rotors.

'I saw it,' Latif said between breaths. 'I saw that I hurt them.' He reached down into his pocket and grabbed me. He thought of the body lying in the field and the part of it, separated and even closer. Then he thought of the men who'd walked so close to him and he was scared again.

'Can we go now?' he asked.

'Have you still the battery?'

Latif passed me to Aktar.

'They nearly found me. I was almost discovered.'

'You did well. It was God's will. Tell me later.' Aktar looked down at me. 'Get on, the others are waiting.' And then he tossed me away.

I rotated end over end and plopped into an irrigation ditch. I sank into the silt at the bottom and started to corrode.

15

00000111100110l. Switched on. Initialised. I was in an olive-green day-sack. BA5799 crouched over me. He looked at my screen as I recognised the encryption and my digital display changed to the time and date and showed the downloaded frequency. I am designed to digitally network soldiers, and the tone from my headset indicated I was ready to communicate.

BA5799 looked up at the men around him.

'So, be ready to move at zero five hundred tomorrow. We'll meet by the gate, and keep the noise down: we want as much surprise as possible,' he said. 'Everyone should be happy with the changes to the plan. Those who need to radio-check, let's do it now.'

Some of the men started towards a row of tents in the corner of the camp.

'And stay hydrated,' he called after them.

We were on the helicopter landing site in the centre of an open area, surrounded by protective walls. It was dusk. One of the men jogged over to a football left by a wall and they kicked it to each other as they went back to their beds.

BA5799 pulled on my headset and positioned my microphone over his lips with two fingers.

'You ready?' he said. A handful of men knelt or stood around him; one nodded and BA5799 pushed my pressel. He spoke and I converted, encrypted and sent his voice: 'HELLO, THREE

ZERO BRAVO, THIS IS THREE ZERO ALPHA, RADIO CHECK. OVER.'

The other man's lips moved in his microphone. I received, decrypted and emitted it through my headset into BA5799's ear: 'THREE ZERO BRAVO, OKAY. OVER.'

'THREE ZERO ALPHA, OKAY. OUT,' BA5799 sent back and looked up. 'Thanks, Sarnt Dee,' he said. 'You good, Corporal Monk?'

'Still initialising, sir.'

'No problem. Has everyone got enough spare batteries? Likely to be a long one tomorrow.'

Soon all the radios around me had initialised. I sent and received until BA5799 was certain none of us were corrupted and our connections were clear. He thanked everyone and walked back through a gap in the blast walls to a small courtyard of compound walls.

He ducked under a washing line and entered a small room carved out of the wall. Inside were two green camp beds covered with mosquito nets. At the back of the room were empty ration boxes and two black grips, a pile of paperbacks and an out-of-date calendar. He dragged one of the beds out of the trapped heat into the evening air and sat down on it.

He leant his body armour against the foot of the bed and placed his helmet next to it. He opened his magazine pouches, tested the ammunition and picked up his rifle, pulled back the cocking handle and looked in through the breech. There was a bottle of water under the sleeping bag and he fished it out and drank. The first stars had appeared and he looked at them. Then he put the day-sack down and reached in with his thumb and finger to twist my switch. 100101011111100000.

000001111001101. It was colder and dark. My digital display read 0453 and my headset indicated that I had finished initialising. My microphone protruded from under BA5799's helmet. He pulled the drawstring on the day-sack and my body and spare batteries drew together with a bladder of water, a smoke grenade and a green plastic bag of ammunition.

He clipped the lid shut so my antenna stood upright, then swung the bag up onto his back and pulled the straps tight. My pressel was attached by his shoulder. He lifted his left hand up and depressed it. I emitted: 'ZERO, THIS IS THREE ZERO ALPHA, RADIO CHECK. OVER,' he said.

'ZERO, OKAY. OVER,' I received.

'OKAY. OUT.'

We were near the front gate. Heavy-wheeled vehicles had churned the ground to powder in deep trenches that led up to an opening in the wall, spanned by a spiral of concertina wire. BA5799 stood to one side of a single file of waiting men, all helmeted and weighed down by equipment. Weapons jutted from their shadows. Antennas and aerials swayed and night-vision goggles cantilevered off helmets. Cigarettes glowed and were thrown into the dust. A couple of men yawned and BA5799 walked along the line to the front. One said good morning to him; BA5799 recognised his voice and returned the greeting.

A squat man approached through the dark, holding his rifle down at his side.

'All ready when you are, sir,' he said, looking back at the line of men. 'Twenty-three including you.'

'Thanks, Sergeant Dee,' BA5799 said. 'How did you sleep?'

'I'll sleep when I'm dead, boss.'

'That bad?'

'Someone has to make sure we've got enough bombs and bullets.'

'I'll just log out with the ops room.' BA5799 activated me. 'HELLO ZERO, THIS IS THREE ZERO ALPHA, MY CALLSIGN NOW READY TO MOVE DOWN ROUTE HAMMER. OVER?'

I broadcast the metallic reply in his ear, 'ZERO, ROGER. JUST CLEARING WITH HIGHER. WAIT. OUT.'

We waited. BA5799 had been busy since he'd unzipped the mosquito net and tugged his kit on, but his nerves were surging now. He thought about the mission again: where he'd be and what else might happen, about his teams moving off down the corridors of his plan and what he needed to coordinate. He hadn't slept well and his eyes scratched as he blinked.

I received: 'THREE ZERO ALPHA, ZERO. YOU CAN MOVE NOW. OVER.'

'ROGER. OUT,' I sent. BA5799 puffed his cheeks and silently exhaled as we moved up to the front. He slotted into the line and tapped the shoulder of the man ahead. 'We're on, Corporal Carr,' he said.

The man in front nodded and whispered up the line, 'Pssst, Jez, good to go, mate.'

The concertina wire was pulled aside and the lead soldier disappeared around the wall and up onto the road. The next paused, then followed him out.

The line shuffled forward and each man waited before stepping through the gap. And soon they were all moving onto the road. Those in front had already spaced out into two staggered files. They were dark shadows against the pale road. BA5799 could tell each of his men by his gait. He smiled, then spun around and saw the single files lengthen as the rest of his platoon appeared behind him.

We passed the high watchtower at the corner of the camp and headed into the horizontal lines of landscape, receding into the night away from safety. It felt hostile, but this is what it's all about, BA5799 thought, the reason he'd joined up. His soldiers bristled with weapons and moved without orders. They knew the plan, what to do when the plan changed – they knew how to switch to sudden violence.

His breathing deepened under the weight of the kit and condensation formed on the gauze of my microphone.

Then the men in front knelt down, and the action rippled along the line until they were all static. They unbent metal detectors and moved into position so the first four were in a box formation. They started to sweep the detectors over the road. Behind him another team stepped over a ditch and disappeared into the dark fields. BA5799 flicked down night-vision goggles to watch them enact his plan.

It was slow work and the men in front were careful. If the detectors alarmed, they stopped and lay down prone so they could prod with rods or dig at the road with their hands. A band of light bled from the horizon and BA5799 could see his team across the field. They had turned and now walked parallel to the road we were on.

I was mostly silent but he sent updates of our progress as they passed buildings. I received terse acknowledgements. One team asked him if they could proceed through a derelict compound and I sent a message telling them to stay to the south of it.

We moved slowly over a bridge and BA5799 was relieved to have cleared the first obstacle. The land seemed less malevolent as the day brightened and light gave perspective to the shadows. We weren't alone: a group of farmers had appeared with the dawn. They leant on their tools and stared, then went back to work and ignored the soldiers. Another team pushed out, as BA5799 had demonstrated on the model, and he watched them move diagonally past the farmers towards a compound.

Only eight men were on the road now. The rest had dissolved into the fields, using ditches and hedges and crumbling walls for cover. BA5799 activated me to keep in contact with them and held a picture of their positions in his head.

The four men continued to wave their detectors across the road, which soon squeezed between two high-walled compounds. BA5799 was tense. The team slowed as they channelled through them, stopping at the smallest signal and scraping the ground with their fingertips, gently feeling for triggers or batteries or bombs. They swept up and down the vertical walls, knowing that danger could be hidden anywhere.

Another team moved around the buildings, checking them. Once they'd finished, one of the men walked over.

'All clear, sir,' he said. 'Don't look lived in.'

'Thanks,' BA5799 said and then he spoke into me. 'ZERO, THREE ZERO ALPHA, THAT'S ROUTE HAMMER UP TO LIMA THREE THREE AND THREE FOUR CLEARED. MY THREE ONE CHARLIE CALLSIGN NOW COMPLETE AT MIKE ONE THREE, GRID 824 463. OVER.'

'ZERO, ROGER. MANY THANKS, OUT TO YOU. HELLO, FOUR ZERO ALPHA, THIS IS ZERO, ACKNOWLEDGE. OVER.'

'FOUR ZERO, ROGER. MOVING NOW. OUT.'

The team ahead continued to sweep the road, and we were followed by four large-wheeled trucks, covered in armour and with small, thick windows in the cab. On top, a helmet barely showed behind heavy machine guns that scanned across the landscape. BA5799 watched them come down the route and hoped we hadn't missed anything that would detonate under their wheels.

The vehicles approached and then stopped. I received:

'HELLO THREE ZERO ALPHA, THIS IS FOUR ZERO ALPHA. I'M GOING STATIC HERE UNTIL YOU'VE CLEARED YOUR AREA. OVER.'

'ROGER, SHOULDN'T BE LONG NOW, TWO HUNDRED METRES OR SO TO GO. ARE YOU HAPPY WITH THREE ONE CHARLIE'S LOCATION AT MIKE ONE THREE? OVER,' I sent.

'YES, I'VE GOT VISUAL. OUT.'

'HELLO ZERO, TWO ZERO ALPHA, I'M LEAVING YOUR LOCATION NOW. OVER.' A new callsign had entered the network.

'ZERO, ROGER. OUT.'

Even though the milky sun was still large on the horizon, it was hot. BA5799 sweated into my headband and his ear was red in my plastic earpiece. On one knee at the edge of the road, he took a map from a pouch on the front of his body armour and pulled a GPS from his pocket. He looked up at the features around him and confirmed his position.

A few hundred metres ahead, trees lined the track to a crossroads where a gated building stood in one corner. Beyond, walls divided the fields into a maze of rectangles.

'Corporal Carr, you can stop there. This is the eighty-third easting,' BA5799 said to the man in front. 'Good effort. Once Six

Platoon are through, we'll move back and secure Lima Three Three.'

'Roger, sir.' The man looked relieved and turned to his team. 'Go firm, lads. Jez, that's far enough. Well done, mucker.'

BA5799 stood and gazed back down the road. Behind the vehicles, a line of soldiers floated on the mirages. 'CHARLIE CHARLIE ONE, THIS IS THREE ZERO ALPHA. ROUTE HAMMER NOW SECURE TO THE EIGHTY-THIRD EASTING,' he said into my microphone. 'ZERO, ACKNOWLEDGE. OVER.'

My emission was lost in the atmosphere and there was a distorted response: 'NO, SAY AGAIN, YOU'RE DIFFICULT. OVER.'

'ZERO, THIS IS FOUR ZERO. I RELAY. FROM THREE ZERO ALPHA: ROUTE HAMMER NOW CLEARED TO THE EIGHTY-THIRD EASTING. OVER.'

'ZERO, ROGER. THAT'S CLEAR. MANY THANKS; OUT TO YOU. HELLO TWO ZERO, ACKNOWLEDGE FOUR ZERO'S LAST. OVER.'

'ROGER, MOVING WEST ALONG HAMMER NOW. WILL LET YOU KNOW WHEN I'M IN POSITION. OUT.'

The truck's engine pulsed as they stopped beside us and men dismounted to fan out across the fields and surround the crossroads. BA5799 waved to the man up on the truck.

The man leant out and pulled an ear defender away. 'You didn't find anything, Tom?' he said over the engine noise.

'No, Dan. Most of the road's in sight of the camp, though.'

'True, let's hope it continues.' The man looked towards the junction.

A team of riflemen stepped down from the back of the truck.

'Morning, boss,' one of them said as he filed up to us. 'Our turn for a bit of tiptoe.'

'Morning, Rifleman Plunkett, we wouldn't want to hog all the fun,' BA5799 said, then walked back to the two buildings that straddled the road.

I continued to play transmissions in BA5799's ear as the other stations of the network pushed farther up the road. He arranged the men around the buildings and moved between them, talking them through the countryside in front and where they were in relation to one another. He used me to tell the network that his teams were now in position.

He knelt in an area of shade, drank from the tube over his shoulder and removed his helmet. His hair was matted against his skull and he scratched his scalp and adjusted my headband before clipping it back on. We waited. The sun was high, the air vibrating. He looked ahead at the platoon that was moving slowly through the junction, checking in ditches and sluices and spreading wide to clear the compounds. The trucks marked their progress as they followed. BA5799 was glad that his part of the task was done for now.

He walked between the men and joked with them. They talked about the operation and how long it was likely to take. He said he didn't know, but the logistics convoy had left and was now heading east.

He dropped into a ditch beside another man. 'You okay, Rifleman Johns?'

'Not too bad, boss. What do you make of that?' The man pointed over his machine gun, propped on its bipod in front of him. 'That geezer just rode down the road from the north.'

BA5799 held his rifle up and looked through the sight. In the distance a man sat upright and still on a motorbike. He wore a black turban and black boots that were planted on either side of the bike. His arms were crossed as he watched.

'Looks dodgy as sin,' BA5799 said.

'That's what I thought.'

'Keep an eye on him.' Then he pressed me: 'THREE ONE CHARLIE, THIS IS THREE ZERO ALPHA. OVER.'

'THREE ONE, SEND. OVER.'

'CAN YOU SEE THE FIGHTING-AGED MALE ON THE BIKE? OVER.'

'YES, JUST APPEARED FROM VICINITY OF OXFORD. HE'S UNARMED BUT HE'S WATCHING THE JUNCTION. ABOUT THREE HUNDRED METRES FROM MY LOCATION. OVER.'

'ROGER, KEEP EYES ON. OUT.'

BA5799 looked again through his sight at the figure framed in the black circle and swore under his breath. It could be nothing, he thought, but then he activated me again. 'HELLO, FOUR ZERO ALPHA, THIS IS THREE ZERO ALPHA, BE AWARE YOU'RE BEING WATCHED BY A LONE MALE IN THE VICINITY OF COMPOUND MIKE TWO FOUR. OVER.'

'FOUR ZERO ALPHA, ROGER. OVER.'

'THREE ZERO ALPHA, THE FARMERS IN MY AREA ARE ALSO MOVING AWAY, NOT GOOD ATMOSPHERICS. OVER,' BA5799 said, as he watched the farmers in the fields to his right.

'ROGER, NOT GOOD AT ALL. HELLO, ALL TWO ZERO CALLSIGNS, STAY ALERT, LOOKS LIKE WE'RE BEING WATCHED. OUT.'

BA5799 stood and walked up onto the road but the rifleman called back, 'He's buggering off, sir.'

BA5799 turned just as the man on the bike skidded his rear wheel around and a cone of dust lifted as he rode away. 'Keep your eyes open and give me a shout if he returns.'

BA5799 waited with a group of his men. They fidgeted in the heat and sweat dripped from their noses. He took off his day-sack, twisted a clip and replaced my battery. Somebody complained it was taking forever, and BA5799 said it would take as long as it took; this was a dangerous part of the operation.

He listened absent-mindedly to the messages I emitted as the other platoons used the network. BA5799 updated the men around him, telling them how Six Platoon had nearly cleared Cambridge and were starting up Hammer. He explained that the road narrowed beyond the crossroads and they had to direct the trucks through the tight sections. A soldier grunted about rubbish driving.

They ducked in unison at the bang. BA5799 looked around at the crossroads and saw the explosion mushrooming up into the sky. The sound echoed through the fields and a bird flapped away. They'd all heard explosions before, but one of them still cursed in the silence after it.

'Cover your arcs,' BA5799 said. 'And look for firing points, there could be follow-up.' He stepped onto the road, his hand poised over my pressel. There was nothing he could do; he was too far away. He hated this moment. He could hear the shouts of the men up the road, trying to make sense of the situation.

He wondered if anyone had been hurt. The blast site was still obscured by dust but men were beneath it, swallowed by the instant cloud and showered in debris – perhaps surrounded by twisted metal, their hearing pierced by a monotone ring and their breath punched out of them – perhaps worse than hurt. He hoped it had been a lucky escape, as it so often seemed to be.

And then I transmitted in his ear.

'ZERO, FOUR ZERO ALPHA, CONTACT IED. WAIT. OUT.'

BA5799 knew his friend's voice. From his tone, he knew they hadn't been lucky. And then an angry shout carried to him: 'Medic, medic. Get a fucking medic up here!'

Men ran through the dust to the stricken truck and pulled the rear doors open to help. BA5799 waited in silence with the men around him.

Then my speaker vibrated in his ear: 'ZERO, FOUR ZERO ALPHA, CONTACT IED ON VEHICLE TWENTY METRES EAST OF CROSSROADS AT CAMBRIDGE. LINE THREE: ONE CAT A, ZAP DA6721, AND ONE CAT B, PL9804. SUGGEST EMERGENCY HLS IN THREE ZERO'S AO. OVER.'

BA5799 watched the soldiers working on a body in the field, then turned to the men around him. 'Sounds like there's two casualties, fellas,' he said. 'One Cat A, one Cat B.' He stood up. 'Let's get ready to move. We need to secure the HLS.'

And then I was emitting again: 'ZERO, ROGER, HOW LONG UNTIL YOU CAN HAVE THE CASUALTIES THERE? OVER.'

'TWO ZERO, JUST WITH THE CASUALTIES NOW. WE'LL MOVE THEM BY VEHICLE. I RECKON IT'LL TAKE FIVE MINUTES. OVER.'

'CHARLIE CHARLIE ONE, MEDEVAC IN THE AIR.

EHLS AT THREE ZERO ALPHA'S LOCATION. THREE ZERO ALPHA, ACKNOWLEDGE. OVER.'

BA5799 pressed my switch again: 'THREE ZERO, ROGER. SECURING IT NOW. OUT.'

We jumped a ditch to run out into the field and I bounced around on BA5799's back. He was glad to have some influence on the situation, to have something to do. He beckoned to a group of men and told them to clear a section of field and they started waving their detectors over the ground. He shouted at a rifle-man to cover them, then spoke through me to the team at Mike 13, instructing them to fan out and secure the north edge of the landing site.

BA5799's face was livid beneath his helmet. He watched his platoon morph around the new area and his team commanders move into position. He dropped the day-sack off his shoulder and grabbed the smoke grenade, then swung me up onto his back and pushed my pressel. 'ZERO, THREE ZERO ALPHA, EHLS NOW SECURE, GRID 825 460, THREE HUNDRED METRES SOUTH OF MIKE ONE THREE, I'LL MARK WITH RED SMOKE. OVER.'

'ZERO, ROGER, RED SMOKE. OUT.'

One of the trucks drove down the road towards us. It rocked in the potholes and stopped.

'CHARLIE CHARLIE ONE, THIS IS ZERO, HELI ETA THREE MINUTES. THREE ZERO ALPHA, ACKNOWLEDGE. OVER.'

'THREE ZERO ALPHA, ROGER. OUT,' I sent.

They pulled a stretcher from the truck and carried it to the field followed by a man supported between two others, dragging his legs, his face pulled back in pain. They crouched there at the edge of the field, waiting. Someone readied the stretcher and another held a clear bag above it. BA5799 walked out into the open area and knelt down.

The sound of the helicopter was distant and then burst above us as the aircraft banked low over the field, its two rotors beating through the air. BA5799 pulled the pin from the grenade and it clicked and fizzed. He threw it onto the ground and powdery red smoke spurted from its base.

The helicopter circled up and around as the cone of red smoke built across the field. It reared its nose as it descended, slowing over the road and ditches. BA5799 watched it disappear inside the fountain of dust streaming towards us; the wind buffeted and then we were engulfed. He turned his head away as the downdraught curled the smoke up and the grass flattened and shimmered.

They hurried with the stretcher to the back of the aircraft, ducked below the rotors and passed it inside. The other casualty was helped up the rear ramp to the medical crew. Then they crouched into a huddle as the ramp began to close and the aircraft lifted away.

The grenade had left a dark red burn on the earth. It was quiet and the men walked back up to the road and down towards the junction.

The logistics convoy had to detour around the stricken truck and the crater blocking the road. I sent and received messages as they cleared the new route. One of them ordered BA5799 to spread his platoon more thinly. He moved some of his men up to the crossroads and we waited with them in the shade of the trees. They asked how bad the casualties had been. BA5799 said they'd have to wait for news from headquarters, but he knew it was bad from the way the stretcher-bearers had walked off as the sound of the helicopter had receded.

Farmers came back to the fields as the afternoon cooled. BA5799 felt safer with them close. It was dusk when the six logistics trucks wallowed down the potholed road and turned the corner at the crossroads. One of the men joked about meals on wheels and they all wondered if there was any post for them on board.

BA5799 pushed my switch: 'ZERO, THREE ZERO ALPHA, THAT'S THE CONVOY PASSING ME AT CAMBRIDGE. HEADING DOWN ROUTE HAMMER TOWARDS YOUR LOCATION NOW. OUT.'

That should have been the end of the mission but they struggled to lift the damaged truck from the ditch. BA5799 yawned as tiredness took hold. He had to change my battery again as we waited. One of the men pulled a foil packet from his day-sack and squeezed cold hotpot into his mouth, then offered some to the others. The setting sun bruised the sky and a man said softly that it was the end of another day in paradise.

Headlights from a vehicle cast long shadows from the soldiers who worked around the blast site, creating a small theatre of light in the dark. Their voices and the clank of metal carried as they attached cables and waved recovery vehicles into position. In a rush of activity, the broken truck was pulled out of the ditch. They hitched it up behind another vehicle and dragged it back to camp. As it passed the crossroads, BA5799 could see the warped front end and thought of the energy needed to twist and deform metal like that.

A message came through me that they should collapse back

onto the road behind the trucks. BA5799 watched the other platoons trudge past before he ordered his teams in and they followed the track marks. His men swayed with exhaustion as they walked home.

We entered camp through the gap. The logistics convoy was being unloaded and a forklift swivelled between the containers. His platoon gathered to one side and waited silently; their eyes were bloodshot and sweat had washed clean streaks down their dirty faces. They unloaded their weapons as a man told them what they needed to do in the morning, and finally they trudged off to their tents. BA5799 watched them go and felt hollow.

He lifted his day-sack off with a groan. 'We'd better go to the debrief, Sergeant Dee,' he said.

'That was a long one.' The man was looking at his watch. 'Nearly twenty hours. I'm just going to dump my kit and make sure they get their batteries on charge before they all hit their gonk-bags.'

'Sure, I'll meet you at the model.' BA5799 reached into his bag and felt for my switch. 100101011111100000.

16

You struggled with consciousness. The concoction of drugs played with your mind. Your body had been battered: infection had showered through it and all of it was compromised and weak. You'd been damaged again; by doctors this time. They'd had to do it to save you.

You didn't know this yet. They were trying to wake you up but you weren't ready. I hung over you. I'm a mix of red and white blood cells, clotting factors, plasma and platelets. Gravity fed my contents down a tube. It dripped through the cylinder flow-regulator and cannula, down into you to replace what you lost when they disfigured you.

I hung on a stand attached to your bed. Four of them were wheeling us along corridors to the intensive care unit, and one looked down at you and was worried. She told the others you were still delirious.

You mumbled. You weren't where they were: not yet in the hospital corridor with the strip lights pulsing above. You were on a table back in camp, and they were pushing you through your room and past the TV room and the dining room and the boot room, and then into a house where your family were waiting. Your friends – all the people you served with, all your brothers – were pushing you through the corridors and laughing at you and you laughed with them. But you were scared and wanted them to stop, but they wouldn't. You didn't want to play this game any more – it wasn't funny.

You mouthed words and then your head rolled from side to side and you furrowed your brow.

'Don't,' you said, 'please don't.'

Something was wrong but you were safe with your friends. And then there was another voice, coming from somewhere else and starting to penetrate. You couldn't understand that it was saying your name from above and telling you something – you knew it wasn't a friend.

'Tom,' it said, 'Tom.'

It was the woman pushing the back of the bed. I was next to her, swinging from a hook. She wore blue scrubs and had pulled her mask down around her neck.

'He's away with the fairies,' she told the nurses. 'Completely delirious.'

'What's he saying?' one of them said, as she pushed the front of the bed around a corner.

'Not sure. He's mumbling.'

'Well, it would be good if he looked less shell-shocked by the time we get to the ICU,' she said. 'His parents are waiting to see him.'

You looked hot below me and your face was greasy.

You could still hear them all laughing at you and you couldn't stop. You wanted to stop but you kept going faster and faster through the rooms.

'Tom, Tom,' the voice cut in again. 'Listen to me.'

You couldn't tell whose it was, but it was harsh and unfriendly.

'Tom, my name is Sarah, I'm a doctor. You have been blown up. You stepped on an IED. We've just had to amputate your second leg.'

This information hammered through you. You wanted to be back in camp, or anywhere else, but you knew it was true and you remembered. You opened your eyes. You were in the corridor and you looked up at them and the ceiling flashing past. You saw me suspended above you and the blurred tube connecting us. The doctor's upside-down head stared down at you. All your friends had gone.

'Tom, can you hear me?' she said and smiled.

You nodded below me.

'Do you understand?'

You nodded again.

They wheeled us through automatic double doors and we were in a ward where the bays were filled with beds and broken bodies and machines that winked above them. A nurse walked past with a kidney dish.

A man approached us.

'He's in this bay, over here,' he said.

We were wheeled next to the window. You were unconscious again when the nurses started to plug you into new machines. They placed a plastic peg on your finger and stuck round elec-trodes to your chest. The machine above faltered and then charted your heart. One of the nurses looked at the displays and noted the readings in a file. Another squeezed me.

'Still on blood?' she said.

'Dr Pearson wants him to have one more after this,' the doc-tor who brought us in answered. 'And also get him started on AmBisome, for the fungal infection.'

'Has that been added to his prescription?'

'Should be. I'll check. He'll need monitoring. It was touch and go in surgery earlier.'

'We heard.'

Soon only one nurse was left adjusting the machines. Then she went too and you were on your own. I was still above you, feeding into your arm. You mumbled once but were mostly still.

The nurse came back with a man and a woman. They stood by the bed and looked down at you, then glanced at me and the digital displays behind. They were worried but relieved you were back.

They saw where the doctors had worked on you and marvelled at the change. Then they looked at your face and smiled, even though you had no life in your skin. The nurse told them the plan: the new medications you were on, and how you would be monitored until they were sure the infection had been managed. She pointed at me and said I was just a precaution to get you back up to speed. She explained they could talk to you, that you'd been conscious since surgery.

The woman put a red handbag on the windowsill and reached for your hand.

'Tom,' she said, 'Tom? It's okay now. We're here.'

You didn't move and they pulled up chairs and waited. The man went to get a drink of water and came back and they sat together. They were gazing across the ward staring into space when you came round and spoke.

'I'm hot,' you said and tried to lift away the blanket. 'Can I have some water?'

She looked down at you and smiled.

'Hello, Tom,' she said. 'It's us.'

'How are you feeling?' the man asked.

'I'm really hot.'

'I'll go and find you a nurse.'

When he left you looked at her and smiled. You still felt odd. Worse than the other times you'd come out of surgery. She smiled and told you it would be okay now.

He returned.

'Someone's just going to get you something, Tom,' he said. 'You've been through the wars again, I'm afraid.'

'Sorry,' you said.

'Don't be silly. The doctors reckon it's all for the best. You're back in intensive care as a precaution, just until the infection's gone.'

'He never should've gone up to that other ward,' she said. 'Not with that infection.'

He placed a hand on her arm. 'Well, they've caught it now,' he said.

'How are you?' you asked them, but closed your eyes and slept.

I was nearly empty when you woke. They were still there and you smiled at them and the man held the plastic cup to your mouth. A nurse came over, asked if you wanted to sit up and helped arrange the pillows behind you.

You felt disembodied. Everything was somehow abstract. You looked down and they watched your reaction. You saw where the blue thermal blanket dropped down flat to the mattress. There was no longer the bulge of a foot. With your knee gone it was shorter than the other leg. It shocked you, but it wasn't you yet and you smiled at them and said you were all right.

'It was very badly damaged anyway, Tom,' the man said. 'You'll probably be more mobile this way.'

'And we spoke to Dr Pearson,' she said. 'He said you'll have no problems with prosthetics. They were very pleased with the operation.'

You slept again. She left and he stayed all night and watched you, willing you to get better. A nurse told him he should go in the morning. When you woke you looked around. You'd been here before but it seemed different. It was sunny outside and the window was full of green leaves. The tree was in the corner of a breezeblock courtyard. A man was loading cages of laundry into a van among the central-heating pipes. There was a green and pleasant land out there, you thought, but it felt very far away.

You looked at where you now finished. You would never feel a foot on the floor again, but it didn't matter yet. Somehow you knew you were still on the edge, you needed to survive and feet didn't matter. You just needed to endure. You looked at a passing nurse and hoped they would protect you from the pain or getting worse and having to have more cut away.

I was empty; my plastic walls had collapsed together and red showed only around my seals. The rest of the blood I'd carried since a young man donated it after a lecture, joking with a mate in the queue, was now in you.

17

Aktar looked down at me and thought about the boy: Latif would be useful if he survived. But he needed praise. Not like the others, who understood already. Latif was preoccupied with his family and cared too much about what they thought. Like so many in this land, he was too concerned with honour.

Well, at least the boy was doing his will. He was expendable, like the one last season. That boy had been useful while he lasted. If Latif survived, he might learn to forget and give himself to the cause.

He looked down at me again, his deep eyes shadowed in his hard face. A loose end from his black turban was wrapped around his neck. My display read 12:08.57. I am a digital watch. Made in Thailand. I'm water-resistant and my stainless-steel back rested against the fine black hairs of his wrist.

He crossed his arms and peered at the junction. He could see them moving up the track, waving their detectors. He knew more of them would be hidden in the ditches. There was a group near the two empty dwellings by the road. He had also laid a bomb there but it hadn't detonated. Maybe the trigger was broken or a wire had come loose. Then a man walked right past where it was buried. Why wouldn't it go off?

At least Latif could trigger the one by the water pump. He saw another infidel in the ditch behind a machine gun. They would be watching him.

The phone buzzed in his pocket. He reached to get it, read the message and looked towards their camp. More infidels were moving down the Nalay road. The farmers had started to leave the fields. Having seen us on the bike, they knew what was coming.

Family and tribe and politics would be our undoing. And he thought about his father returning to their house in the mountains. It was the only time he remembered seeing him. He had hidden behind his mother. His father's cloak had snow on it and he'd leant his gun next to the door. Aktar couldn't decide which to stare at: his father or the rusty rifle propped against the wall.

And then he had gone. He never saw his father again but a man had come to speak to his mother and she had sobbed. He hadn't known what to do, so he went to play with his friends. That was a different war, but it was the same fight. Maybe his mother was now dead too. It didn't matter.

One of the infidels on the road had lifted his weapon and was pointing it at him. He knew they wouldn't shoot: he was unarmed. He smiled at their rules. The soldiers were constrained as long as they weren't threatened, but they could also bring death suddenly in the night. It was so hypocritical.

He glanced at me again – 12:21.23 – and then held the handles of the bike. He looked over at the crossroads. They were getting closer to the water pump. He prayed they wouldn't find the bomb. He'd been careful making it and used his best materials.

Something glinted. The infidels were moving in the field where Latif would be. The boy could be replaced but he hoped they wouldn't find the wire. And then he noticed men nearer to him and he was surprised they were so close, lying on top of a building and watching him. He was scared when he saw their foreshortened barrels and the radio aerials.

Then he calmed himself. They wouldn't attack him if he wasn't a threat.

It was nearly time. He would like to see the infidels being sent to hell, but once the bomb went off they would be jumpy. Their rules always changed and bent once they were attacked.

I was over the red petrol tank and he twisted the key. He kicked down and the engine started. His fingers released the lever in front of me and the rear wheel skidded around. The wind sang around me as we rode away. He rocked the handle-bars from side to side to avoid potholes and the suspension sucked and hissed below me as the wheel mapped the rough track. His turban flapped out behind us.

In a gap between houses he caught a glimpse of the junction, then it flashed into view again with the truck. They were nearly there. Go on, Latif, he thought.

Suddenly he heard it over the sound of the bike and the dust cloud rose above the bushes we sped past. He muttered, 'God is greatest,' and hoped that it had damaged them. He was thankful for how good the new equipment was from across the border. He wondered if Hassan would be pleased.

We rode on and turned down beside a wall onto a single track and his tendons tensed next to my strap as he pulled the lever. We stopped. He let the engine idle and twisted his wrist to glance at me. I displayed 12:32.02. He waited for gunshots or shouts but it was quiet. And then the boy Latif came around the cor-ner, breathing hard. He stopped, put his hands on his knees and looked down at his trainers.

Aktar smiled at the boy.

'Well done, Latif,' he said. 'Listen, one of their helicopters is coming. That means we have really hurt them.' He checked me again and thought how quickly the helicopter had arrived.

'I saw it,' Latif said, looking up. His face was pale. His top lip had the fuzz of first hair. 'I saw that I hurt them.' He glanced back down the track. 'Can we go now?'

'Have you still the battery?' Aktar held out the arm I was on and the boy passed him a battery.

'They nearly found me,' Latif said. 'I was almost discovered.'

'You did well. It was God's will. Tell me later,' Aktar said. 'Get on, the others are waiting.' He looked down at the battery in his hand and then threw it into a ditch.

We rode away. Latif's arms were clasped around Aktar's waist and the wind and the engine noise rushed around us. We stopped and Aktar stepped from the bike to feel around under a pile of dried poppy stalks beside the road. Their ends scratched against my face. He pulled out a radio and the weapon that I was so used to being next to. He handed the gun to Latif and switched on the radio.

'Paugi, Paugi, are you there?' he said into it and looked at the boy. 'Do not worry, Latif. They will not follow us this far.'

'Hello, Aktar, is that you?' the radio crackled faintly.

'Yes, we are leaving the funeral now. You should leave too,' he said, then held the radio to his ear so I was by his neck.

'Yes, I am leaving too. I saw the cloud. It looked successful.' The voice was excited.

'Yes, God gives victory to the holy warriors.'

When Aktar next glanced at me, it was dark and my face reflected the blue flame of a stove. We were in a room with tiled walls and men sitting all around him, cross-legged or relaxed on mattresses. He told them that it was time to change lookout, pointed at one of them and ordered him to go.

'But it's Latif's turn,' the man said. He wore his woollen hat far back on his wide forehead.

'Not tonight. You go.'

'I'm always doing it, Aktar,' he said, and the other men laughed.

The boy was in the corner, grinning nervously as they congratulated him again.

The men went to sleep and Aktar took me off and rubbed his wrist where my strap had left a sticky indent. He placed me next to the rifle and lay down on the mat.

The first time he had seen me was when Hassan had taken me from the lifeless wrist of my previous owner and handed me to him. It had taken Aktar a while to understand how I worked, but he had needed to know if he was to command.

He checked me one last time, pressing my light button so I glowed 21:47.34 at him.

The men's breathing whistled around the room. He stared at the ceiling and thought of his trip into the mountains last winter and how proud he was that the council had picked him. The hardships in the training camp had changed him. Everything he learnt had set him apart from these men: they looked up to him now. He took pride in that, and hoped Hassan knew everything he had achieved with them.

He remembered Hassan's anger; the workbenches where they learnt to mix explosives; the cold and the puffs of snow when they missed their targets; the whooping and joking with other students once he detonated his first bomb. He thought of feeling jealous for not being considered the best – he would make up for that now. And then his breathing settled and he slept.

18

He took me from the top of the day-sack. He'd kept me there because he thought there was a chance I might be good luck. I had been there for a while and had flattened. The last time he'd used me, he'd poured ammunition into me in a rush.

He pushed me open and looked at the faint words, *TOM BARNES*, that he'd drawn on my lining. He had used Tipp-Ex to write it after I'd been given to him at the end of training. He pulled me onto his head, smoothed my side down flat and adjusted my cap badge above his left eye.

He was sitting in a small room on a Z-framed camp bed. Attached to it was a domed mosquito net. The other man in the room found his one of me in a grip and pulled it on.

They walked through a courtyard and across the camp. The hot afternoon sun pressed down on my green wool. We went under a camouflage net raised on poles and out into an open area enclosed by the perimeter of the base. To one side vehicles and trucks were parked in rows on the oil-stained sand.

Men gathered. They had kicked up a cloud of dust that hung at knee level. Slowly they found their positions, forming three sides of a square as commanders quietly jostled them into straight lines. Most of them wore berets like me, with the cap badge of a bugle over the left eye.

We stood apart from them. He adjusted me on his head and

waited, his eyes squinting against the low sun.

A padre walked up to the open side of the square and looked at the three blocks of formed men. Crosses were sewn on his collar and a dark cloth hung over his shoulders and down the front of his camouflaged uniform.

He spoke to them of remembrance and loss, and said they should pray. He told them about a conqueror of death, here in their time of need, who in the presence of death comforts those who mourn.

I tilted forward as he listened to the padre. He wanted to remember and to register the loss but he didn't feel anything. He inched his head up and looked at the men across the square, friends of the man who'd died. They could feel it; he could see it on their faces. He didn't want the loss to weaken him, though, couldn't let himself imagine it was something that might happen to him. That would paralyse him.

The padre continued talking and his mind drifted and he thought about the patrol tomorrow, how best to tell them the plan during orders. His men were doing well but he didn't want to let up on them; it was too soon and they still had so much to achieve.

They were told to pray together and my leather band flexed around his skull as he mouthed the familiar words. He knew the prayer without thinking and the words hummed out along with those of the men around him.

He wondered if they would encounter the enemy tomorrow; he wanted to be tested and he imagined fighting along a ditch and overcoming them. He was jealous of the platoons that had seen more action. He needed his men to be the best, his platoon to be the most respected.

Now the padre was talking about the man who had died, and

he wanted to feel sad but instead felt empty. He didn't care. All that mattered was scrawled on the orders sheet in his pocket.

The padre finished talking and a man standing to one side lifted a bugle to his lips and played a piercing tune they all knew. His hand jerked up and the end of his second finger touched my wool and he held it there in a salute. The bugle sounded again and they all started to walk away.

As we headed back towards the camouflage netting, someone asked if he wanted a brew. He took me off and sat beneath a tarpaulin on a wooden plank behind a table. He folded me in on myself and laid me on the plastic table cover. They talked and sipped from metal mugs. The sky turned orange and he thought how much like a hotel by the Mediterranean it was. Soon they were playing cards.

Later, after they had boiled foil bags of food and poured Tabasco into them, after they'd passed a satellite phone around so each of them could walk to a private corner of the camp and call home, he went to the room and zipped me back in the top of his day-sack. He hoped he wouldn't have to take me out again.

19

There were three nurses over you, looking down and smiling. They'd worked around the bay and now it was your turn. One of them talked to you about how you were feeling and what the weather was like. Another said your parents would be back at eleven. They joked and you laughed with them about how one of the nurses had dented her car that morning. The laughing hurt.

One of them dissolved colourful pills into a pink slurry and squirted it from a syringe into a feeding tube that looped into your nose and down to your stomach. You felt the chalky liquid inside you.

I went into you too. I fed into your penis and up your urethra to your bladder. They had pushed me inside when you were unconscious. That was in another country. You were very ill then. They inflated my balloon in your bladder and it held me tight. Your urine trickled out down my silicone tube and collected in a bag at my other end. The bag was replaced every time it was full.

If it wasn't for me, you'd be lying in a patch of your own piss.

The nurses pulled the sheets from you and started to wash you with flannels. Tender but efficient, they started with your face before washing around the dressings that covered your stumps and your arms and your left hand. They washed under your armpits and then held me up and washed around where I entered you. You could feel me, solid and foreign down its middle. You weren't embarrassed: there was no other option.

Two of them lifted one side of you, then the other, and washed your back. They pulled away the old clammy sheet and replaced it. You grimaced and one asked you if you were okay and said it wouldn't be long. You breathed through clenched teeth as the pain seared from your stump. They pulled the fresh sheet beneath you and tucked it under the mattress.

Another attached a bag of brown food to a hook above and the sludge started to slip down the feeding tube through your nose. They checked where the cannula entered a vein in your arm and pushed the plunger on a syringe to give you more relief. They passed you a glass of water and your hand shook as you craned your neck forward to drink. Before moving on, they hooked up a bag full of bright yellow drugs that dripped into you to stop an infection from taking hold. It made you feel horrid.

You thanked them.

They went to the next bed, talking to one another but not joking any more. Whoever was in that bay wasn't conscious and the curtain stayed closed. You'd been like that when they first cleaned you.

You looked out the window. The air couldn't hold the heat of summer and the clouds were piling up, it would rain and perhaps thunder. But you fell asleep. Your mother and father came later, your brother was with them too. You woke up and talked with them. After a while, your parents went for coffee and said they were seeing one of the doctors at twelve.

Your brother pulled up a chair between you and the window and said, 'How are you, Tom?'

'Fine, thanks. Slightly painful today,' you told him.

'Where?'

'Don't worry, it's nothing.'

'Let me see if I can get someone.' He looked around the bay.

'Honestly, it's nothing.'

You watched him; he'd become so determined. He knew everything about your injuries, every medical term, everything they planned to do to you, what it meant and what the outcomes would be, every last percentage, and he wouldn't let the doctors and nurses rest or not give a straight answer. You loved him for it.

'Please, David. I'm fine. It'll pass.'

'Won't be long,' he said and went for help.

A nurse came back with him.

'Are you okay, Tom?' she said.

'I'm slightly uncomfortable. My leg hurts, and my back. I'll manage, though.'

'I've told you before, Tom, this isn't an endurance test. No one's judging you on how much you can tough out. You don't need to be in any pain.' She was smiling while studying your notes. 'The pain is optional, and if I were you, I'd opt for none.'

She gave you something, you didn't really register how but it wrapped around you and the pain went and it was wonderful. She said she might have given you a bit more than she should and winked.

Your brother told you about the family and how everyone was thinking of you. You told him about the future and what you would achieve. The drugs gave you confidence and you talked to him about where you'd been and what it had been like.

The drugs made you sway from euphoria to nausea. They'd separated you from your body; it was unnatural but better than the pain. The energy that let you talk was suddenly gone and you needed to sleep, so your brother left.

The bag hanging at the end of me was full, and while you slept a nurse came to unplug it and attach a new one. I'd been in you for three weeks now, during all your surgeries, when they washed your wounds and cut more of you away. Afterwards, I had been wiped clean of blood and bone dust.

When you next woke, the ward was quiet. You were uncomfortable and looked out of the window. You tried to move but the muscles you strained were either damaged or fixed in new, unnatural positions. Some were severed, others didn't exist any more and synapses fired at nothing. Shocks speared back from the confusion of cut nerve endings among the trauma. You lay still as your foot was peeled open and salt was poured in and you looked down at the empty space of flat blanket where the pain bolted from.

You waited for it to pass. You could feel me snaking from your groin across your abdomen and you counted the cords and pipes that fed in or out of you, each one invading your sense of self. You would die in a sloppy pool of your own excrement and agony if you weren't plugged into this wall of machines, if we weren't here to take away discharge and feed the drugs and medicines into you. You understood how completely dependent you were.

While you'd slept, someone new had been brought into the bay. He was conscious and sitting up as his family and the doctors talked tenderly to him. They surrounded him and you watched them. White cotton pads were taped over his eyes and his head swept from side to side in disorientation. His family seemed worried and the doctors tried to explain.

Later, after the physiotherapist had told you how to squeeze a rubber ball with your only undamaged limb, after your parents had given you a cold yogurt, the lights were dimmed in the ward.

The man who had just arrived was silent but upright, leaning against a stack of pillows. You wondered if he was asleep. And then he moved.

'Colonel, is that you?' he said. 'I'm going, Colonel.'

He moved his head and you watched him and wondered who he was talking to.

'Are you okay, mate?' you said. But your voice was still damaged and he didn't hear you.

'Zero Alpha, this is One Zero Delta, I'm moving. Over,' he said. His head rolled. He chopped his arm down.

'Where are they? No, don't. Don't do that,' he said and was quiet for a while.

You pressed your help button and a nurse came over.

'You okay, Tom?' she said.

'That new bloke has been saying a few odd things to himself.'

She looked over at him. 'He's been a bit confused since he got here, poor thing.' She walked over and rested a hand on his arm. 'John, it's Mel, I'm a nurse—'

'What? Get back,' he said and lashed out blindly. She moved away.

'John, it's okay. You're safe now. You're in hospital in England.'

'I need to get to the patrol base.'

They tried to calm him down but drugs and trauma kept him from the truth. They asked if you'd talk to him. You tried to call across the bay but your voice wouldn't carry. They released the brakes on your bed and wheeled you over to him.

I hung down between the beds. He had one of me as well and you talked to him above us.

'John, my name's Tom,' you said.

'Who's that?' he said. 'I need to speak to the colonel. Something's gone wrong.' The white pads stared past you.

'I know, John. Can you hear me?'

'I don't know you. I must speak to the colonel. It's dreadful. We must get back or he won't make it.'

'I know. I'm Tom Barnes. I'm a captain. Do you understand?'

'Yes,' he said.

'Okay. Listen to me. You've been injured. Do you realise that?'

'Yes.'

'You are home now, John. You've been flown back,' you said. 'We're in hospital.'

'I understand,' he said. His head had dropped.

'The colonel isn't here. But everyone's helping you now. You're safe. Do you understand?'

'Yes. Thank you, Captain Tom,' he said. There were red pockmarks across his face and his lip was held together by black stitches. 'I'm sorry. I was just confused.'

'No worries, John. I'm injured too. They give us ketamine and other drugs that can make you see strange things. It's not real. You're safe now. I'm just across the ward from you. Give me a shout if you want to talk.'

The nurses wheeled you back and mouthed thank-yous and smiled. It had exhausted you.

In the morning they replaced my bag again and washed around your penis, holding me out so it was like a piece of meat on a skewer. You marvelled again at the deep purple bruise on it and wondered how much that must have hurt.

The doctors came and stood at the end of the bed to discuss you. It felt odd being below them, their notepads open as they talked about your injuries. You were flat and helpless and not part of it. One of them said you would be moving back up to L4 soon. You were ready; they were just waiting for a bed.

The man on the other side of the room was asleep when they came for us. They wheeled us through the corridors and my bag, half full of your piss, swayed beside the bed. People were moving around the hospital, normal people who'd come in through the front door: a decrepit man heading for a cigarette, rolling a drip beside him; a fat woman in a wheelchair complaining to a nurse, she was quiet when she saw you; and a bald child who never stopped staring. You felt odd being among people who noticed you were different.

We waited in the lift and then were in the new ward. We had been here before; you'd been very dehydrated and the urine that passed along me had been brown. You'd been in pain and they hadn't realised how ill you were. That was before they had to cut away your remaining leg. I'd been there for that.

We were taken to a bay where four men were sitting on their beds or in wheelchairs. The nurses pushed you to a free space in the corner. One man was missing a leg and his stump was so short it didn't cover the cushion he sat on. He's had it bad, you thought.

You were introduced to each of them and they all said hello. One said they'd been waiting for a double amputee to come to their bay. He said between them they had five legs and eight arms, they were now beating bay 4. You smiled.

During visiting hours, the ward filled with people; friends and family of the other men. They all introduced themselves and said they were happy to have a new member of the team. They offered fruit and sweets and magazines. A shiny helium balloon floated over one of the tables.

But then nurses hooked the yellow bag of drugs to you again and it flushed through your blood and made you feel desperate. The light was too bright and the noise too loud. Your father was there and you asked him to close the curtains. You listened to the throb of voices and laughter from behind the blue curtain as you sweated and waited for the side effects to pass.

I stayed in you for another week. We went down to theatre for more surgery and you were knocked out again by anaesthetic. They smiled down at you and you joked with them as they held the gases over you and told you to count to ten and you were obliterated before you got to four. Once more, they opened your bandages and were happy that the infection had disappeared; they stripped layers of skin from your thighs and applied them over open raw wounds. These grafts took and the doctors were pleased with your progress.

A nurse came and said it was time to take me out. You sat up and watched as she deflated my balloon, which collapsed in your bladder. She held your penis out straight, pulled, and I scratched down your urethra causing a sharp pain. You flinched, sucking your stomach in, and finally I was free.

20

A man came up the aisle I was in looking at his phone. He wanted me but hadn't spotted me yet. He stopped to type a message into his phone and put it away in his jacket pocket. Then he saw me, reached up and lifted me off the hook. He found the can farther down the shelf. He went to the counter and paid, and I was in a plastic bag with the can as he walked out of the shop.

When he took me out of the bag, he was sitting by his son's bed and he put me on a table. A blue curtain surrounded them. It was quiet, the lights dim.

'How are you, Tom?' he said.

'I'm fine,' his son said. 'So, how are we going to do this?'

'I'll just go and get some towels and an extra pillow. I'll find a nurse.' He stood up and pushed the curtains apart.

'Don't get thrown out, Dad.'

'No chance. Visiting hours are a bloody nuisance.'

When he came back, he propped his son's head up and pushed a pillow under his neck. 'It's about time, Tom. You look like you've been boozing for a month,' he said. He picked up the can next to me and squirted foam into his hand.

'I feel like I've been boozing for a month,' his son said.

'And your grandparents are visiting tomorrow,' he said as he spread the shaving foam on his son's face with the flat of his hand.

'Yup, we don't want to give them too much of a shock,' his son said. 'No legs and a beard – I'm not sure they'd know where to look.'

'Quite.' He pushed the foam over the chin and up to the ears, then wiped his hands on a towel and picked me up. He dunked me into a plastic mug of hot water and rattled me against its sides. 'Right, hold still, Tom.'

'I'm not going anywhere.'

He held me over the face. It was bent backwards so the neck was exposed. And then I was against his skin and pulling across him, cutting through bristly hairs on his neck that caught in the white soap, collecting on my blades.

'How's that?' he said. I was in the cup again and the hairs washed off me.

'Fine. Feels quite nice actually.'

He used me to clear tracks in the foam and cut the beard away, curving me carefully around the hollows and contours of his son's jaw. He looked down at him and thought how much thinner he seemed – how sickly, disappearing in front of them. The yellow bag of drugs hung beside him, dripping through the needle in his arm. The man knew it was saving his son from infection and he needed to endure it. He would never be the same again and he was terrified about his future and wondered how long they'd need to care for him.

He gently moved his head to one side and then swept me down his cheek before rinsing me in the cup again. God, he was glad it hadn't been worse. They were lucky to have him; he was himself, he could talk, he could see. Unlike some on the other wards. As awful as it was, he thought, they still had him.

'Are you sure I can't get you anything more to eat?' he said.

[134]

'Thanks, Dad, I'm fine.'

'Hold still.' He flicked me down in short strokes along the top lip.

'Adam had a burger brought in today, but it didn't make me want one. I think it's the AmBisome.' His son looked at the bag of yellow drugs. 'The doctors say it's like Domestos.'

'No wonder it makes you feel so shit.' He pulled me down the other side of the face. 'How high do you want these sideburns?'

'Not too high.' His jaw moved below me as he spoke. 'The doctors say I've got to be on it for another week.'

'Stick with it, Tom.'

He dropped me into the cup and the foam and hairs floated off my blades. He took the towel and dabbed his face dry. 'Clean as a whistle,' he said.

'Thanks. It feels good.' His son raised a hand from below the covers and felt his chin.

'I'd better get going. It's gone ten,' he said. He shook me in the cup and left me with the can in a small cupboard by the bed.

'Night, Dad.'

21

I am a Camp Cot, Folding. My NSN is 7105-99-383. I was one of the first to arrive at the base. They unloaded me from an ISO container and threw me in a pile with all the others. Around us, an excavator was filling protective walls with rubble and helmeted men erected antennas by a command post. A watchtower was being constructed on top of an old building.

The camp expanded and a line of tents sprouted along a wall as more men arrived. When helicopters landed, the world turned brown and a thin layer of dust collected on me. The new men were issued kit from the piles and I was picked up and carried to a small room cut into the wall of an old courtyard. A man unfolded me and my canvas stretched taut on my aluminium frame. He attached a dome that held a mosquito net to my four corners. This was the first man I ever supported.

I was used as a goal. I was blown over by the downdraught of helicopters. My legs sank into the mud when the rains came.

After a few months he left and another man replaced him. This one stayed longer. During the months he slept on me, he became lighter and his skin more deeply tanned. Time dragged for him and nerves kept him awake towards the end, when he was so close yet couldn't imagine being safe.

The next man landed in a helicopter, came into the room and dumped his kit beside me. Then the camp was attacked and he ran out to help. Like the others, his days followed a pattern of shifts, meals and attacks. He pulled on his heavy body armour, day-sack and helmet, and walked out with his rifle and was gone for hours. When he came back he was hot and elated or exhausted.

Men nudged him in the night and told him it was his turn to man the ops room. He would sit up on me and push his feet into flip-flops, sigh and walk across the dark courtyard.

He sometimes slept on me during the day, when it was so hot he sweated the shape of his body into my canvas. After he woke, he wrapped a green towel around his waist, filled a red tub and stood in it, pouring water over his head with a mess tin.

When it became even hotter and the room was an oven, he dragged me out into the courtyard and slept under the stars. Sometimes he couldn't sleep and hooked earphones in and looked up through the gauze netting at the sky.

There was another bed like me in the room. His friend slept in that one. When their shifts overlapped, they chatted and laughed, read their post to each other and shared food from parcels. Once he returned and two camel spiders had been dropped on top of me and were crawling over his sleeping bag. He told his friend how funny he was and said he'd get him back.

In the room around me, cardboard boxes were stacked and ripped open. The men delved into them and chose foil packets they took away to eat.

He sat on me and stripped his rifle down to clean it and the gas parts left oil marks on me. He checked and replenished his ammunition. Sometimes he zipped the net closed to make me his private space. He lay on his sleeping bag with a head torch on and read a book.

*

One night, after he had been busy all day and his skin was grimy and he was too exhausted to wash, he removed his combat boots and socks and let his white feet expand and cool on me. He thought about the patrol he'd just finished as he looked up at the endless stars.

He wondered if his men could have outflanked them and he relived pulling the trigger and the puffs as his rounds had slammed into the compound in the distance. The sound of metal travelling through the air filled his head again: the fizzing of ricochets; everyone gasping for breath after he'd sprinted and thrown himself into cover.

He thought about what he'd said on the radio, how he'd commanded his platoon, how he'd described the situation to Zero. He could still hear his men's shouts amidst all the confusion. He remembered crouching in the ditch and trying to work out what was happening, trying to piece the battle together. The enemy had disappeared. He should have followed and caught them but he chose to be cautious since air support was on its way.

He put his hands under his head and against me. There was still dirt between his fingers.

He couldn't stop it all going around in his head. It had been a chance to be bold, to close and kill – but they'd disappeared into the fields and trees among the confusing compounds. He imagined himself being brave among the tight walls and neutralising them at close quarters, leading his men relentlessly forward.

He thought of the jet flying over and the thrill as it disintegrated the wall and one of his men whooping from along the ditch. He replayed everything as he should have fought it, decisively and without hesitation. He promised himself that next time he would.

And then these thoughts merged into details of tomorrow's mission. And he was back out in the network of fields, moving between other houses and locals, and he tried to decide how best he should clear the area. He had so little time to prepare; he'd have to give orders early and his men were exhausted already. He was overwhelmed by it and he reached for his alarm clock to set it an hour earlier. And then he remembered another thing he should tell them about the mission and the planning went on and on in his head.

And as often happened with the men that slept on me, he remembered a place far away that didn't involve any of this. He was sitting on the lawn at his parents' house in the cool sunlight, and the dog was trying to lick him as he laughed and played with it.

Then he was heading into town and he thought of a girl. She wasn't right for him, but somehow, out here, she seemed to be. And he recalled other girls, some that he'd only glanced at, or shyly said hello to over loud music in a club. Some he'd blown it with. He wondered if they were right. Did any of them think about him out here? He hoped so. And he wished he was with one of them.

Finally he slept. It was a deep sleep of fatigue. He hardly moved all night but his ribcage expanded and contracted on me and he sweated. A buzzing mosquito, trapped inside the net, landed to extend its proboscis into him and suck blood up into its abdomen.

The stars twisted across the sky. Someone walked by in the dark and woke up the man in the camp bed next to us. He got dressed and went to keep watch. And we were alone in the courtyard.

He was already waking before his alarm clock rang. It was the brightening sky that made him turn over on me, and the chill that made him pull his sleeping bag up. It was a half-conscious bliss, being elsewhere, and the day ahead didn't exist, only dreams of home that slowly corroded as he woke and realised he was lying on me, inside the netting, and a different sun was rising above him.

He coveted it: the longing to be back where he was safe and didn't have any responsibility and wasn't trained to do any of this. Where he didn't have to lead anyone out of the gate again. He wished he didn't have to. It was his private moment of cowardice before the day became real. He let it fester and was embarrassed, even though no one would ever know.

He hardened himself against it and it was gone, suppressed within him. He unzipped the net and swung his legs out, itched his thigh and left to wash himself and prep his gear, to take his men out there beyond the walls and try to make a difference.

The rhythm of shifts, patrols and downtime went on unbroken and became normal for him. But it did end. It ended before it should have, after he'd encased himself in armour, picked up his rifle and walked away from me one evening.

He never returned. Someone else came and cleared all his belongings from around me. They took the sleeping bag that smelt of him and packed it with everything else into a cardboard box. The man in the other bed was still there and he felt the absence.

After a few weeks, another man arrived to take his place and the rhythm continued. When he left, others came and I supported them one after the other. They were excited at first, apprehensive as they struggled to understand, sometimes disillusioned or resigned and always superstitious in the weeks before they were replaced.

Much later, after they'd gone and the sun had bleached my cloth, other men started to use me. They spoke another language and their uniform was different and they didn't think of this as a distant country.

22

I was in a pack of fifty in a drawer. A man opened it and lifted me and six others out onto the table. He turned on the machine, which flashed, whirred and clunked. He sat and looked at a screen and pressed the trackpad. Then he slid us into the guides of the tray.

Rollers caught the first of us and pulled it down into the machine and the cartridge jerked across its surface. This happened four times and then I was at the top. The rollers dragged me in and I was under the printer head as it swept across me.

It propelled tiny jets of ink onto my surface, forced out of the cartridge by superheated explosions. It fired millions of these from its microscopic nozzles in spurts of primary colour that grouped to form an image on me. At first it was hard to know as I lurched down and each new strip appeared on me, but then I was ejected into the out-tray.

The ink dried quickly on my glossy surface. I was a photo now. The man sitting at the desk and switching off the printer was in me, dancing in a dark room with lights that had flared around the lens of the camera that had taken me. In me he looked younger. There was another man with him. They both were dancing and smiling at each other.

He pushed me together with the other photos, looked at his watch and walked out of the building to a car. He laid me on the passenger seat with his phone and started the ignition.

He drove quickly. He was worried about how he'd react when he saw his friend. He'd been dreading it. He had heard from his friend's brother that it was bad, that Tom had now lost the other one as well. He wondered if Tom would still be like he was before, when they were best mates. He looked down at me and remembered the night I was taken. He smiled. God, he'd been a dick that night. They both had – she wasn't worth it – and they'd hugged and made up in the morning.

He thought of training; perhaps he should've printed one of them together during training. It didn't matter. He hoped I'd cheer him up.

It was bright, so he put on sunglasses and turned up the radio.

He was apprehensive as he walked into the hospital, holding me in his hand. He asked for directions at a desk and went down more corridors. He hated the smell of hospitals.

A woman called out to him and he hugged her. She explained that visiting hours hadn't started yet, so they went to a chrome canteen and queued for a coffee. When she opened a red handbag he insisted on paying. He didn't like coffee but drank one with her anyway.

She told him how it was all going. She looked tired, he thought. He showed her me across the metal table and she smiled, and said what a good picture I was, but didn't look properly. He told her again that he would do anything they needed. He'd been wonderful for Tom, she said, he was really looking forward to the visit. But she had to go now: half the extended family was coming today and she needed to control them. Tom found visitors quite trying.

He wondered if Tom would find his visit trying.

And then he was in the ward. A nurse smiled and led him past bays that were already filling with visitors. He saw the wounded. He knew they were soldiers, like him; he could tell by the way they looked and joked. He thought about the place that had damaged them; he would have to go back there soon.

The nurse pointed to the corner where Tom was sitting in a bed by a window. He looked over and smiled and then grinned.

Tom grinned back.

It was the other man printed on me but he was so thin and fragile that it didn't look like he'd be able to dance now.

He wanted to give him a hug but he was scared of damaging him; his skinny arms and neck made his head seem skull-like. So he sat down next to him. 'Hello, mate,' he said.

'Hello, mucker. It's good to see you,' Tom said. He squeezed a rubber ball in one hand. The other hand was under the blanket. He had the bed sheet up to his waist. His top half was bare and he was sweating.

'Hot in here, then, or are you just trying to trap one of the nurses with your hunky body?'

Tom smiled and glanced over at the nurses' station. 'Haven't fallen in love with any of them yet. I get a bit of a fever with the anti-fungal drug they have me on,' he said, pointing at a yellow bag that hung from a hook. 'It makes me feel pretty awful actually.'

'Yeah, your mum said. I just had a coffee with her.'

'How did you think she was?'

'Seemed fine, mate. But what do you expect? You've really given her a bit of a nightmare, haven't you?' He smiled. He didn't want to turn away from his friend's face but he could sense the gap where his legs should have been.

'Do you want to see?' Tom said. He'd noticed his discomfort.

'No, don't worry.'

'It's no problem. Here, look.' He leant forward with a grunt and drew the sheet back. 'This one was the traumatic amputation during the incident.' The left leg stopped below the knee. It was covered in plastic and swollen under the dressing. A tube snaked out from under the plastic. 'The pipe there pulls all the gunk out of the wound. It's meant to promote healing and prevent infection.' Tom nodded at a machine hanging by the bed next to a bag of urine. 'That thing sucks it out. See the canister of blood and pus?'

'Nice, mate.'

'Yup. And this one they had to amputate a couple of weeks ago. It was badly infected. That's why I'm still on this anti-fungal treatment.' He placed his good hand on a mass of white bandages that ended above the knee.

'We heard all about it, mate. You were the talk of the town.' He stared at it and the pipes that led up from his groin. There was a whiff of antiseptic.

They chatted. He could tell his friend was weak and supported by medication. His mum had hinted as much. She'd said he could be confused but was fighting hard and sometimes seemed surprisingly lucid.

But he was still Tom and asked questions about outside. He wanted to know all about his pre-deployment training and his girlfriend, and what everyone had been up to. So he told him about a party and said they'd all asked after him. They talked for an hour and when Tom started to look tired he said he'd better be off. He didn't want to incur the wrath of his mum.

'Please stay, mate,' Tom said. 'It's good to see you.'

'Just a bit then. Hey, I brought you these.' He held me up and handed him the pile I was in. I was in Tom's hand and he shuffled through us slowly, resting each on his stomach. He picked me up and paused.

'Thanks, mate,' Tom said but his voice caught.

'What's up, mucker? Are you okay?'

'Nothing. Could you pull the curtain, please,' Tom said quietly and twisted away. I bent under his thumb as he held me.

'Sorry, mate. I thought . . .' He stood and pulled the curtain whooshing around on its rail. It blocked out the laughing and chatting of the other visitors.

'It's not your fault,' Tom said. He tried to look away, embarrassed, and his eyes filled and glistened.

'I'm really sorry, mate.' He sat back down next to the bed and clasped his hands in front of him. 'I thought they might make you remember better times.'

'They do, mate. They do. Thank you.' He had turned his head away and glanced down at me as a tear trickled across the bridge of his nose and dripped onto the sheets. 'It's just hard,' he said. 'And I'm stuck in here with all these people helping me that I never wanted to meet. I didn't want their help. I'm stuck in this fucking bed.' His voice nearly broke and he shook silently.

'Sorry, buddy. I should've thought it through.'

'It's fine, mucker. I suppose I hadn't been forced to think about it yet, that's all. This is all so unreal, mate. It's not me, this broken body, it's just not me. Not yet.' Tom turned back to his friend. There were wet tracks down his face. He smiled. 'I'm the bloke in this photo – dancing. I'm a runner, a soldier . . .' and his voice faded and the smile crumpled into a sob. 'Not this cripple,' he managed to say and gestured down the bed.

'Mate, you're no cripple.' He rested his hand on his friend's bandaged arm.

'No? You want to see me try and take a piss? That pipe does it for me now.' Tom smiled and sniffed.

'They can do amazing things these days, Tom. And if anyone can get over this, it's you. You're the toughest bloke I know.'

'I don't feel particularly tough at the moment.' He put me back with the others on a bedside table and wiped his eyes. He laughed. 'Look at the state of me: not particularly brave.'

'A cry will do you good,' he said.

'I can't show any weakness in here. I need to set an example, but it's such hard work.' He wiped his eyes again.

'I know, mate, you always were a stubborn bastard.'

He stayed for a bit longer. Before leaving, he promised his friend they'd be out dancing together before he knew it. Tom didn't believe him, but laughed. 'That's something that would sell tickets,' he said.

I stayed on the cupboard beside his bed for a while. A glass of water was put on me and left a ring. Tom never looked at me again, he just lay in the bed and measured time by the daily ward round, the yellow drugs dripping into him and the visiting hours after lunch.

They took Tom away in a wheelchair. His brother packed up all the things that had accumulated around his bed. He picked me up and looked at them dancing together in me then dropped me in a cardboard box with hundreds of letters and cards.

23

BA5799 pulled me out of the small pouch attached to the front of his body armour where I was kept next to a compass and a notepad. He was kneeling just off a path next to green bushes and reeds and his camouflage merged into the mottled shade. A field stretched out to his left, its young wheat a block of green before a strip of wall pink in the heat.

He looked down, deciphered the information on me instinctively and fixed his position.

I'm an aerial photograph taken from a satellite, depicting a network of ditches and walls. Most of me is covered in fields crossed with roads and bridges over blue rivers and paths that ghost into the desert. I show the shadows of walls and compounds. Each building has a round dot imposed over it and labelled with an alphanumerical indicator. A grid of northings and eastings is laid over all of it and each kilometre counts up and across me.

He pushed me back down into the pouch, pressed a button and reported our location. He turned to the interpreter and asked if he was okay. The man reclined beside the path, his hands behind his head, and chewed a piece of grass. He grinned.

BA5799's men were waiting for him along the track and he beckoned to them. He stepped over the path and headed diagonally across the field, the crop scrubbing against his boots. He looked at the dried mud through the young leaves and tried to guess what was below the surface.

It's always someone else, he thought. It never happens to you. But he watched his boots press onto the ground and was scared. It was affecting him more often, as patrolling this land became routine. It held him now, each step bringing him closer – increasing the odds – until he'd taken one too many and he trod on the inevitable. But he couldn't show any sign of it, couldn't think about odds and chance. His men were following him and he spun around and watched them crossing the field.

His radio emitted in his ear and the distraction was gone as he began to work out the best route into the village.

It could never happen to him.

He led his platoon down a track that cut through the first sparse compounds of the village, past windowless walls that each contained a family unit. A young man was standing on the next corner. He was peering around a wall with his back to us. BA5799 swept his arm down and the men behind him moved into cover. When he called hello in the local language, the man spun around in surprise. He was backing away so BA5799 pushed his rifle behind him on its sling.

'Peace be upon you,' he said awkwardly. And then he waved the interpreter up and they walked towards the young man.

'Tell him we want to talk to him,' he said.

The young man's eyes were heavy with mistrust. He wore a long green shirt under a sleeveless cream jacket and dirty trainers that were too big for him.

'Ask him to open his jacket so we can check he's not armed,' BA5799 said to the interpreter.

The man slowly parted the jacket and pulled up his long shirt, exposing his smooth stomach above loose trousers tied with a drawstring. He had done this many times before.

BA5799 smiled and asked him his name and where he was from, then took the notepad from beside me and started to write.

'He says his name is Mohammad,' the interpreter said. 'He says he lives some way from Nalay.'

The young man flicked his head to indicate a direction.

'Ask why he is north of Nalay,' BA5799 said.

'He is helping service the ditches for Kushan Hhan. He helps them at this time of year.'

'I've heard of Kushan Hhan. He's one of the Nalay elders. Find out if he's still opening the school.'

The interpreter spoke to the young man for a long time and became agitated.

'What's he saying?' BA5799 interrupted.

'He claims not to know much of Kushan Hhan or his business. But I do not believe him.'

BA5799 felt for the young man. His furry top lip showed his age. He imagined him willing it to sprout into a proper beard so he could be respected.

'This person is not good,' the interpreter told BA5799, as the young man averted his eyes. 'He is lying. Look at his shoes. He is dressed like a terrorist.'

The young man shifted and then said something.

'What did he say?'

'He says he needs to go back to work. I do not think there is any work. Only not good work.'

So BA5799 called up two of his men and they searched the young man. He had a phone in a pocket and they said they had to take it from him. They put it in a plastic bag and gave him a slip of paper as a receipt with instructions on how to claim compensation.

The young man glanced at the paper. It meant nothing to him and he was frightened. They let him go and he walked away, turning back and staring at the soldiers. The interpreter was annoyed and said they should have arrested him but BA5799 told him that a pair of trainers, a phone and a bit of attitude was not enough evidence; they would send the phone in for forensics.

He pulled me out and wrote with a permanent marker on my laminated surface. Many traces of ink were still on me: report lines, boundaries, named areas of interest and the codes of past operations, with new information written over them. He slotted me back next to the notepad and walked farther into the village.

BA5799's men spread out around the crossroads. They stood and knelt in pairs by oil barrels or in doorways, slipping into shadows and covering the market. The local people watched them. Some went about their business as if his men weren't there, reaching under awnings to inspect green-blue melons or buying eggs from piled trays.

Under the awnings, shopkeepers crouched on mats beside their goods. Farm tools were stacked behind them and bags of crisps hung from wooden posts above piles of sweets, spices and cans of fruit. They grew cautious as BA5799 walked forward, his antenna and the following interpreter marking him as the leader.

BA5799 looked at his watch and started talking to them. Some ignored him but others spoke. One gesticulated up the road and complained about the craters. When would they be fixed? The produce could not get through. And BA5799 told the interpreter to say they planned to do it soon. Others smiled and joked and a few said that bombs from his planes had burnt their crops.

BA5799 told them to come to the base for compensation, but they said it was too dangerous to be seen going there.

Children gathered in an alley, having heard the foreigners had come. They sniggered and hid behind one another. A little girl waddled up to a crouching soldier and asked, wide-eyed, for food. She motioned to her mouth. He said he couldn't help but she didn't understand and kept begging. Another soldier smiled and took out his camera. The children lined up for a picture and looked serious, then craned over each other to see as he turned the digital display towards them. When they saw themselves they ran away laughing.

BA5799 needed information about the balance of influence. He asked them about the insurgents, but they all replied there were none here; they were good people and wanted a peaceful country. He asked them if they'd seen any men digging mines into the roads near the village, but they said they knew nothing about it.

He took me out and noted something down after one conversation. And then the atmosphere changed and no one was willing to talk any more. BA5799 looked up the road and saw a group of men standing around a motorbike, watching. He thought the young man from earlier was among them but couldn't be sure. Those in the market drifted away and a shopkeeper began to lift his produce inside, then rolled up his sunshade.

BA5799 looked at his watch and decided it was time to move on. His men emerged from their cover and followed him out of the village. He wanted to get a strip of trees between his platoon and the village, so he took me out and traced his finger across my surface to work out the safest route back. He sent a message to the camp reporting his location and intentions. In the operations room, a small blue sticker labelled *B30* was moved across a map pinned to the wall. That map was identical to me.

They walked back to the patrol base that was marked near my centre in blue. He used a metal detector to lead them over a bridge and then they cut across a field. He looked at me once more to report his location but soon he could see the camp and didn't need me any more.

When one of his men said he'd seen movement behind us, BA5799 commanded a team to go static and protect the rest of the platoon. He stayed with them, focusing on a motorbike in the distance before we collapsed back to safety.

When they were all back in the camp, BA5799 removed his helmet and sighed. He was hot and thirsty and went to get some water, where he met a man who asked him how it had gone. He took me out and described the patrol, hovering a pen over my grid lines, and talked about the suspicious young man, the atmospherics in the market, and how they'd been followed by a motorbike as they returned.

And then the camp was attacked.

'Deep joy,' BA5799 said, put me away in my pouch and jogged for cover.

24

My warps were strung vertically on a loom. Three women worked on me. They hooked out my upright threads and knotted dyed wool to them, cutting away the loose ends with a flick of a knife. They threaded weft horizontally to hold me together and banged me down with a heavy comb to compact my knots. I slowly grew up from the ground.

Sometimes the women talked but for most of the day they were silent. They checked a design on the wall, matching red, orange, ivory and deep blue to its tiny squares and knotting the colours into me.

My deep crimson pattern of encircling leaves and stepped diagonals piled up until, on the forty-second day, I was finished.

My fringe was cut from the loom and the women were paid. I was taken across the road, placed in a drum and spun so wooden battens beat me and settled my pile. I was dragged out and men pulled me flat and I was shorn with electric clippers that cut my threads short and sharpened my pattern. A hand checked the smoothness of my soft surface and two boys laid me out on the floor, soaked me and pushed brooms across me. Soap foamed through me and my colours shone.

I was hung and dried. Two weeks later I was folded, covered in plastic and stacked with others on the back of a truck. I was driven from the village and into the green valleys, through mountains along a road that clung to the rock and weaved a course down the steep spurs and finally onto flat plains. The truck stopped in a city that night and the driver sat with others by a fire and drank. And then we drove on west across a desert, past villages and camel trains, burnt tanks rusted and scrawled with graffiti and convoys of white lorries.

The road became congested and the traffic shimmered around us as we crept forward. In a town crowds thronged around administrative buildings and queued in lines that blocked the street. Some had purple dye on their right index fingers and were excited.

We then arrived in a large city, where I was unloaded into a warehouse and waited.

Weeks later, a man pulled me from the stack and I flopped on the concrete floor, spiralling dust up into the air. He pulled out others and threw them down next to me. Another man knelt down and ran the flat of his hand over me. He studied the others and then he chose me. They discussed whether payment should be made in the new currency or dollars.

I was folded and taken out by one of the men. He put me on a cart with rubber tyres and a pony pulled us out of the city into the fields. We stopped by a high, long compound wall that shadowed the road. The driver stepped down from the cart and knocked on a tall, black gate. Kushan Hhan opened the door and greeted him and came out onto the road to look at me. He was pleased and put his arm around the man in thanks.

He called over two boys who were out in the field, running as fast as they could, trying to make a kite fly, and laughing.

'Faridun, this is Noor Hhan,' Kushan Hhan said, introducing the driver. 'We are working together on a new venture.' He put an arm on the boy's shoulder and pointed at me. 'Look what he has given me.'

'It is wonderful, Father,' Faridun said.

'It is from the north,' the driver said. 'It is a very fine carpet.'

'My father says the best carpets are from there,' the other boy said.

'It is a generous gift,' Kushan Hhan said. 'Now, Faridun, can you and Latif take it into the house, please? I need to speak with Noor Hhan.'

'He is a handsome boy, Kushan,' the driver said as the boys lifted me up.

'He should be working, not playing with his friends. He's nearly a man.'

They watched the boys take me through the gate into a court-yard. It was an oasis of green and colourful flowers, many the same red as me. Water trickled down a channel and clear white stone paths cut between pergolas and wooden frames of lush vines. Tulips and herbs scented the cool air. The boys stepped up onto a veranda and into a clean painted room and put me down on the floor.

'Where do you think?' Latif said, pulling me along by a corner. 'Here?'

'I'm not sure,' Faridun said. 'Mother will know where to put it.' He had his hands on his hips and looked down at me. There were two other carpets in the room around a small gas stove and a few bowls. To one side was a low table and cushions. 'Shall we fly the kite again? We could use my new bike to get more speed.'

'I want to try first.'

'It was my idea and it is my bike,' Faridun said and ran out.

*

The family had meals together, sprawled on me and the cushions around the room. Some of them slept on me and they all walked on me. The children learnt to crawl and took their first steps across me. Sometimes the family celebrated and the men danced to music, their bare feet jumping up and down on me as they leapt in a circle and clapped.

I stayed in that room and every few months I was taken into the garden, held up while the dust was thumped from me and then returned to the endless pattern of daily existence as the family revolved around the house. Rains came and the garden cycled through the seasons outside.

A few times a year, men gathered around me to discuss the land and irrigation and what crops to grow, to argue about the government and the governor. Kushan Hhan led the debates. He sat on me and tea was brought out for his guests as they talked.

One summer, gunfire and explosions sounded in the distance. When the men now met they talked about the arrival of the foreign soldiers and their helicopters. They argued over the sale of a compound at the edge of the village where they had erected new watchtowers and walls. Their voices deepened as they discussed the shadow of the old government and the men who came from the mountains to fight the soldiers.

The family noticed the changes too. Whenever gunfire could be heard crackling in the distance they hid in the corner of the room. But this soon became normal: now they listened to work out how far away the danger was and often continued what they were doing.

Kushan Hhan's meetings grew strained and he worked hard to lead the men through the suddenly painful discussions. The fair division of water into the ditches of their fields was no longer the most important subject. Now the balance of power across the land had split them. Many blamed the foreigners and told Kushan Hhan that everything had been fine before they came, so why were they here? And what of the constant explosions?

Kushan Hhan urged them to stay calm about this foreign presence: it was for the good of the country. But some said that a good country would do nothing and that the fighting was ruining them, scorching their fields and stopping trade. He told them that the foreign soldiers needed time to bring peace.

That same night, Kushan Hhan sat cross-legged on me with his family all around him and watched Faridun eat his soup. He was now old enough to fight, to be caught up in it, and Kushan Hhan prayed he was leading his people in the right direction.

One afternoon after the next harvest, when the days were getting hotter, Faridun came home limping and with a bloody lip. Kushan Hhan brought him over and they sat down on me.

'What happened, my son?' he said.

'There was a checkpoint on the way back – I could not avoid it,' Faridun said. 'I am sorry, Father. They took your fertiliser.'

'Was it a government checkpoint? Did the soldiers hurt you?'

'It was some of Hassan's men, I think. One of them was from the mountains.' He licked his swollen lip and looked down at his cut ankle. 'Latif was with them.'

'Aadela,' Kushan Hhan called into the next room, 'can you bring some water and ointment please? Faridun is hurt.'

'Why, what happened?' she said, coming in. 'What have you done now, Faridun?'

'Nothing, Mother. I'm sorry about the fertiliser.'

'That doesn't matter,' his father said. 'Why did they hurt you?'

'They pushed me over and threatened me.'

'Why?'

'Latif was there with them – he must be working with them all the time now.'

His father crouched beside him. 'Why would they threaten you, Faridun?'

'They said it was because you work for the infidels.' He looked at his father. 'They said they would—'

'Would what, Faridun?' his mother said, sitting down in front of him with a bowl.

'They said if Father continues to work with the foreigners they will behead Lalma.'

'What is that meant to mean?' She looked at her husband and then glanced at the doorway and spoke more quietly. 'What is that meant to mean, Kushan? How can they come here and threaten us like that?' She was angry and stared at him. 'You must go and see the governor.'

'It is not a problem, Aadela,' he said and stood. 'I'm sorry you were hurt, Faridun.'

She looked up at him. 'It is a problem, Kushan.'

'They try to intimidate us. It is the school, and perhaps the wedding,' he said, gazing into his garden through the window. 'We must not let them.'

'You will speak to Hassan, then. He has gone too far this time.'

'It is not possible, Aadela. Things have changed.'

'Hold still, Faridun.' His mother dabbed his lip with a cloth, and water dripped onto me. 'Well, you have to do something.'

Faridun brushed away her hand. 'I'm fine, Mother. Please, give me a moment.'

'I will not let you put this family in danger, Kushan,' she said, pressing the cloth back on Faridun's lip.

'I will talk to Latif's father again,' Kushan Hhan said.

'Latif doesn't matter. That foolish boy has made his choice now. How could he do this to Faridun, to us? After everything we have done for his family. Did you not give him a job last harvest?'

'I will discuss the checkpoints at our next meeting.' He was dark against the window.

'Your stupid meetings,' she said. 'Nothing ever gets done, you men just sit around like statues and do nothing. I'll go and talk to Latif's mother.'

But my owner had gone back into his garden.

In the following weeks Faridun's lip healed. He came back from the fields each night and ate with the family. They were preparing for his younger sister's wedding and the women sat around the room and on me sewing silks and threading jewels.

One day the women were singing softly, stitching the bridal dress, when Faridun came home early from work.

'Where is Father?' he said.

'In the back field,' his mother said. 'Why?'

'The soldiers are here. They want to speak to him.'

'What do you mean, here?' She pulled a thread through the silk in her lap.

'They're outside now. Right here, Mother.'

'Did you bring them here, Faridun?'

But he had already left.

'We should finish,' she said.

She made the women and girls leave the room, tidied all the fabrics and needles from me and waited.

Kushan Hhan came back with his son.

'What is happening?' she said as they entered.

'The British soldiers are here, Aadela,' my owner said. 'They have come to speak to me.'

She held a length of fabric to her chest. 'Why are you here, then? Go out and see them.'

'I have invited them in,' he told her.

'You will not, Kushan, I will not let you bring them into this house.'

'They have asked to see me. We cannot forget our traditions, Aadela.' He looked out of the door.

She was frightened. 'It means nothing to them.'

'Go and make tea, Aadela,' he said firmly. 'And do not show yourself.'

'Do you do this for power, Kushan? It is reckless.'

'Go,' he said. 'Please.' He glanced at his son. 'Faridun, bring in the foreigners.'

The boy brought the soldiers in. There were only three of them. The first walked in after Faridun. He was dark and massive and his aerial rattled off the top of the doorway. Once he'd taken his helmet off and pulled a band from his head and smiled, he didn't seem so huge and strange. He placed his equipment and his rifle down by the door.

Kushan Hhan beckoned him over and they sat on me across from each other. Another soldier waited outside the door and the third man came in and sat with them. He spoke first.

'This is Captain Tom. I am his translator,' he said. 'He thanks you for allowing him into your home. It is very generous of you.'

'Tell him he is welcome,' Kushan Hhan said and smiled, touching his hand to his chest.

The young soldier nodded. He was hot and his trousers were damp with sweat. He spoke to the translator.

'He says he has placed his men around the house for our protection. He is sorry to have to do this. He hopes it does not mark you out.'

'It is fine: I understand.'

'Captain Tom is from the base beyond the village.'

'Tell him I know the base well. I have been there before to meet with them,' Kushan Hhan said. 'But each time I go there it is a different man in uniform I speak to. I have never seen your captain. How long has he been here?'

The interpreter and the soldier talked.

'He has been here for two months. He apologises that they are always changing, but it is beyond his control. I myself have had to speak for three different groups since I have worked with them. They never stay for very long.'

'Where are you from?' Kushan Hhan asked the interpreter.

'From the capital. I learnt English there.'

'You take a great risk.'

'As do you,' the interpreter replied and Kushan Hhan smiled.

While the young man talked to his interpreter, my owner studied another soldier guarding the door into his garden.

'Captain Tom would like to hear about the school you have opened,' the interpreter said. 'He says he wants to support you in this.'

Kushan Hhan still looked out of the door but then turned to the soldier sitting on the other side of me. The man was smiling but Kushan Hhan could tell he wasn't comfortable being here. 'Tell the captain that there will be time for talk of schools and government and bombs. Tell him I will bring tea for us to drink together.'

He motioned to Faridun, who went through the back door and returned with a tray holding three small cups of tea, which he put down on me. Kushan Hhan leant forward to drink. The captain did the same, twisting awkwardly in his armour to pick up his cup.

'He thanks you,' the interpreter said. 'He says it is refreshing.' They all sipped tea and waited.

Kushan Hhan let the silence fill and listened to the water running in the channels through his garden.

Suddenly the captain started talking to his translator. He seemed to mean well but was impatient. He would want to do business quickly – like everything else they did. Fix it and then move on. Build, repair, leave. He looked straight at Kushan Hhan as the interpreter spoke.

'He is very interested in the school, if you would like to talk about it?' he said.

Kushan Hhan sighed and put his cup back down on the tray. 'Ask the captain how many children he has.'

The two men spoke, then the interpreter said, 'He is not yet married, but hopes that one day he might be.'

'Not married? How old is he?'

'I told him you were surprised,' the interpreter said after speaking to the captain again. 'He is twenty-five. He has yet to meet the right woman. Their traditions are very different.'

'His father has not found a woman for him?'

'He says he wishes it was that simple.' The interpreter smiled. 'He has to do all the hard work himself.' The young man grinned as his words were translated.

'It should be simple,' Kushan Hhan said, 'but rarely is. Still, it makes for strong families.' He pointed at his son. 'This is my son, Faridun. He is seventeen. I will have to find him a bride soon.'

Faridun sat by the window. He did not smile but stared at the captain's strange clothes and the armour that encased him.

'The captain says he likes your garden,' the interpreter said. 'It is the most beautiful thing he has seen since he has been here. It reminds him of his father's garden.'

'Your father has a garden like this?' Kushan Hhan said.

'The captain says it helps his father think after work.'

'Yes.' Kushan Hhan looked out into the courtyard. 'It is the one thing I have some control over here. And who my children marry, of course.'

The young man smiled at the translation.

They continued to talk about the garden, the surrounding fields and what the farmers were growing. The captain asked about the harvest and how good it had been. Then they talked of family and the men Kushan Hhan was close to. They discussed the village and how the market was doing and he told the soldier how the bombs under the road made everything difficult for them.

The captain fidgeted on me and had to stretch out his legs. My owner smiled at his discomfort and suggested he should get used to sitting on the floor. He could tell the man wanted to leave; without his weapon he was worried and he glanced at his watch and then at the soldier guarding the door.

So Kushan Hhan told him about the school.

'The building has been destroyed and it is too difficult to rebuild without any security,' he said. 'I have tried, but I lack the support of the other families. They feel threatened.'

'The captain understands,' the interpreter told him. 'He will do what he can to help but he is aware of the difficulties. He feels the school is important for the area. He has funds.'

Kushan Hhan looked down at me and rubbed my pile. 'It is always about money.' He was angry. 'Funds do not keep them from beating the children who attend the school, or ripping out doors and windows, or setting fire to the roof. You think dollars will solve all our problems.'

'He says they will do everything they can. He understands it is not easy for you. But we must be going soon or our journey back to the base will be more dangerous. He thanks you for the tea,' the interpreter said, putting his cup down on me.

'Tell him that he will walk out of here, back to his base, and before sunset I will be visited by them. They will come in here, sit where he has been sitting and ask me what the soldier wanted and what I said. Tell your captain that.'

The soldier looked at him and spoke slowly to his interpreter.

'He says he hopes you have not taken too grave a risk.'

'We will talk more of the school when we next meet,' Kushan Hhan said. 'If he is still here and it is not some other captain.'

'He hopes he can continue to talk to you. Captain Tom says he realises how hard it is for you to invite him into your home and he is thankful,' the interpreter said.

'For each time I speak to a captain or a major like him, and hear their promises about security and education and bridges and new roads, about money, I have to speak to the insurgents five times.' Kushan Hhan stood up. 'The insurgents come here to tell me how I should lead my people and to threaten me and my family. They will punish me for inviting you in here today.'

'I understand,' the interpreter said.

'But does he understand?' Kushan Hhan pointed at the captain, then called over his shoulder, 'Lalma, come here.'

There were whispers from behind the back door and then

Lalma walked in. She stood next to him, her bare feet on me. She glanced up at the soldier, then looked down and pulled her green headscarf up to her eyes. Faridun shifted in the corner.

'This is my daughter. She is to be married,' Kushan Hhan said. 'They have threatened to hurt her if I talk to these foreigners.'

He held the soldier's gaze as the translator explained what he had said.

The captain nodded and put his equipment and helmet back on. He looked at Kushan Hhan with his beautiful daughter standing beside him and said he hoped they would meet again soon. Kushan Hhan watched him pick up his rifle and step out into the courtyard; he looked aggressive again with his eyes shadowed by his helmet and his weapon at his side. He wondered if the man's father really did have a garden like his.

When they had gone his wife came in through the back door and hugged Lalma close to her. She watched him silhouetted by the window. 'How was it, Kushan?'

'You know how it was, Aadela,' he said softly. 'You were listening to every word.'

'I thought it went well. Perhaps they might help us – maybe they do have money?'

'Maybe,' he said.

'And you didn't promise them anything, Kushan. I think Hassan will understand that you had no choice.'

Kushan Hhan wasn't sure that Hassan would understand and he walked across me and went to sit on the veranda and look at his garden.

25

I had been on her table for over a week. She'd tried to write on me but never got beyond *Dear Tom*.

She was back now, leaning over me and reflected in the mirror. Yawning, she put on her makeup, brushed her hair and tied it back. She slipped her earrings in and glanced down at me and then out of the window at the rusted blue gas-storage tower by the park beyond the flats. A train cut through the rooflines and the bin truck's lights flashed as it crawled up the wet street.

She felt excited whenever she thought of him and how she'd smiled at him when they met. They had talked but other friends were there too and he wasn't interested, so they'd circled around the party at a distance – she couldn't stop looking at him. He won't want to hear from me, she thought. He was abroad and wouldn't be back for months. But he had smiled back and lingered near her before leaving with his mates.

And then she picked up the biro and started to write. She wrote fast and the pen looped across me. She smiled once and put the end of the pen to her mouth before turning me over and continuing down my other side. When she had nearly covered me, she paused and then wrote: *With love from Anna. x*

She looked at her watch and rushed to fold me in three. Her tongue licked my tabs, wetting my glue, and she pressed down my edges. Then she wrote his rank, name and address on the front of me. It occurred to her how strange it was that the four-digit number could deliver me all the way to where he was.

At the postbox she looked at me again and paused, suddenly nervous at the thought of him reading me, and then she said what the hell under her breath and I dropped through the dark slot.

I was taken to a sorting office and fed through a machine that recognised the letters and numbers she'd written on my front, and I was pulled down a track of belts and wheels and fell into a bucket. Next a man picked me up and put me in a sack.

I was projected across the world by trucks and planes and sorted again, then I went on a helicopter and was thrown off the back through a cloud of dust. The bag was opened outside a small mud building under camouflage netting and I was put in a pile with a parcel and three others the same as me.

A man was handed all of it and he smiled and walked over to a camp bed, where he sat down and sifted through us. He opened the parcel first, ripping through the cardboard and examining the bottle of chilli sauce, nuts, oatcakes, the tin of pate and the chocolate bars. He had a bite of chocolate as he read a card and smiled.

He picked me up and frowned at the handwriting. Then a friend called to him, so he tossed me aside and jogged out of the courtyard.

There were shouts and laughter. A ball arced into the courtyard and bounced around, and he ran back to pick it up from between jerry cans. He threw it over the wall and disappeared again.

He returned with another man and their T-shirts were dark with ovals of sweat. They sat opposite each other on their beds and talked. He offered him something from the parcel and then started to read me.

Dear Tom,

*I read an article in the paper about where you are. It sounds really awful
and, well, I thought I'd write. I know we've only met a few times but I
asked Jess for your address. I hope you don't mind!?*
*The last time was at her party – do you remember, we talked for a while?
I'm not sure what about but I enjoyed meeting you. I think it was a few
weeks before you went. It must be so difficult leaving it all and heading out
there. No one really talks about it; we just carry on at work or in the pub.
Just so you know, I have thought about you.*
*It seems odd. I'm about to walk to the bus and go to work. It looks like
it's going to rain again and I will probably be late (I'm always late!) and
the biggest decision of my day is what sandwich I have for lunch. I can't
imagine what you're doing except that the sun is probably out and it's hot
and you probably wish it wasn't. The article made it sound like it is getting
harder and we don't know what we've let ourselves in for being there, and
more people than we realise get hurt – I had no idea really.*
*Don't write back if you don't want, but it would be nice to see you when
you're home. Jess says it won't be for a few months – maybe not until
Christmastime. Could we have a Christmas drink? I love that time of year.
I best get to the bus stop before it's so crammed I have to spend my journey
in someone's armpit. Stay safe, Tom.*

With love from Anna. x

*PS. Long blonde hair, quite short and stared at you a lot during Jess's party
– if you can't remember!*

He put me down on the bed under the mosquito net and continued to eat from the parcel and thought about the girl.

Over the next few weeks he tried to write back. And he read
me over and over, but all he could manage was *Dear Anna, thank
you for your letter* before he had to head out again or fell asleep or
didn't know what else to write. And then he didn't come back
and I was packed away into a cardboard box.

26

I am made in China. My body was stamped from sheet metal, my barrel extruded, my stock and grip carved from wood and I was assembled and riveted together. I was packed off the production line in 1978.

I was sold by dealers to capitalists and became hot in a cold war.

I was fired at soldiers. I was fired into the air to celebrate weddings. I might or might not have killed anyone. For years I hung off the shoulder of a shepherd in the mountains and I seized up. But I was found and cleaned and given to Aktar.

I was where he often kept me, wrapped in a cloth, stuffed between the split water tank and the wall. The men pulled me out with the other weapons and unwrapped me. They crouched and waited in the shade. The weapons were handed out and they pulled the magazines clear, checked and reinserted them. One man tossed a bag of loose ammunition to another. They shrugged on assault vests that hung loose around them.

I was placed next to Aktar. He was peering through a gap in the trees and holding a radio in his hand. He spoke into it but it was silent and then fuzzed.

'He is not responding,' he said and looked at his watch.

He picked me up and wiped away grit that had collected on me and then blew more from the groove between my trigger housing and stock.

'We take no risks. Just the same as last time,' he said. 'Abdul, Latif, we will go forward to the edge of the buildings. Paugi, be ready with the rocket. And then we meet back here and hide the weapons.'

The four men looked at each other. One sat on his haunches, holding the grenade launcher, and grinned yellow teeth at Latif. Aktar glanced down at the radio again and then held it to his mouth. 'Karmal, are you there? Can you see the entrance?' Again there was no reply and he pushed the radio into his vest. 'Let's go,' he said to them.

Aktar carried me by his side. He pushed through the branches and walked out towards a track that led us between old walls. The others followed behind, half-crouched with their weapons across their stomachs. Aktar knelt down and looked carefully over a wall that was only waist high. He could see the flag flapping lazily above the camp and the horizontal slit of the watchtower.

'It seems quiet,' he said, then dropped down to crawl past the opening.

The boy Latif followed behind him.

Aktar walked on, keeping close to a wall until he was pressing his back against it, sidestepping, and my stock scraped against the dry stone. Then he leant forward and there was the watchtower again, now much closer.

The three others were lined up next to him.

'One at a time,' he said.

Aktar smoothly stepped around the exposed wall and back into the shadows of a doorway. They followed him in and waited for the bullets to come, but the watchtowers were silent. One of them blew out a silent whistle.

Aktar checked around the frame, which seemed untouched. He held his breath and pushed the door open, afraid it might squeak. The men went with him into the compound and across to the other side. The far wall was destroyed and lay in craters and piles of rubble. He moved into a corner and propped me against the loose masonry. The others grouped together with him and squatted down. They looked nervous. One itched his forehead under his hat.

Aktar shuffled out on his belly and scanned across the camp and then the desert that climbed up beyond the river by the cemetery. There was no movement.

'Latif and I will fire at the tower on the left,' he said as he studied the camp. 'Abdul, take the one on the right, through the trees. Try to conserve your ammunition, all of you.'

He crawled over to pick me up. He worked my cocking handle, compressing and then releasing my spring, and my bolt carrier sprang forward, collecting the top round from the magazine and sliding it into my breech. My bolt rotated into position behind it.

'We should spread out,' he said. 'You first, Latif.'

Latif crawled out past Aktar's boots and around the craters and rubble until he could hide behind a stack of bricks. He anxiously glanced back at them and cocked his weapon.

Aktar flicked his head at the next man, who slid out, dragging himself beyond the boy until they were spaced out along the wall.

Aktar clasped my grip and clicked my safety lever down with his finger. He knelt behind the wall and checked to make sure the others were ready. Their weapons were poised in front of them and they waited for his command.

Aktar nodded and held me up to his shoulder. He pulled me closer and twisted his chest out from behind the wall until I was pointing at the watchtower. His finger hardened on me. He swayed, my sights looping around the target. Then his breath exhaled onto my stock and we settled. He gently squeezed my trigger.

My hammer was released, leapt up and slapped into the back of my bolt, sending my firing pin forward into the base of the first round. I fired and the bullet left my barrel, forced out by the explosion in my breech. The expanding gas worked my piston and flung my extractor back. The empty case spun out of me in a copper whirr as I punched up and sideways into Aktar's shoulder.

My bolt carrier flung forward and lifted another round into my breech. I was ready.

He adjusted his aim and jerked my trigger back again, and again, and I bucked in his arms each time. The others were firing too and Aktar's eyes sparkled next to me. He saw a burst of debris lift from the infidels' watchtower as one of my rounds hit. Then another struck right below the slit. He glanced to his right.

'Well done, Abdul. Keep firing at the tower,' he shouted over the noise, excited now. 'Send them to hell, Latif. God is greatest.'

And then a jagged yellow cross strobed silently in the black slit. They were being shot at. Noise and violence suddenly cracked the air around us in piercing clips that beat through the sky. Aktar ducked behind the wall and grinned at the others.

Latif was reloading, dropped his magazine, then fumbled to pick it up and looked back at Aktar. 'God is greatest,' the boy said but his words were lost in the shock of metal tearing through the air above.

'Keep firing, Latif,' Aktar said in a lull. 'Just a few more moments.'

[173]

He switched me to automatic and held me out around the wall, firing me blindly. I spewed bullets and my barrel heated and bucked and my action blurred as it sawed back and forward inside me. Phosphorus-tipped rounds traced bright ephemeral lines out into the haze. My magazine chunked empty and Aktar stepped back into shelter. He worked my magazine release catch and pushed the empty into his vest, replaced it and cocked me. Then I was firing again.

Dust jumped from the wall in front of Latif as bullets slammed into it. He held his weapon above his head and fired back until the cloud engulfed him and he ducked away, covered in dirt and rubble.

Aktar looked over and laughed at him. 'Are you okay, Latif? Keep firing.'

'God is greatest,' he shouted back, laughing too, and fired over the wall again.

Then the pitch of the cracks changed as different weapons fired at them. The higher-calibre rounds smacked new notes overhead, lodging in walls or deflecting up and ricocheting into the sky.

On the far side of the wall the man was crouched in cover. 'Aktar, I have nearly run out,' he shouted and pointed at his magazine.

Aktar looked around. He pulled the shirt of the man next to him. 'Now, Paugi. Make it count,' he said over the noise.

The man ran out and held the launcher on his shoulder. He paused, the green cone of the grenade wobbling as he aimed it. He steadied himself as a round puffed beside his foot, and then another, closer.

'Come on, Paugi,' Aktar said. 'Fire.'

Then his grenade hammered away in an instant cloud of propellant. He shouted that God was greatest through the smoke as
the projectile fizzed into the chaos and exploded in the distance.

Suddenly rounds stripped across the wall, tracked over the
open ground and through the man and he was on the floor, the
firing tube clattering beside him. Aktar ducked back into cover
and held me across his chest.

'Paugi,' the boy yelled and slid down into shelter.

'Keep firing, Latif. Keep firing at them,' Aktar shouted and
watched the injured man. He was holding his thigh and blood
showed between his fingers. His mouth gulped up and down as
he hissed and clawed at the ground.

'Paugi, can you crawl here?' Aktar called. 'Crawl over here.
You will be hit again if you remain there.' A round made a stone
jump next to the man. Something was wrong. The noise was
wrong; it was never normally this violent. Aktar held me in his
shoulder and looked around the corner at the base. And now he
saw them, out to the left in the desert, spread out near the cemetery and firing.

'Latif, get back,' he shouted. 'They're on the hill as well. To our
left.' He was scared, his tongue dry in his mouth.

'What?' the boy said and dragged his weapon back to him.

'There, up on the hill now – they've left the camp to outflank
us.' Aktar beckoned above the wall. 'You are exposed. Get down.'

'How did they get there?' Latif started to crawl away. A burst
of automatic fire clicked over us.

Aktar slung my strap over his shoulder and paused, looking at
the heaving body of the man. He noticed a shard of rock flick up
and a blade of grass stir. And then we were moving and he didn't
feel anything and his head was hot and he ran out as a tunnel of

sound wrapped around us. His legs pushed us on, tingling under him until we were next to the man.

We skidded down beside him and Aktar grabbed his arms. The man screamed in pain as he was dragged. Bullets cracked past us. I fell from his shoulder and down to his elbow and dangled awkwardly on my sling, knocking into the head of the injured man as Aktar pulled him into cover.

Aktar gasped for air and leant back against the stones. The injured man was below him, breathing through clenched teeth in the lee of the wall. And then the other men crawled over.

'What do we do, Aktar?'

'We need to get him back to the road,' Aktar said between breaths.

'We can't get him across the field,' Latif said. 'They will cut us down.'

'Latif, you will help me carry him,' Aktar said. 'Abdul, make sure they aren't trying to encircle us.'

'Aktar, it is too dangerous – we will be too slow with him.' The man looked out around the wall. A bullet kicked up dust to his left and another clapped past and struck the wall at the far side of the compound. 'They are up on the hill now.'

'I know, Abdul. But we must get him back to the road.' Aktar stared at him over the groaning man. 'We cannot leave him here. You need to cover us.'

I banged against Aktar's back on my strap as he supported the hurt man. Latif was on the other side and their arms were wrapped around him. The man's head lolled forward and his legs dragged through the dirt. They carried him out of the compound. The sky still cracked and the weapons echoed and thumped in the distance. We moved down the wall, past an exposed corner and there was a sudden burst of fire.

'Faster, Latif,' Aktar said, and they stumbled on under the weight. He was angry with fear and his back crawled with the certainty that a bullet was about to thud into it. 'Abdul, fire back.'

Behind us the man raised his rifle above a wall and sprayed countless rounds.

'This way, Aktar,' Latif said. He was tiring. 'It will be quicker if we cross to the trees here.'

Aktar swore. 'No, Latif, that is where we laid the bombs. We must follow this track.'

He was angry that he couldn't take the short route now, that his bombs made him vulnerable, and angry that he was going to die. He wanted to drop the body and run, or turn and fire. And I made him angry, banging impotently against his back as he carried the wounded man. He was angry that he hadn't seen them up on the hill and he was angry with Karmal for not being there on the radio.

We kept on down the track to the road. The firing had stopped and all he could hear was their breathing and the effort pounding in his ears. The man's leg was soaked with blood and he left a dark trail behind us. He was whimpering.

'We should stop soon, Aktar,' the boy said. 'I don't think Paugi can take any more.'

'A bit farther, Latif. We need to get beyond where they will follow us. Beyond the bridge,' Aktar said, trying to glance back. 'Are they still following, Abdul?'

'I cannot see them.'

'We should cross into this field, Latif,' Aktar said.

They stepped over an irrigation ditch, awkwardly pulling his legs across, and moved along the edge of the field. Then bullets started clipping the thigh-high leaves around us.

'Fire back, Abdul,' Aktar grunted.

'I can't see where they are.'

'Fire anyway. Just keep shooting.'

And he fired his weapon back towards the camp in a long automatic burst and the red tracer drifted away to the horizon.

'Get to shelter,' Aktar said.

They staggered down a path thick with foliage and came out next to a wall. A young man was sitting against it. His bicycle was propped next to him and he was eating dried apricots. He looked up as we appeared.

'You. Come here, we need help,' Aktar said as he saw him.

The young man stood and backed away towards a green bicycle.

'I said come here, boy.'

'Latif?' he said.

'How do you know Latif?' Aktar studied him. 'Quick, you can help us. We need to get this man to safety.'

The boy looked at Latif, who was bent under the weight of the injured man. 'Are you okay, Latif?' he said. 'I know a place that's not far. Follow me.' He reached out for Latif's weapon, then me, and slung us on the handlebars of his bike.

He pushed the bicycle beside him as he led them across the field. I swung off the handlebars as it rolled through the wheat to a small building edged by irrigation ditches. They all rested against the wall as the boy took a key from his pocket and opened the door.

'You will be safe in here,' he said.

'Thank you,' Latif said.

They edged the man sideways through the door and into a dark storage room filled with cans of fuel, bags of grease and buckets among stacked tools and farming equipment. They gently laid the man down on the concrete floor.

'What should we do with Paugi?' the boy said. He put his hands on his knees and coughed. 'He might die.'

'I will go for the doctor,' Aktar said, then unhooked my strap from the handlebars and held my grip.

'You must stop the blood leaving him,' the other boy said. 'Here, let me.' He crouched down beside the body, tore a strip of cloth from his shirt, wrapped it around the thigh and pulled it tight.

'Thank you, Faridun,' Latif said and joined him, tearing his own shirt and wrapping another cloth around the leg.

Aktar looked at the injured man. 'He might survive, so do what you can. I will be back soon.' He stepped towards the door. 'Abdul, come out here. You must keep guard.'

'How long will you be, Aktar?' he said as they walked out and he knelt beside the building.

'Not long, Abdul. I will return from that direction.' Aktar pointed towards the road. 'The infidels shouldn't come this far, but keep watch. Here, take this,' he said and unclipped the magazine from me and threw it to him.

He held me at his side as he ran across the field back to the road. We dropped down to the water tank and he swung his leg onto his motorbike. He slipped his head through my sling so I was across his back, then kicked down on the bike and powered it up onto the road. His turban fluttered against me as we sped away and the wind whistled on my barrel.

He was pleased by how well the boy Latif had done.

But something flashed off to his right and caught his eye – a mushroom of grey dust that lifted out from among the trees. He knew there was no longer any need for a doctor before the shock-wave of the explosion passed through him.

He thought he should go and check if any of them had survived, but fear paralysed him and he imagined another missile dropping towards him. He clenched low over the petrol tank and drove on, his eyes watering in the wind.

27

'This is for you, Tom,' the nurse said as she wheeled me up to your bed. You pushed yourself up on your elbows.

'Great,' you said and looked down at me. 'About time.'

'Do you want to try it?'

'Sure,' you said and started to pull yourself from the bed with a grunt.

'Wait, Tom, not so fast.' She laughed. 'You'll need this until you're stronger.' She reached for a wooden board propped by the wall and balanced one end on the bed and the other on my seat.

'Now, slide slowly onto the board.' She put her hands under your arms and helped you inch across. 'That's it. No rush.'

You were thin and weak and your arms trembled as you pulled yourself into me. You puffed out your cheeks.

'Are you okay?' she said.

'Just a bit dizzy.'

'That's normal. You haven't done much exercise for a few weeks.'

'Five, it must be now,' you said.

'Right, have a quick try.'

You placed your hands on my rings and pushed my wheels around and reversed me away from the bed. Then you pushed down with your left hand, my castors flicked around and I turned to the right and rolled into the centre of the bay.

'Aha, look who's got new wheels,' a man said from one of the other beds. He dropped a magazine into his lap.

'How am I doing?' you said.

'Pretty pathetic, I'm afraid, mate. I'm not sure you'll make it to the pub.'

'Well that's a blessing, Adam. I won't have to listen to your chat.' You pushed the tops of my wheels forward and I glided across the lino.

'I'll let you have a few days, Tom, and then I'll race you. We'll see if you can make it onto the hot-laps leaderboard.'

'Adam, there'll be no more wheelchair racing. The ward manager isn't at all happy about it.'

'John's currently winning, but he's cheating as he's only blind in one eye. Maybe we need to develop a new handicap system. What do you think, Sister?'

'And deaf in one ear,' a man shouted from another bed.

'Speak up, John. We can't hear you.'

'What?' The man cupped a hand around his ear.

'Adam, it's not funny, somebody'll get hurt,' the nurse said. 'And leave John alone.'

'We'll make it non-contact from now on,' he said, blew the nurse a kiss and hopped into his wheelchair.

'Come on, Tom, I'll show you the rest of the world.'

You pushed forward again and we followed the man out of the bay and along the ward. He waved and joked and introduced you to someone, who laughed, and you gently shook his two-fingered left hand. We wheeled on and the nurse called after us and told you not to go far. We went on out of the ward and farther into the hospital.

'Where are we going, Adam?' you asked as we coasted around a corner past a doctor.

'For a fag,' he said, pulling his chair forward with loping strides of his one remaining leg.

'I don't smoke.'

'The fresh air will do you good, mate.'

We freewheeled down a slope and into a lift.

'Come on, how long's it been since you were outside?'

'Fair enough,' you said.

We rolled out of the hospital and you leaned on my brakes and were just able to clip them on. 'I'm so weak.'

'It'll come back.' He sucked on a cigarette and dropped the pack on his seat in the space where his other leg should have been. 'Sure you won't have one?'

'I've definitely wasted away.' You were looking at your arms. 'No thanks, last thing I need is to start smoking now. All the doctors say it's terrible for wound healing.'

'God, don't you start, mate – or I'll fucking shove you off into the city.'

You looked down the hill, past the parked cars and the bus stop. The sky was clear above the red-brick buildings. You breathed in. We stayed for a while and spoke to another man who asked if you were in the army and talked about bravery. He tried handing you some money but you wouldn't take it.

He had to have another cigarette and said this way he only had to come out half as often. So you waited and then flicked off my brakes and we headed back inside.

You came to a ramp and couldn't push me up it. You called to the man ahead pulling himself forward with his leg. 'Adam, mate, wait up. I'm struggling here.' You strained forward on my wheels, your arms burnt and you leant your weight forward but I still didn't budge against the slope.

'Bloody hell, you are weak,' he said. 'You've managed all of about two foot.' He was looking back down from the top. 'Try a run-up.'

So we reversed back and the man at the top made a beeping noise. You pushed me forward in fast stabbing flicks and you gritted your teeth as we hit the ramp, but I was too heavy and we stalled halfway up. I veered into the wall with a clunk as you lost control of me.

'For God's sake,' you said.

'No dramas,' he was drifting down towards you. 'Hold on to the back of my chair.'

A man walked past. 'Do you need a hand, guys?' he said. 'I'll give you a push.'

'No thanks, mate,' you said. 'We'll be fine, thanks.'

'Are you sure? It's no problem at all.'

'I'm positive, thanks.'

He walked on down the corridor and glanced back at us.

'That's the spirit, Tom, fuck 'em all. We'll manage without them,' he said, laughing as he positioned himself in front of us. 'Right, hold on to my back rest.'

You gripped with your good hand and he pulled forward with his one leg and we jerked slowly up the ramp as he towed us behind him.

'Thanks, Adam.'

'You may be thin,' he said at the top, breathless, 'but you still weigh a bit.'

'That's all the fags, mate.'

'Oh, sod off,' he said and raced away, and you tried to keep up.

I stayed by your bed and you waited to heal. You joked with the other men and talked about who had the worst injuries, whether you'd swap a missing leg for a missing arm and whose scars were the ugliest. One of them drew eyes on his stump with a marker and used a flap of disfigurement to make it talk. A nurse told him off and shook her head as she left, and he made the stump into a sad face.

You told one another to stop being pathetic when they came to clean your wounds and you winced. When anybody groaned or gasped in pain, another would ask if he'd been shot by the phantom sniper. You'd laugh through the pain and tell everybody to piss off. And you drank in the morphine that made you euphoric and then sick. You shared food and read articles from the papers aloud to each other and slept.

Visitors filled the ward with presents and chocolates and magazines and noise. They would sit in me and look over you. Some found it difficult and you led the conversation and helped them through it. They twisted their hands together and didn't know what to say, it was hard seeing you like this. You were embarrassed when people you didn't really know visited. They came because they thought it was the right thing to do, but you hated being seen broken in the bed.

You were reading a magazine when she came. Her hair was shorter and it took you a moment to recognise her.

'Hi, Tom,' she said. 'Jess told me not to come, but I couldn't . . .'

You remembered her and the parties and how you'd ignored her. How you'd hoped some unspoken attraction would bring you together without you having to do anything. And you thought of the letter you hadn't replied to, which you'd reread a hundred times when you were still out there.

'Hi,' you said.

'I'm Anna. I just thought I should – I couldn't not come.'

'Yes, Anna – sorry, I know that. Sit down,' you said.

You pulled the sheet farther over yourself as she sat down in me. You were ashamed. You wanted to run away from her. You couldn't be disinterested and ignore her now, couldn't marvel at the pangs of excitement each time your eyes met across a room. She was next to you and you couldn't look away and pretend you hadn't been staring at her all along. She could see how damaged you were, how much you'd been changed, but she didn't look at it. She only looked into your face.

'Thank you for the letter,' you said. 'Sorry I didn't reply.' Your heart was racing and your chest was tight with panic. You wanted her to leave.

'I brought you this.' She put a bag on the table.

'Thanks, Anna.'

'Open it later,' she said.

'Thanks.'

'It's nothing, just chocolates.'

You asked how she was and about the friends you both knew. She seemed worried and asked how you were. She was nervous too and her fingers played against my cushion. You heard only some of what she said and it was awkward when she told you a story about people she thought you knew but you didn't.

You interrupted her before you meant to, when you couldn't take the embarrassment of it any more. 'I'm sorry,' you said, 'visiting hours are nearly over.'

You managed to thank her for the letter again before she left; you said it meant a lot. But she was already walking across the ward and away from us. She looked like she was going to cry and you knew you had pushed her away. You thought she was

[186]

crying because of the way you had been changed.

You put your hand on my cushion where she'd been sitting and breathed in her scent and thought how perfect she was. You were glad she had gone.

When you were well enough to leave they started to pack up your things. You pulled yourself across the board and into me, using my armrests to shuffle your bottom back. A nurse was behind you, ready to help, but you did it yourself. You waved to the others in the bay and said you'd see them soon, and they told you to break a leg.

We wheeled out to the car park. You held on to the top of the front door and shifted yourself into the passenger seat. You looked down into the empty footwell. A man folded me up and put me on the back seat, then drove us away from the hospital.

The lampposts flicked past and the ducking power lines swept together, aligned and then retreated. You looked at the cars around us as they swapped places down the motorway and the people behind the wheels. A few of them glanced at you but couldn't tell anything was wrong with you through the door. You talked to the driver because you thought you should.

The white lines that throbbed under the car made you want to sleep but you were also excited. You were out of the hospital and heading for the next place; it was progress. You'd been in this country for six weeks but hadn't seen it yet, and even though the land around was familiar you were experiencing it for the first time.

We turned off the motorway and passed through suburbia, then pulled through gates down a gravel track and stopped at the back of a building. I was reassembled and pushed up to the front seat and you slid yourself into me.

The gravel was too rough for my wheels, so the driver grabbed my handles and pushed us through it. Nurses greeted you and wheeled us down green corridors to a ward. They showed you to a space in the corner. It was like the last hospital except there were fewer machines above the bed or stands to hold up bags of drugs.

The other men limped or wheeled over to shake your hand. They were in sports kit and looked strong. You didn't want to talk yet, so you pulled the curtain around your bed and slept and I waited there, empty.

The next day you started your rehabilitation. It was gentle at first. We wheeled around the centre and you met all the people who would tell you what to do next. It was the first day at school and everyone noticed we were new. A physiotherapist introduced herself and gave you a piece of paper. It told you where to be during every hour of the day. You folded it up and stuffed it between my cushion and armrest.

She gave you exercises to do and we rolled to the gym, where others were sitting on the floor waving their limbs in the air or standing on one leg and lifting weights. You lowered yourself off me onto a blue mat and sat with your little stumps out in front of you, working them against a resistance band until they ached. An instructor handed you pink weights, the only ones you could lift, and they shook in your hands as you tried to extend them above your head.

And then we wheeled on to the next session. In the corridor you passed another man in a chair like me. You were shocked by his injuries and thought how strange he looked as he glided past, suspended up in his chair without any legs. He nodded at you and you nodded back. You felt sorry for him and didn't want to stare. You wheeled around a corner and two therapists walked past and stopped to tell you where the next session was, bending over you and talking gently.

You met a man who told you how they'd get you walking so you wouldn't have to rely on me. He asked how tall you'd been and what size shoes you'd worn. He explained the casting process and promised they'd have you standing in a couple of weeks.

He went to get equipment to measure your stumps. While you waited, another man went past. He had no legs, like you, except he was walking on prosthetics, flicking them forward and arching his back. He was red-faced, his arms swinging around him for balance. You didn't want him to see you looking but wondered how he did it and couldn't imagine being able to do it yourself.

Others called you over at lunch and asked you to sit with them. You felt dazed and sick after the morning's effort and they could see it in your face. They told you that it got easier, that you'd look back and be amazed by your progress. Just be patient. And then you pulled out the piece of paper and saw you were already late. You hated being late and pushed my wheels hard to hurry to your next session.

The physiotherapist started working on you, moving your damaged stumps and examining your muscles with her thumbs, mobilising them while you flinched and stared at the floor through the hole in the treatment table. You talked her through all your wounds and she inspected them under the bandages. You enjoyed talking to her and laughed at the pain she inflicted and how hard she made you work. She told you she'd get you walking soon.

At the end of each day you chatted in deep sofas with the others and balanced cups of tea between your stumps or on armrests. You watched TV with them and then you went to your bed and slept.

[189]

For two weeks we wheeled around the centre, always pulling the piece of paper from under my cushion before we rolled on to the next session. You became stronger, I went faster. You started to know those who were helping you and you loved them for it. They cast your legs and prepared the equipment that would make me obsolete.

Some friends came to see you at the weekend and we went into the garden. They walked slowly alongside you and you tried to act as if nothing had happened; you tried to hide the effort of wheeling me. You were self-conscious being at waist height and looking up at people who once had to look up at you. You tried to hide your stumps from them with a jumper in your lap but as you pushed me it kept falling off and it frustrated you.

You gently lowered yourself off me onto the grass. They watched you do it and looked at where you no longer had legs and at the white bandages, stained with secretions from your wounds, poking from your shorts.

They'd brought you beer. It was normal for a while. They talked about what they'd been up to, about other friends and how well you were doing. But then your left stump started to hurt. You wanted to go inside and get some drugs – to be alone.

You nearly fell as you pulled yourself up into me. They wanted to help but didn't know how to say it. So they followed as you wheeled yourself back towards the centre along the path. You thought they were watching you from behind so you pushed me faster.

And then my front castor was trapped. You pushed forward and pulled back on my rings but couldn't get over the lip – you blamed me for this – and then my rear wheel dropped into a gap between paving stones and we were stuck. You became frustrated and embarrassed and groaned. You tried to rock me out and swore when you couldn't.

We fell back until my anti-topple bars caught us. But you didn't trust me and thought we were going to fall and you flailed out, reaching forward as I tipped over. You put your foot out to stop yourself, but you had no foot and you dropped down onto your stump. It banged hard on the ground. The unnatural pain shot through the cut bone. You contained yourself from shouting out in front of them but the shock showed as tears in your eyes. You sat there with your head bowed, as the stain on your bandage grew with fresh blood. I was next to you on my side. You were suddenly exhausted.

One of your friends grabbed hold of me and another lifted you tenderly into me and your head slumped forward as your friend pushed us over the path. The bumps and jerking made you feel nauseous and you wished he'd stop but he wheeled us out of the garden and back to the centre.

28

I was screwed to a wall by workmen in a new disabled toilet at a rehabilitation centre that needed more capacity. I reflected the handrails, basin, dryer and shiny toilet. A red panic cord hung down from the ceiling.

Many of them came in, often on crutches or in wheelchairs, and I reflected them as they awkwardly pulled the door shut. They held the rails, flushed and used the sink. Some didn't need to sit on the toilet and emptied urine out of a tube.

A new man appeared. At the start a nurse came with him and helped wipe, but after a few weeks he had the strength to do it on his own.

Now he was back and pulled himself from the chair onto the toilet seat, his stumps jutting out in front of him. He wore a T-shirt and shorts and looked down between his stumps as he went. Once he had finished, he flushed and then wheeled up to the door.

But this time he caught his reflection in me and stopped. What I showed was different from how he imagined himself. He saw the freakishly short limbs and the space between them and the floor, where he used to exist. He knew I reflected what others saw, and it shocked him. He shook his head in disbelief. He was unnatural, created by violence and saved by soldiers and medics: he'd survived the unsurvivable and it showed. He felt disgusted.

He pulled his shorts off and then his T-shirt and dropped them on the floor. Naked, he stared into me and down at himself and shook his head again without wanting to. He saw the grotesque scars and folds of flesh and the pink skin grafts that covered his wounds. He saw the violence of the bomb. Who could love that, he thought. Then he closed his eyes and started.

It hurt, but less than everything else, and his expression didn't change and there was no pleasure. When he'd finished, his severed nerves buzzed and he bent down his head and breathed. His semen was brown with blood from the trauma and he looked at it in surprise.

He went to the tissue dispenser, flushed again, put his clothes back on and left. He never looked in me again.

29

I was spilt with twenty identical others from the cardboard box we were packaged in. I clinked against them as we rolled out across the green mattress.

BA5799 lined us up into rows of ten and then thirty and pushed us one by one into a magazine. He held me between his thumb and finger and rolled me through the jaws, sliding me back so I could descend and depress the spring. I was fifth from the top, one above a tracer round tipped with red.

We rattled as the magazine was dropped and hurriedly packed away.

When the magazine was attached to a weapon, we lifted up one position as the top round was loaded into the chamber; now I was fourth. After a few hours, the magazine was removed and the top round reinserted, pushing me back down. But once the rifle kicked above us, I jumped up a place and then another. After a pause we jumped again and the bolt carrier was above me. I was next.

The excitement stopped; it wasn't my turn yet. I descended as the magazine was replenished by four more like me.

One day BA5799 removed us and I was sliding up the magazine again. His thumb dragged me out and he added me to a row on a table. The table was covered with graffiti, and I rested in the groove of a cap badge that had been carved into its surface. He bent over me and the other rows of bullets on parade.

At the end of the table was a stripped-down rifle. He picked it up and started to clean it, pulling a string down its barrel and pushing a cloth into its breech. He leant back into a decaying sofa.

We were in a gap between two buildings, in the shade of a tarpaulin sagging over us. A board rested on the back of the sofa behind him, pinned with pictures of women and letters. A wooden sign was nailed in the corner. It said *TWO WAY RANGE* and pointed towards the gate of the camp, out across the yard trembling in the heat.

BA5799 picked up another piece of the weapon and flicked at the dust caught in its mechanism with a brush. A man looked over a partition at the end of the sofa. His hair was plastered down his forehead and he ducked to pour more water over his head with a bowl. Water ran over his mouth and he blew droplets of it out.

'I need to do mine too,' he said before dropping again to scoop up some water.

BA5799 peered into a weapon part, clicked the trigger forward and looked up from the sofa. 'I had a stoppage.'

'Never nice,' the man said. He stepped from behind the partition, tucking a green towel around his waist. 'Back in a sec.'

BA5799 reassembled the weapon, pressing bolts together and propping it against the end of the sofa.

The man came back wearing flip-flops and shorts and sat in a plastic garden chair across from him. 'I needed that,' he said, running his fingers through his hair. 'When's Six Platoon due back in?'

'Not sure.'

'I wish he'd get on with it.'

'Should be any minute,' BA5799 said and started to scrape carbon from a black cylinder.

'God, it's hot today. Take a shower and you're pissing sweat two minutes later.' He leant forward, grabbed a paper from a chair, opened it, then threw it back down. He looked around. 'Do we know when the next helicopter's scheduled?'

'No news. Two, three days, maybe.'

'Feels like they've forgotten all about us. I need some post. And these papers are two weeks out now.'

'It's busy up north,' BA5799 said, then slid the cylinder onto the rifle and cleaned the magazines, blowing out the dust and wiping them down. He took a round from the table, twisted it through his fingers to remove dirt and pushed it back into its slot. 'I heard they're sending fresh on the next one.'

'Who said that?'

'One of the CQ staff.'

'Well, it better be more than a couple of manky oranges,' the man said, crossing his arms and leaning back on his plastic chair.

'I quite enjoyed those,' BA5799 said.

In the distance gunfire crackled. BA5799 held the bullet over the jaws of the magazine and looked at the other man. 'Too far away?'

'That has to be up in PB50's area,' the man said and they listened as the gunfire sounded again.

'Definitely too far away,' BA5799 said.

They relaxed. Two figures, translucent in the heat, crossed the camp above dark shadows. The man picked up the paper and then threw it down again, sighing. 'Got anything to read?' he said.

'If you look under my bed there's a few magazines. Got sent them last week.'

'Dirty ones?'

'Afraid not. They're from my mum.'

BA5799 clipped each round away and the rows disappeared from the table.

Then a man dressed in his armour and carrying a weapon walked out of the vertical sunlight into the shade. He unclipped his helmet.

'Move over, Dan,' he said, pulling another chair into the shade and slumping down. 'Getting hotter out there.'

'Nothing?' BA5799 said.

'Few farmers beyond Lima Three Three, but they didn't want to talk.'

'Is that everyone in, then?'

'Yup, shop's shut for the day.' He lifted his armour over his head and drank some water.

The three men talked as BA5799 cleaned and refilled another magazine. One of the men went out and came back with a bottle of shampoo.

'Not more contraband, I hope, Dan?'

The man smiled and prised the blue lid off. He tipped it up and a small bottle of whiskey rolled out across the table, knocking apart the row I was in. 'The girlfriend sent it,' he said. 'Want some?'

'Sure, everyone's back in,' BA5799 said. He was on the final row, wiping down each round and then pressing us back into a magazine. A glass was placed down and brown liquid was poured. BA5799 was cleaning me and he picked up the glass with the same hand and I was next to his mouth as he drank. He forced a cough from his throat and smiled at the others. 'Thanks, Dan.'

'Not very much, I'm afraid.'

'I've got more,' BA5799 said.

'You kept that quiet, Tom.'

'I'll just get it. Been saving it for a special occasion.' He pressed me through the jaws of the magazine and I was back in the dark, zigzagging stack of rounds.

The next time I climbed up the magazine, the rifle bucked twice and then we were moving and the bottom of the magazine was crunching in the dirt. It fired again and I was below the dull metal of the weapon, pushed up by the spring and ready to work. We bucked again and the bolt carrier ejected my predecessor, recoiling to sweep me from the top of the magazine and ram me into the chamber.

Ahead, a small hole of light shone at the end of a silver right-hand spiral. The weapon wobbled, then steadied, and my cap was hit by the firing pin. My propellant charge ignited, burnt and split me in two, sending the front half down the barrel.

The weapon worked around me and extracted the empty part of me, which glinted as it fell onto the soil next to BA5799. He was in a line of men with his elbows pushed into the dust.

The other half of me accelerated down the spiral towards the light. The grooves of rifling melted into me, scarring my jacket and spinning me. I burst out of the barrel at 940 metres per second, away from the weapon with BA5799 tucked behind it, and his soldiers all firing and sweating beneath their helmets on the hill by the cemetery.

In an instant they vanished away behind me.

My trajectory was predetermined: gravity, atmospheric pressure, a gentle southerly wind and the world spinning on its axis, all acted on me. Friction heated me to 276 degrees as I ripped a silent hole through the air, building a centre of pressure in front of me. The constant bang I made trailed behind in a cone of noise and turbulence, spreading out to shock everything in my wake.

Many others were in motion around me, churning the air with kinetic energy. Some slapped past but most were ahead or behind and converging on our target. I flew in a flat arc towards my terminal event. An irrigation ditch flashed below me, and then another and another as the fields whipped brown, green, brown and then I was over the ruins of compounds.

The round that had been below me in the magazine was in the air now, following behind, its tip glowing red. Friction sapped my energy and my arc deepened as I started to drop.

My target was ahead but he pulled away and I silently passed him before my noise cracked against his eardrum.

I travelled to the far side of the derelict building, where I slammed into a mud wall. I dragged my shockwave in after me and it lifted flecks of stone and rock up in an explosion of pressure.

30

The room I was in looked over the garden. I wasn't used much, only when guests came to stay.

Your father and brother stripped my mattress and twisted me through the door and down the stairs. They took me across a hall into a room that was used at Christmastime and smelled of fire and scented candles. I was positioned against the wall.

Your mother was there, moving tables and rearranging ornaments on the mantelpiece. The men helped her with the sheets and blankets and she plumped the pillows and pulled my duvet flat. She took a few things away and brought in some others.

Your father looked around and told her to stop fussing, then they went and I was on my own. The shadows of trees swayed across the windows that overlooked the garden and squares of sunlight tracked over the cream carpet.

A car crunched over the gravel drive and the dog barked with excitement. Your mother brought you in and you rolled up to me in your wheelchair.

'Do you think this will be okay, Tom?' she said as she put your bag on the sofa.

'Of course, Mum, it's great,' you said.

'How about a nice cup of tea?'

'Great. Thanks,' you said and hopped onto me, my springs bouncing under you. 'You didn't need to bring the TV in.'

'We thought it would help, just for a bit. You don't want to keep wheeling around the house.'

You pulled yourself up on me and looked at your phone and then around the room and thought about the last time you'd been in here. There had been ripped wrapping paper and a fire; your grandparents had been drinking sherry.

She came back with a tray, passed you a mug and sat at the end of me. 'I hope it's okay. We just thought it would be easier than trying to get upstairs.'

'It's fine, Mum.'

'The occupational therapist inspected the house last week. She said this was the right thing to do. It won't be ideal with the shower but we'll have to make do.'

'Mum, it's great. It's just good to be home,' you said. 'The garden looks nice.'

'Your father's been at it any chance he gets. You know what he's like. He should be back soon,' she said. 'Biscuit?'

'Thanks. And is David still coming?'

'He should be back for supper. I've cooked your favourite.'

'Thanks, Mum, I can't wait. The food's been okay but I've been looking forward to coming home.'

'I thought we could drive up the hill to the woods if you wanted. Freddie needs a walk. You could sit in the car. I'll just give him a quick run.'

'Great.'

You left with her and struggled to push your chair across the thick carpet. When she asked if you needed a hand, you said you'd manage.

When you came back you were tired and pulled yourself into me and under my covers. You felt safe in me and you slept deeply.

Your father came and sat on the edge of me and turned to look down at your face. You seemed untroubled and stronger and he smiled. He placed his hand on your shoulder.

'Tom,' he said. 'Would you like some food?'

You rolled onto your back, opened your eyes and stretched. 'Hello, Dad.' You smiled. 'God, that was a nice kip.'

'Do you want something to eat? It's seven o'clock. David's back.'

'Sure.'

He pushed your chair closer and you transferred into it and followed him out. The sun set and it was dark. The garden was quiet but there was laughter from another room and the sound of family and food.

But when you came back you were drained and pale. You hauled yourself onto me and stared at the ceiling.

Your mother came in. 'Are you okay, Tom?' she said.

'That was delicious, Mum. Thank you.'

'I hope it wasn't too much.'

'No, I'm just tired. It was so great to be with you all. I started to feel a bit odd.'

'In what way?' She sat down on me.

'Please, Mum, it's nothing. I just need a good night's sleep.'

'I'll go and get you a bowl,' she said.

She came back with a blue plastic bowl and a flannel and put them on my covers. You pulled off your T-shirt and shorts and started to wash yourself.

'I'm going to let Freddie out,' she said.

You dunked the flannel in the bowl and wiped it under your armpits, then across the back of your neck, over your body and down around your stumps and groin.

Tears filled your eyes as you started to wash your face, and you wiped at them with the flannel. You leant forward and held your face in your hands. The flannel was pressing against it and water dripped onto my covers. You sobbed, the sadness overwhelming you, and your whole body heaved. You slapped your hand down on me with all your strength and grunted in frustration.

'Stop it,' you said, 'for fuck's sake, stop it,' and pulled the flannel hard against your skin.

But sobs shook you and she came back in. 'Tom?' she said, then walked over and gently sat on the edge of me. 'Oh, darling. It's okay.'

'Please, don't,' you said, but you were crying now and couldn't fight through the tears to speak. 'Please. I'm fine,' you whispered.

You held the flannel to your face and cried into it. Your face creased up and your mouth pulled down with saliva strung across it.

Your father and brother came and sat next to her. Your whole family was on me.

'I'm sorry,' you said. 'It's pathetic.'

She put her hand on your shoulder. 'Tom, don't worry. This is normal.'

The three of them looked at you.

'It was so nice tonight at supper, and I forgot all about it,' you said. 'It was just all of us together.' A sob fought up through you and stopped you speaking and they waited. 'It was so nice,' you whispered, 'being back here at home with everyone around the table. And I'd forgotten. But when I slipped at the table it suddenly reminded me of what's happened.' You sniffed. 'I've been stuck in a hospital, in this weird existence. It's all been so unreal and suddenly I'm here. And it is real. This is me.'

'It will get better,' she said, her face sad.

'I've got no legs. That will never get better.' You cried again and then spoke through the tears. 'I used to go out that door and run up on the hills. And now I can hardly get across this carpet.'

You wept and covered your face with the flannel again and bent forward so your head was between your stumps.

'Let it out, Tom,' your father said. 'You've got to go through this. If you didn't, something would be wrong.'

'It's all wrong.' You smiled at him and laughed through a moan. 'It's all wrong. I feel like I've been chosen for a main part I never wanted to play and everyone's come to watch. They're all watching me, looking to see what's happened, what's gone wrong. Half of them I don't even know. I don't want them to see. They should mind their own fucking business.'

'People just care about you. About us,' your brother said.

'I know, David,' you said. 'But it's such hard work. I can't pretend it's all okay. It's too much effort. Oh, look at Tom, isn't he doing well, poor thing – and then I have to live up to always doing well and getting better. What happens if I don't?'

Your father laughed. 'No one thinks it's all okay, Tom. They're rooting for you. And we'll be here to help you through it.'

'I'll never run again, or dance or do anything normal – like help bring the shopping in.'

'You never did that anyway,' your brother said, and you all laughed despite the tears running down your face.

'Well, I'll probably still be more help than you, David,' you said.

You sniffed away the tears and started to wipe the back of your neck again and your father gave you a toothbrush.

'Thanks, Dad,' you said and gave your mother the flannel.

'We're all in this together. People really do care.'

'I know, I'm sorry. It's bloody self-pity. I'm sorry, I shouldn't be so pathetic.'

'You're mourning a loss, Tom. I know it feels like you're not the same,' he said, moving closer up me and looking at you. 'To us you are the same. We feel so lucky that it's still you in there, that you're still here. You might never run, or bring in the bloody shopping, but you'll – we'll – get through this.'

You started to brush your teeth and closed your eyes and the tears had stopped.

'I know, I was just being silly,' you mouthed around the toothbrush.

'It's not silly at all,' your mother said.

'You're the one at the centre of this and none of us can imagine what you're going through,' your father added.

'You're doing so well, all the doctors and physios are really pleased.' Your mother held out a cup for you to spit into.

'I know.' You passed the cup back. 'I suppose being back here, at home, just made everything seem so stark. I've been a sick person in a bed, with no legs, broken in hospital. Now I'm getting stronger, I'm becoming a normal person with no legs—'

'It'll take time,' she said. 'You're getting better every day.'

'—I'm back in the real world and I suddenly remember what I used to be able to do, what I might have achieved – and it feels like all that's been taken away.'

'You will still achieve,' she said.

'You're determined, mate,' your brother said. 'There are so many things you can accomplish; it just may not be in the same ways.'

'And we're here to help you, Tom.'

The sobs still gripped you, but you all talked together and laughed. You felt lucky again.

'I'm sure I'm fine, you should all go to bed,' you said finally. 'I feel much better for it. I needed a good blub. It's hard in hospital with so many people around. And you don't want to let the side down.'

They smiled, said goodnight and left. The pills didn't let you dwell on it and you fell asleep, despite the nerve pain and the discomfort in your arm and all the thoughts in your head.

At dawn you woke and the drugs held you in a daze and made your eyelids heavy. The birds were singing and you reached for a bottle, manoeuvred yourself over the edge of me and urinated into it. You fell asleep again and dreamed of running. You were running through tents and the grass was long and made it hard but you needed to get to the school on time. Lines appeared on your legs, cut with an invisible scalpel, deep around your calves, and they were red and started to bleed down to your feet and made running harder. The lines became deeper but you managed to keep going and then there was no one to save.

You woke slowly and I was the most comfortable thing you'd experienced for a long time. My white duvet cocooned you; you knew you were at home but didn't know why. It was familiar and you felt safe. Your nerves fired from your feet and you could feel them under my duvet but they felt cold. Why were they cold? You tried to move them. Then you were absolutely awake and remembered why you were in me, downstairs in the room where Christmas happened, and not in that other place.

Your mother knocked on the door and brought in your breakfast. You sat up and took the mug of tea while she opened the curtains and you looked out at the early autumn morning.

Later, you went out into the garden and lay on the grass and the dog's tail wagged as he tried to lick you and you pushed him away.

The next day, you were on me reading a paper when she knocked and brought a man in. She introduced him and said he'd come to talk to you. He wheeled himself over with confident thrusts of a chair like yours. She left and the two of you talked. He told you how he had been hurt and how long it had taken to recover and what it was like always being in a wheelchair. He said you would be much more mobile. You saw he was broken but found it hard to relate to him.

He told you about his wife and children and how he'd overcome the despair and what he had achieved. He said he now appreciated every day and was making the most of life. He told you what had happened would make you appreciate life more.

You nodded and smiled but didn't believe him. You couldn't see how what had happened to you could be in any way good. Before leaving he turned and said that you probably didn't understand it yet, but one day you would. You thanked him for coming, rolled over in me, pressed the remote and watched a programme about antiques.

Your mother helped you pack your things and you left. I was empty for a few weeks and waited for you to return. When you did, you were stronger and you briskly wheeled yourself in and she propped two mechanical legs against the sofa. They stayed there and you often glanced at them and wondered if you should put them on and practise but you were too tired. At night, when it was dark and you were asleep, they rested there motionless and it looked like someone might be standing among the shadows with us.

I stayed downstairs and you came back every few weeks and your mother looked after you. You became stronger and spent less time in me. And you put the legs on and went past the window with jerking steps, leaning on the walking sticks you held in each hand.

One morning she came in with a cup of tea and pulled the curtains and the brown leaves blew across the garden.

'I wouldn't change it,' you said to her.

'Sorry, Tom?' She turned around and glanced at my covers. 'What needs changing?'

'I wouldn't change it.' You took a sip from the mug. 'Any of it.'

She came and sat on me and looked at you. 'I don't understand.'

'I wouldn't change what happened to me.'

'Of course you would.' Her brow was creased. 'You don't have to say that, Tom.'

'I mean it. It's part of me now. I know I can't change it anyway, so it's a stupid thing to say, but if someone walked in and asked me if I wanted to go back and for it never to have happened, I'd say I wouldn't want to.'

She shook her head. 'You don't mean that.'

'I do.' You grinned at her. 'It's hard to explain but it's already too much a part of who I am. Life's changed and it's been grim, but I'm experiencing so much.'

After that visit, you didn't need me in that room any more and I was taken back upstairs.

31

I was ridden around a city that pulsed with the fumes of stationary traffic and the incessant horns of tuktuks. A man rode me through this to work but one day I was stolen and loaded onto a truck with many others like me. We were driven a great distance, the air became cooler and we waited while a mountain pass was cleared, then we crossed over and down into a new country. I was sold at market to a man who took me home and gave me to his son, Faridun.

I had a green steel frame and a red plastic saddle; I had a bell that rattled through potholes. I was too big for Faridun when I was first given to him; he couldn't reach my saddle so he pedalled me standing up. His father jogged alongside holding us as Faridun smiled and steered me in small circles around the road outside their compound. Finally his father pushed me off and watched us wobble away down the road until I veered into a ditch and Faridun catapulted over me.

But he learnt to ride me for the sheer pleasure of speed and freedom. He pedalled me as fast as he could with a kite fluttering behind. His friend Latif ran alongside, both of them laughing. He shouted at him to go faster until he couldn't keep up. They got bored with the kite and the lack of wind. So his friend sat on my saddle and Faridun pedalled me to a river and I lay in the reeds while they swam.

Faridun did grow into me as his father said he would. And I carried him around the district when he ran errands for his family.

Faridun's father controlled the network of irrigation that kept the land green for the farmers. He decided which sluices should be opened and whose fields the water should slosh into. He told Faridun it was difficult to be fair and how in some dry years men came open-handed and pleaded with him.

When Faridun was becoming a man, his father began explaining how he governed the fragile web of water. He sent Faridun out to work and he rode me to one of the ditches and met older men who worked for his father. They would stand in the muddy channels and shovel silt into wheelbarrows or pile it up at the edges of fields.

Faridun propped me in the shade of a tree, rolled up his trousers and worked with them. When the men stopped for lunch, they didn't invite Faridun to sit with them, so he sat with me under the tree. He tried to listen to what they were saying and sometimes thought he heard them talking about his father.

Every few days his father came to inspect the work they'd done and to pay the men. He dropped down into the channel and checked its depth, then told them to dig deeper or widen the channel and remove rotten wood. He gave them more instructions and told them where they should work next. He never looked at Faridun, who listened to the men muttering to one another after his father had gone.

Sometimes they would joke and laugh with each other and sit around in the heat doing nothing. Faridun wanted to tell them to do what his father was paying them for, but he was frightened so kept working alone, ignoring them, and each new scoop of mud fuelled the ache in his back.

The fighting each summer was more intense than the last and the distant popping of gunfire made them lean on their tools and look around. Sometimes it was close by and they would run away, back to their houses, and Faridun would jump on me and cycle home.

Bombs were hidden under the roads more frequently, and Faridun became careful of the paths he steered me on. His father told him where he could go and his mother worried anyway. Whole stretches of road were riddled and everyone knew not to use them. But Faridun always skirted around the little piles of rock or creases in the road surface that didn't look right.

More checkpoints barred the roads and he couldn't avoid them all. He would show his papers and we would ride on. But sometimes he had to give money and once a man at a roadblock pushed me over and my sprocket caught and tore open Faridun's ankle as he fell. They forced a weapon deep into his mouth and stole the sack I'd carried from the market. They laughed at Faridun as he limped home, pushing me beside him, worrying about his family and his sister and angry with Latif.

After a day spent clearing a channel, Faridun was riding me home, his wet trousers clinging to his legs. He turned a corner and saw soldiers walking towards him. He was frightened but there was nowhere else to go, so he pedalled me on down the centre of them. One smiled below his helmet and then jeered, making another laugh. He thought he might be able to ride straight through the column and home, but one of them called in his own language, 'Hey, young man. Wait. Peace be upon you.'

Faridun pulled my brake lever, my pads pinched my rims

and I stopped. He looked back. The soldiers were sinking down to kneel. One was walking towards him. He spoke through an interpreter who wore sunglasses and cloth tied around his head.

'Peace be upon you,' the interpreter said. 'May we speak with you?'

'I am just on my way home,' Faridun said. 'I have been working in the fields.'

The interpreter talked to the soldier, who smiled and then told him something and nodded out across the fields.

'We are looking for a man who lives around here. His name is Kushan Hhan. We need to talk to him,' the translator said.

Faridun twisted his thigh over my crossbar and looked at them. He glanced down and fidgeted with my stem.

'I do not know this country well,' he said. 'I am just here to work.'

The interpreter spoke to the soldier, who was holding a map and writing on it.

'I just told this captain what you said; then I told him you were lying.' He smiled at Faridun. 'I know where you're from, and I know you're a bad liar. Your eyes are too honest, young man.'

The soldier started to interrupt but the translator held up his hand for more time.

'This captain is a good man. He means no harm,' he said and grinned. 'You should help us – you know that, don't you? The government of the republic would want you to help us.'

Faridun looked across the field in the direction the soldier had nodded. It was his house and he knew his father would be there. He knew his father didn't think much of the government but had worked with the soldiers before.

'I know where he is,' Faridun said and looked at the interpreter.

The soldier looked surprised when his words were translated.

'Can you take us to him?' the interpreter asked.

As soon as Faridun started to push me down the road with them following behind, strung out in a column, he wished he hadn't agreed to help. He wanted to shrink away before anyone saw him with them. He felt vulnerable and stared out across the fields. Please don't be watching, he thought. But he knew they would be; they always watched the soldiers.

It wasn't far and he turned me down the track to the complex of walls that huddled around the main compound he lived in. He thought of his family sitting on the carpets around the stove and chatting. He wished even more that he hadn't agreed.

The soldiers spread out around the compound and Faridun leant me next to the tall, black gate.

'Wait here,' he said and went in.

The soldiers were moving across the front field and a group dropped down by a thicket of bushes. Another team was pushing out along the main wall, crouching beside it and across the road. The soldier closest to me was talking into a radio, then said something in his foreign tongue and the interpreter shrugged.

Faridun's father walked towards us down the road from the back field. He had seen the soldiers arrive. He saw me and thought of Faridun and hoped he was all right.

He put his hand over his heart and spoke to the interpreter, who stood next to the lead soldier. 'May peace be upon you, what brings you to my house?'

'And upon you be peace,' the man said and nodded his head respectfully. 'We are looking for Kushan Hhan.'

'You have found him,' Faridun's father said and smiled. 'How may I help you?'

'My captain would like to speak with you.'

The soldier spoke to the translator and offered his hand to Faridun's father, who shook it.

'He apologises for coming to your home, but he wants to resume the dialogue that the security forces once had with the elders in this area.'

The gate opened and Faridun came out and saw his father. 'These men want to see you, Father,' he said.

'I know, son. I have just heard.' He smiled at him and turned to the soldier. 'Please wait for one moment,' he said. 'I need to make sure my house is ready. Then we shall talk.'

Faridun grabbed hold of my handlebars, wheeled me through the gate and propped me against the post of an awning at the edge of the garden. His father signalled that the women were not visible, and Faridun led three of the soldiers inside the large room at the end of the compound, beyond the veranda.

When they had finished talking and the men were gone, Faridun's father came into the garden and sat on a low bench near where I waited.

Faridun followed him at a distance. 'I am sorry, Father,' he said softly and twisted a vine leaf in his fingers. 'I should not have brought them. But I thought, with their weapons and power and money – I thought you might want to talk to them.'

'It is done now, Faridun.'

Faridun looked over at him. 'Will they punish us? Will Lalma be okay?'

'I don't know, Faridun,' he said. 'We will have to wait. God willing it will be of some use.'

Faridun crouched down and dangled his fingers in the water that trickled along a concrete gutter into the garden, disturbing the small track of silt at the bottom. 'Are they winning now?'

'Winning?'

'Will the soldiers make us safer? There seem to be more of them, and they come farther into our land. Are they pushing Hassan and his people away?'

'It's not just Hassan, Faridun. It is complex. The elders will want to know what I have said as well.'

He stared through the lattice of green that hung from the pergola: if he didn't focus, it was a shifting emerald blur. Conflict had always raged beyond his walls but he and his family had only ever known peace in this compound. However, the world outside was encroaching now. He looked at his son.

'What I do know,' he said, 'is that no one wins.'

Faridun rode me to work each day and the dread that he'd endangered his sister and family twisted through him. He wished he'd stayed quiet and lied to the soldiers. A bark of frustration burst out of him as he pedalled me and he shook his head, grasping his fingers tightly around my grips.

He returned home and expected that Hassan's men had visited. As we rode down the track to the compound he imagined what they'd done to his family. He prepared himself to see his sister's headless body and his dead father and mother, the rest of his family all slaughtered around them. He'd been told that's what they could do. But everyone was fine and welcomed him in and he sat with them as they prepared for the wedding.

A few weeks later, Faridun's father sent us up to the edge of the desert that had been abandoned when the soldiers arrived. Their base was attacked most days and the buildings and compounds were punctured with holes and strike marks. Many had collapsed and entire sections of wall had been destroyed. His father told Faridun that they had to keep the channels clear for when the people returned, for when the fighting was over. It was their duty, he said as he waved us off.

Faridun cycled me up to one of his father's small buildings. The men were waiting and grunted at him. I was against the wall and he opened the door with the key his father had given him. The men filed in, took tools from the stacks by the walls and pushed a wheelbarrow out, then walked across a wheat field and started dredging a ditch.

That afternoon, I was flat in the dry grass beside Faridun. He was sitting on his haunches, loosening the jammed slat of a sluice gate, banging it with a hammer until it crunched free. Then he worked it up and down, untied a grimy bag of grease and spread it into the gate's notches.

He looked up when the firing started, then over at the other men, who had also paused. There were trees blocking their view, but it was close and from the direction of the soldiers' base. Faridun wiped his hands on the grass, lifted me up and pushed me towards the men.

'It is near?' one of them said.

'From the base,' Faridun called back. He wheeled me down the path next to the channel. The gunfire stuttered and then built again.

'What do you think?' Faridun said as he pushed me up to an old wall that ran alongside the ditch the men were clearing. They stepped up onto the path, drips from their clothes darkening the dust.

'They are too close,' one said. 'I am going home.' He picked up a shovel, put it in the wheelbarrow and walked away. The others followed.

'Wait, it might be over soon,' Faridun said.

One of them dismissed him with a wave and said it was nearly the end of the day anyway.

They began running when the air above started to crack. The sound sprayed across the sky as they sprinted in a crouch for the small building. Faridun saw them chuck the tools down by the door and sighed. They disappeared through the trees and down the road. They won't be back today, he thought.

Faridun rested me beside the wall and slid down until he was leaning against it. With the wall between us and the firing he was safe and waited, listening to the bullets and looking up at the sky as it ruptured above him. There was no visible sign of the noise. He thought how odd that was but knew the tiny bits of metal would travel far into the district before they landed and kicked up a puff of dust in a field. He'd seen that several times.

The sound subsided and only the occasional bullet snapped overhead. Then it roared in a crescendo and he heard the whine of a ricochet sail up through the constant cracks. He didn't feel frightened behind the wall, and told himself the firing would stop soon, the attackers would drift away and the soldiers would wait in their towers again.

But it went on much longer than Faridun expected and he took some dried apricots from his pocket and started eating. There was one last burst of gunfire and finally it was silent. He was about to get up and pack away the equipment when he heard shuffling through the foliage next to the wall, a hiss of breath and murmuring. Then they came around the corner and Faridun stood up and reached for me.

The injured man's chin was flat against his chest and his grey trousers were dark with blood. He was held between two men.

Faridun knew them all and he backed away. These were Hassan's men and Latif was with them. They have come to punish me, Faridun thought.

'You. Come here, we need help,' one of them said. His accent was foreign.

It was the man who had pushed us over at the checkpoint. The weapon he had forced into Faridun's mouth was slung across his back and the eyes that had threatened his sister flashed up at him. He didn't seem to recognise Faridun and was less frightening now. His turban had been knocked back, exposing his forehead, and he stooped under the weight of the bleeding man, his expression desperate.

Faridun stepped away and held my handlebars.

'I said come here, boy,' the man said again, trying to be forceful through the strain.

Faridun didn't move. He looked at Latif under the other arm of the hurt man. He was struggling to control his breathing, which came in faltering wheezes.

'Latif?' Faridun said. He was concerned for him.

'How do you know Latif?' the man said. He tried to heft the injured man up. 'Quick, you can help us. We need to get this man to safety.'

'Are you okay, Latif?' Faridun said but the young man didn't reply. Faridun pushed me out from the wall. 'I know a place that's not far. Follow me,' he said, taking their weapons and hanging them from my handlebars. They dangled down beside me as I was wheeled across the field back towards the small building. They carried the injured man behind us, stumbling through the wheat and over the hard clumps of earth. A fourth man was with them and kept checking behind to make sure they weren't being followed.

Faridun unlocked the door and pushed me into the small room. 'You will be safe in here,' he said.

'Thank you,' Latif said. He coughed and looked up at Faridun.

They came in and lowered the injured man down onto the slab floor. Faridun saw Latif stagger away towards the wall and crash into a stack of shovels. He steadied himself.

'What should we do with Paugi? He might die,' Latif said still coughing.

'I will go for the doctor,' the man said. He came over to me and unhooked one of the weapons from my handlebars. He was in the doorway now with his weapon and glanced back down at the body but didn't seem to know what to say.

Faridun went over to the injured man and crouched beside him. 'You must stop the blood leaving him. Here, let me,' he said and tore off a piece of his shirt. He lifted the leg up and fed the cloth under, wrapping it around the thigh. He pulled it tight and tied it off.

'Thank you, Faridun,' Latif said and joined him, ripping his own shirt.

The man who'd threatened Faridun and kicked me over at the checkpoint looked down at Latif and Faridun tending to the bleeding man and told them to do what they could. He stepped out of the door and the other man went with him to guard the hut.

They tore more strips and helped each other wrap the man's leg but he had stopped moving and his breathing was shallow; they didn't know what else they could do. They sat back against the wall between the upright tools and waited, their shoulders touching, each feeling the other's body heat. Neither spoke for a while.

'Do you remember when we used to ride that bike to the river?' Latif finally said.

Faridun looked at me and thought of all the times they had spent together when they were young. When they were best friends.

'Why did you join them, Latif?' he said.

'Why do you not?' He looked across at him. 'Do not judge me, Faridun. I have family duty to them.'

'But at the checkpoint? After everything?'

'I am sorry,' Latif said.

In the silence they both gazed at me over the dying man and Faridun remembered the time they'd tied a kite to me, trying to make it fly.

The guard came in from outside and nodded at the man on the floor. 'How is Paugi?'

'I cannot tell, Abdul,' Latif said. 'I don't know what to do.'

'Aktar will soon return with the doctor,' the man said. 'He may survive that long. It is quiet out here, the infidels haven't followed,' he said and ducked back out.

'I am scared, Faridun.'

'You will be safe here.' He reached for his friend's hand and held it between them.

'I am always scared. I am scared of what they think of me and whether I will be able to live up to what they expect. And I am scared when they send me to dig bombs under the roads or shoot at the infidels. I am scared of them when they have been trained in the mountains and are hard and know only fighting and God.'

'You must leave them,' Faridun said.

'Today I didn't think I could shoot at the camp again. We try and do it every day, but this time I was so scared I could hardly walk. Other times I make peace with it, with God.' He fidgeted with his assault vest and spoke slowly. 'I do not mind dying. It would be an honour to be martyred. I have lived and it would not matter if it were all over. But today I could hardly lift my weapon or follow them and my legs went forward without me. I wanted to be anywhere else. And then the fighting started and it was breathtaking. I was with them and I loved them. It is so exciting, Faridun.'

'You are safe now, Latif,' Faridun said, releasing his hand. The room had grown darker and the horizon was silhouetted through the door. 'I should go home. You can stay here until your friend returns,' he said as he stood up.

'No, please stay, for just a minute; it is good to talk to you.'

'You have your friends now. I have to go to my family.'

'These are not bad people. They are better than the government. They just want what is best. I have tried to make sure they won't hurt your family, Faridun. But your father—'

'I must go, Latif. If this ends, maybe we shall talk again.'

'It will never end,' he said and looked down at his lap.

Faridun stepped over to the injured man, crouched and rested his hand on his chest. 'Your friend is dead,' he said.

'I know,' Latif said, his eyes following Faridun over to me.

Faridun placed his hands on my grips and wheeled me towards the door, then looked back.

'Peace be upon you, Latif.'

The young man inhaled to reply.

Faridun held me and was staring at his friend. In a flash, his existence became a dot, deprived of anything physical, and he couldn't comprehend the extent of his body as his consciousness churned over, folding on itself, and slammed into a final moment.

There was no time for pain but confusion turned to loneliness and the despair of knowing was complete.

I was ripped away from him in the vacuum and the walls smacked together with the farming equipment and humans and then thumped outwards in an explosion of dust and debris. I was flung into the air and cartwheeled away with rock and mud and landed in the field on my rear wheel. It buckled and I bounced on and then my front wheel broke free and rolled across the field through the dust, wobbling from side to side before it slowed and fell.

I was bent and dented and broken in two. The dust drifted away as my spinning rear wheel slowed and its squeaking stopped and the mound where the building had been settled in on itself.

The last glow of dusk was replaced by night and it was still.

The torch flashed across the field and then was switched off. Two figures were hurrying down the road. One of them had to run every few steps to keep up with the taller figure striding quickly towards me. It was Faridun's father, the man who had bought me five years earlier. He was with Latif's mother. He turned the torch back on and walked off the road into the edge of the field.

'Oh God, oh God, oh God. Please, no,' she was saying as she stumbled into the wheat. Faridun's father stopped to help her to her feet.

'It could be all right,' he said. 'Please, do not panic. Aktar might be playing with us.'

'He was not lying this time. I could see it in his eyes.'

'Try to be strong.'

'Oh God,' she said again. 'I cannot bear it.'

The two figures were dark against the field as they approached the destroyed building they couldn't yet see.

'It is just over here,' he said to her and swept the torch around the field. He saw the dark clods of earth and frowned and then the oval of light glinted on my spokes and he shone it over my wheel and recognised me. Faridun's father knew it would not be all right.

They walked past my bent frame and the beam of light tunnelled through the dark, flecked with insects and dust. Then Latif's mother saw the pile of rubble, let out a wail and ran ahead. He called for her to be careful but she climbed over the scattered debris and broken wall and started scrabbling at the earth.

'My son,' she cried. 'Latif.'

They pulled the rock and earth away and flashed the torch into the gaps. They kept digging for the rest of the night. They found an older man they didn't recognise and they hoped there might be some confusion. But then they found Faridun and hugged each other and sobbed together. There was another body and they shone the light over his distorted face. They didn't know him either. It was dawn when they found Latif's body and she wailed again for her son.

32

You pressed your stump into me and we became one for the first time. A man was crouched in front of you and guided us together.

'That's it,' he said. 'Push down. Can you feel the bottom of the socket?'

'I'm not sure.'

You were sitting on a treatment bed and held its edge as you leant forward. Your stump was covered in a white sock. As it descended into my foam insert, filling my interior, I cupped around you.

'It all feels fairly odd,' you said. A nerve tingled in the side of your knee as I squashed your soft tissue.

'It will for a bit. Here, you pull up this suspension sleeve.' He pulled the grey silicone sleeve up from me and rolled it over your knee and around your thigh. Now we were securely joined together.

'How does it feel?'

'There's quite a lot of pressure on the sides,' you said.

I was pressing painfully into your medial condyle and the head of your fibula.

The man ran his thumbs along where my plastic and foam curved in and you could feel his fingers through the silicone. 'We need this area for lateral support, I'm afraid,' he said. 'I can always push it out a bit. Getting the sockets just right will be a balance of comfort and support. The more we shave off here, for instance, where it's digging in, the less support the socket will give you.'

'It's not too bad, Mike. Let's see how I get on, if that's how it's meant to be.'

'I can always adjust it later.'

He walked over to a collection of other legs propped up by a mirror, each topped with a different-shaped socket moulded to fit the stumps of broken people like you. He picked one out and brought it over.

'Now let's try the above-knee socket,' he said. 'We'll try you on this mechanical knee to start.'

You pulled a white sock up around your stump and took the end of the plastic socket from him.

There was no symmetry to your injuries. The other socket was bigger than mine and plugged around your stump up to the base of your pelvis. The metal frame and cylinder of the knee joint knocked against me as you adjusted it, grunting as you pushed into the socket and wincing at the unnatural feeling.

'Are you okay?'

'Fine, thanks.'

'You won't need this belt forever, but we normally start people with one, just while they learn. It'll keep the prosthesis on until you can take a better suspension system.' He pulled a strap up from the socket and helped you pass it around your back. You secured the Velcro.

'Want to give it a go?' he said.

'Of course.' You were nervous and shuffled across to your wheelchair. You felt the weight of me pulling down awkwardly on your stump, out in front of the chair. You wheeled forward and positioned us at the end of the parallel bars.

'Wait a second, Tom,' he said. 'I'd better get Kat before we send you off. She's always telling me I'm not qualified. She'll want to be here to make sure you're doing it right.'

'We don't want her missing any of the fun.'

He went and you looked down at us. We made your proportions right again and you smiled. We were metal, a collection of bolts, carbon tubes, plastic and rubber. We didn't fill the space your muscles and flesh used to; we were too thin and hard-edged, but suddenly, at the end of me, there was a shoe. Your nerves fired and you could feel the ghost of your foot, right where you could see it. You could feel what you saw.

You tried to wiggle your toes and almost expected to see the shoe flex, but your feet were frozen in their final moment. You lifted your leg and I pulled forward and the weight of me tugged down, lifeless, and the illusion was painfully broken. You stopped smiling. You ran your fingers over my components, studying how the carbon rod was bolted to the bottom of my socket and holding my foot at its end.

This is what I'm going to be, you thought. This is the beginning.

She came back with him. 'Hi, Tom,' she said. 'Mike says you're ready for lift-off.'

'I didn't want to be responsible for any of your patients doing a face plant, Kat,' he said, spinning an Allen key in his hand and leaning over the bars to look at us.

She stepped around beside you.

'Quite,' she said. 'No face plants on the first day if we can possibly avoid it.'

'We save them for later, do we?' you said.

'Of course,' she said. 'You just wait for your first stairs session, Tom. They're usually very entertaining.'

'I told you, Tom,' he said. 'You lucked out with your physio.'

'Right, hold on to the bars and pull yourself up. No heroics. Just check for comfort.'

You grabbed the two parallel bars that extended towards a mirrored wall in front of us, then pulled forward and levered yourself out of the wheelchair. Your stump squashed down into me as I took your weight.

I was designed to push in against certain areas of you, where there was less damage and scarring, against your patellar tendon below your knee cap and up around the back of what was left of your calf. I pressed in there now and you blew a sharp breath.

'Okay?' she said.

'A bit sore.' You were bearing your weight through your arms and slowly relaxed them so you sank into me, the soft tissue of your stump compacting. We were taking all of your weight and your hands hovered above the rails. You swayed forward and back. And then the mechanical knee beside me collapsed as the geometry passed its breaking point and you grabbed for the rails and sat back heavily into the chair.

'Well caught. Just remember that the above-knee will release if you flex it too much,' she said. 'How did that feel?'

'Not too bad,' you said and looked down at me.

'What about comfort?' the man said. 'Still pressing in?'

'It is a little.'

'No problem,' he said. 'I'll sort that.' He ducked under the bar and knelt in front of you. 'Let's whip it off.'

You rolled down the sleeve that held us together and slid out your stump. The man carried me into a workshop where other men were bent over machines wearing goggles and masks, cutting carbon or moulding sockets around casts. He'd made me in here, forming me around a plaster copy of your stump. And then he'd fastened an adaptor to me and assembled me, bolting on my pylon and attaching my foot. He walked over to a bench now and filed down the lips of my socket, widening my opening.

'Try this,' he said after he'd taken me back into the treatment room.

You pulled me on again. 'Thanks, that feels better already.'

'Stand up,' she said. 'We'll attempt a few steps.'

You pulled yourself back up with a grunt, lowering your weight down into me as you slowly released your grip on the bars.

'Keep holding on, Tom, and then just place your foot forward. The below-knee prosthetic should be a fairly natural action. The above-knee will take more getting used to. It's all about using your bum muscles for control.'

You edged forward, lifted me off the ground and I swung. The weight of me acted like a pendulum, and then my heel touched back onto the ground and you'd taken your first step. You rocked your weight over me and the mechanical knee was swinging past, its hydraulic piston arm sliding gently out among the crossing struts of the knee's polycentric frame.

You gripped the bars and looked up at the mirror and saw yourself standing there, upright and walking. You watched us move forward and took another step.

She was behind us, holding your waist to steady us. 'That's it,' she said and looked around you, smiling.

You saw her in the mirror and smiled back. 'It feels amazing to be up,' you said.

'You're doing well. Try and lengthen your stride a bit. That's it.'

You stepped out again, placing me farther away from you,

and your stump wobbled in me as we impacted with the ground. Then you rolled over me as the other leg swung past. I was hurting you but you concentrated and didn't feel it.

'Well done,' she said. 'Take it easy turning around and then just head back to your chair. You're on your own now.'

She bent under the bar and stood with the man. You shuffled around and noticed how clumsy I was when I wasn't walking forward. I bumped into the right leg and then caught up against it. You were stuck on one foot, my toe trapped behind the pylon of the other leg. You couldn't get me free.

'Do you need a hand?' she said.

'I should be okay.' Your lips were pursed. You looked down and tried to move me as if I was yours but couldn't. I was odd and clumsy and you struggled to animate me, your brain sending signals to muscles that no longer existed, and I wouldn't do what you wanted.

You pulled me free with an exaggerated jerk of your knee. I flicked out and swung around and you nearly fell but grabbed the parallel bars and breathed out with a whistle.

'Well done,' she said.

'That was close,' the man who had made me added. 'You're already getting the hang of it, though. It's good stuff, Tom.'

We shuffled back along the bars to the chair and you carefully lowered yourself into it.

The man ducked back under the bars and pushed his Allen key into one of my bolts and you felt it twist through me. 'I just want to turn your foot out a bit,' he said and loosened a bolt and then another. He adjusted my foot.

'Thanks,' you said. 'That looks better.'

'How did everything else feel?' he asked.

'It slightly feels like I'm falling over the front of the foot, if that makes any sense?'

'Okay, try this.' He rotated another of my bolts and the toe of my foot dropped.

'The above-knee side should be fine at the moment. We've got it on the most stable settings. As you get better we can make it a bit more dynamic.'

You stood again and they watched you walk slowly up and down the bars. She told you not to overdo it but you wanted to keep going. Once you didn't lift me high enough and I scuffed the floor and nearly tripped you over. She told you to concentrate on taking evenly spaced steps, to keep your back straight and think about engaging the muscles in your bottom.

Your knee started to shake in me and you sweated as your back ached and you felt dizzy. You saw how red your face was in the mirror. The pain that had been masked by concentration started to swell and you collapsed in your chair and said you'd had enough.

She sat on a stool next to you. 'Well done, Tom. A good start. When do you next go home?'

'End of the week,' you said, then pulled out a piece of paper and showed it to her.

'Great, we've got three more sessions. Looks like you're almost ready to come out of the bars. Then you can take them home and practise.'

'It was great to be upright. It made me feel so much more human.'

You pulled off the other leg and then me and propped us against the wall. The relief from the pressure throbbed pain-fully and you rubbed your hand up and down your thigh and removed the foam insert from your stump. Underneath, the bottom of the sock was bright red against the white cloth.

'Blimey,' she said and looked down at the end of the stump as a drip of blood fell onto the carpet. 'Did you feel that happening?'

'Not a clue,' you said. 'I don't have much feeling at the end of the stump.'

'Take off the sock and let's have a look. I'll just get a bag.'

You peeled the sock off your knee and the sodden end flopped off your skin. Blood had flattened your hairs and squelched them up around the stump. 'Shit. That's not good, is it?' you said.

'Mike, you'd better come and look at this.' She held out a plastic bag and you dropped the sock into it. She knelt in front and looked at your stump. 'It's bled quite a lot.'

'What do you think?' you said. 'It's the wound that's taken ages to heal, but I thought it was nearly there. Seems to have opened up again. Will it stop me from walking?'

'I'll mark where it is on the inside of the socket,' the man said, 'and we'll see if we can make a bit of room to accommodate the area.'

He picked me up and ran his hand down the inside of me, then took a ruler and measured the position of a dome of blood that was slowly forming into a new drip on the front of your stump. He held a ruler in me and drew a round circle with a blue marker. 'It's about there,' he said. 'I reckon if I make a space, it'll allow more room for the scarring.'

He took me to the workshop again and ground down my surface to create a cavity that would keep me from pressing too hard against your wounds. And then he carried me back to you.

'Don't let it get you down, Tom,' she was saying. 'That's pretty normal. These things take time, and a little bleeding can actually improve healing in the long term.'

'So I can stay at it,' you said.

'Of course. We'll keep an eye on it. You'll need to be careful because you can't feel it, but it's only surface scarring that's been damaged.'

'I made some space in the socket,' he said, handing me to you.

You ran your hand over my plastic and the new gap he'd carved out. 'Thanks, Mike.'

'Best get that seen to upstairs, Tom. One of the nurses will cover it for you.'

'Thanks, Kat. See you tomorrow,' you said.

I was left next to my pair, propped against the wall with all the other legs. You came back the next morning and sat on the bed and looked at me across the room. You were tired and ached. You felt around your stump at the scab that had formed over night. You'd been healing so well and I'd opened you up again to the elements and the chance of infection. You worried about regressing.

She walked in and rubbed alcohol gel on her hands from a dispenser on the wall. 'Hi, Tom. How did you sleep?'

'Bit stiff this morning. I can definitely feel it in my back.'

'You've spent the last ten weeks in bed and a wheelchair, so your body will take some time to adjust,' she said. 'Right, let's get them on.'

You pulled me on and hoped I wouldn't damage you again. You walked me along the bars and managed a few steps without holding on. She handed you two black walking sticks that wobbled under the pressure you leant through them. She told you to come out of the bars and you shuffled a slow circuit of the room, concentrating all the time on controlling me. And then you felt a wetness in me and around the skin of your stump. It was cold and even though it didn't hurt, you knew I was pressing in against the scab and making you bleed again. You tried to ignore it, shuffling on as she gave instructions.

They were pleased with how you'd united with me. The next weekend they let you take me home and told you to practise each day. You showed me to your family and described all my various parts. They were happy for you and saw your excitement. They said how amazing I was, but you didn't put me on.

You lay on a bed that was downstairs and stared at me propped against the sofa, thinking how unfair it was that for you to progress, I had to damage you. You looked down at the scab that was so small on your stump but caused so much anxiety. What if it became infected and you had to go back to hospital? You couldn't bear to be a broken body in hospital again with them all looking down at you. You rolled over and ignored me.

When you got back to the centre she asked how much you'd used me at home. You lied to her. She told you to put me on again and during the following weeks you improved. The feeling of achievement and progress started to overcome the anxiety. There were others at the centre and you wanted to be the best, measuring yourself against them and sacrificing your stump to be quicker and more nimble.

Each time you sat down to remove me, you hoped it would be all right but knew it wouldn't. I always damaged you and you despised me as you prodded the gunky scab and the blood that had soaked the sock again.

But I was too addictive, we went quicker and farther and you kept coming back for more. You walked across a room and you realised you no longer had to think about each action of swinging me forward. It felt like I was part of you.

We fell, as we always did whenever you had a burst of confidence, and I twisted below you and collapsed to the floor. Each time you reacted with a lifetime of learnt experience and your stump jolted inside me as your brain braced your remembered foot out. I sheered away from you, pulling across your stump to an unnatural angle, and then you were in a heap with me bent painfully below you. She was there to help you up.

You went home again and did use me. We staggered through the dead leaves of the garden in slow loops, sweat darkening your T-shirt. Your family watched us out of a window, you bent over the sticks and me kicking up the leaves, and it made them happy. But they hated the damage I did to you even more than you did.

We went back to the centre and it snowed. You decided not to get into your wheelchair one morning and you slid your stump down into me from your bed and walked out of the ward. The automatic doors swung open and you went into the physiotherapy department.

'No chair, Tom?' she said.

'Morning, Kat.'

'Take a seat, I'll be with you in a mo.'

You sat on a treatment table and felt proud of the freedom I'd given you.

'Where's your other stick?' she said as she walked back over.

'Binned it,' you said. 'Thought it was a little geriatric. One stick can be carried with a touch of flair.' You spun the black stick through your fingers, lost control and just managed to catch it before it hit her.

'All right, steady,' she said, shielding herself from the rotating stick. 'We give you two for a reason, Tom. It makes you stable while you learn, keeps you balanced.'

'It's fine, really. I feel ready.'

'Well, it's good you're feeling so confident. I thought we could do a few full flights of stairs today.'

'Great, gravity-assisted work at last,' you said as you followed her out.

We were at the top of the stairs. You dropped me onto the first step and started to place your other leg down but it was so steep you thought you were going to fall. The right leg caught next to me and began to bend too early. You lost control and snatched at the banister.

'Don't lean back,' she said. 'It's like skiing. You'll have more control if you stay above the legs.'

'If it's like skiing, this is definitely a black run,' you said, pushing yourself away from the banister and positioning me in the centre of the step.

'Well there aren't any blue runs, I'm afraid.'

You dropped me down again and jarred into me. I was bending – we were going down too quickly and you jolted through me again and again. Then you leant back away from the fall and the knee buckled out and I twisted. You gasped and grabbed for the handrail.

'Steady, Tom, steady. Hold it there,' she said.

You were sitting down on a step.

She sat down beside you. 'Are you okay?'

'Fine.'

'You really do need to lean forward. It will give you more control and keep you better positioned for the next step. I know it feels strange,' she said. 'But the knee joint needs to clear the previous step and you'll get better resistance from the hydraulics.

Watch,' she said and walked down past you, exaggerating the placement of each foot.

You sat on the step with your hands on your hips. You try bloody leaning forward, you thought. It's easy to do that with real legs, you try doing it with prosthetics. How the hell do you know what it's like? And you were about to tell her this but then stood up and descended more slowly, trying to lean forward.

It was exhausting and you hauled us back up the stairs and descended again. She made you do it until you were breathless and I was so full of a mix of sweat and blood that I started to slip off you. She said you'd done well, and you used your wheelchair for the rest of the day.

You improved on me but you became thinner. The pressure I exerted on you, and the weight you lost from the energy I used, made your stump shrink. I could no longer support you properly and you jarred painfully into the bottom of my socket. After one session, when you told her it was unusually sore, you took me off and she saw that your stump was purple. She took us back to the man who had made me.

I rested next to you as he wrapped plaster strips around your stump and made a new cast for what would become my replacement. That was the beginning of the end of me. Slowly you outgrew all my parts and the man switched them over until I only existed as separate components in a cupboard and you'd progressed to a high-activity leg and a carbon-fibre socket.

33

I was at twenty thousand feet and had been airborne for five hours. I am an unmanned aerial vehicle. I cruised at 165 knots and the wind howled around me. A thermal buffeted me, my aileron twitched and I levelled out in a holding pattern above a grid I'd been sent to because the troops below were in contact. I was there to support them. I had already dropped that afternoon in the north, where other soldiers had needed me.

The ground was pale through the thick atmosphere but the sensor mounted on my bulbous nose could detect through it, magnifying heat signatures into a monotone image I transmitted to my operators. One had just started his shift and had a can of Coke beside my control panels.

I am a communications platform and information bounced through me. The excited soldiers below sent radio signals. I transmitted them on to a satellite above that in turn rebroadcast them to the dish next to the air-conditioned cabin of my ground control station.

My sensor registered the light shapes of the soldiers lined up by a wall and the white heat that splashed from their weapons. They sent a message through me that indicated the enemy's location. After the 1.5 seconds it took for a command to arrive from the control station, my gyroscopically stabilised sensor rotated away from the soldiers and tracked across the grey lines of the fields and cool black channels of water. It settled over a square and the V of a dark shadow. And then my magnification flicked out to show a wider area and the square was one among a patchwork of grey and white walls.

It flicked back in and I circled above and then saw their thermal shapes. Heat streaked off the walls around them. My controller told the soldiers on the ground that he had positively identified the enemy. There were two signatures and I sensed another two as I arced around. He said he'd keep eyes on and the silent battle continued below.

My controller sent me an instruction and the numbers on my readout tumbled as I descended to 7,550 feet. He switched my sensor to white-hot, inverting my image, and now the little figures by the wall showed as black shapes. This wasn't as clear so he switched it back.

A flash of white streaked across my image and then one of the small ghostly figures was flat on the ground. My sensor-operator sent a message that an RPG had been fired and it looked like an insurgent was down. I banked around the area and my sensor zoomed out again and I could see the enemy in relation to the soldiers who needed me. Then I flicked back in and the prone figure was joined by another who pulled him into a dark shadow. And they were all there, huddled in a white blob.

My controllers were restless and one calmly asked the soldiers if they wanted me to engage. They told him to wait and their message was distorted by the background sound of bangs and breathing. The controller informed them that the enemy was breaking contact and he kept my cross-hairs over them as they slowly withdrew. They disappeared behind a wall and I was commanded to swing wider and then I sensed them again. One figure turned and spat heat from his weapon. They crossed into a field and my pilot transmitted that he still had visual.

I tracked them across the field and my operator informed the troops that there was another insurgent and described the bicycle with weapons hanging on it. He said they had moved to a small building tucked under some trees. He took a grid and changed my flight profile so I could maintain a fix.

My sensor zoomed in on the dark doorway and the thermal signature of the man crouching beside it and the hot barrel of his weapon. Another figure ran from the building and I lost it under the trees.

My pilot told them that one enemy had left the building but they still had four confirmed. They discussed rules of engagement and then permission came and I arced around and a command passed through me to the ordnance attached to my fuselage. My camera wobbled as my weight changed and the missile dropped away into the haze. My cross-hairs hovered over the building. One of the white shapes was walking beside the building and then crouched down.

My image flashed and fuzzed and noisy pixels of white burst out. I readjusted. The heat strike was at the centre of where the building had been. They widened my aperture again to show the smoke boiling out of the trees. And then my sensor was turned to focus on the road where a small white speck was moving away and I magnified on it. It was a motorbike travelling down a road, its engine heat building as a sharp white dot.

They reviewed the rules and decided not to engage. Then my sensor array rotated under my nose, back to the impact.

The building no longer had a shadow and earth had been thrown around the strike mark and was dark where it showed against the hot surface of the field. I continued to circle above as the blast area cooled and my sensor operator sent a damage assessment. I loitered and then my turboprop whirred and I climbed away.

Thirty-six minutes later I was needed again, forty-three miles away. My operator clicked a mouse on a grid. I received the command and changed course and flew myself north to help.

34

In the beginning, I was mostly in the Atlantic. I evaporated and travelled as moisture across the ocean towards an island where I formed part of a grey cloud that scudded across winter fields. Soon the fields turned white and were crisscrossed by black lines and dotted with red squares. The temperature changed and I grew too heavy and fell as snow, drifting slowly down until I settled.

A day later two figures came. I was on the ground so they towered towards me. The first walked slowly with a stick in each hand, kicking his legs forward through the snow that squeaked as it compacted. Even though it was cold he was sweating and his breath billowed.

The other figure followed along behind, picking her feet up and folding her arms around herself. She smiled and talked to the man. 'Keep your back straight and push through your glutes. Try not to abduct your right leg. That's it – better,' she said.

The man walked on towards me, leaving dark holes in the snow where he carefully planted each stick.

'Don't flick your leg like that. You're arching your back again.'

'I'm bloody trying,' he said through gritted teeth. 'I'm an amputee, not Scott of the bloody Antarctic.'

And then his foot caught, he teetered for a second and fell forward. His sticks rattled against his metal legs as he landed face down into me.

She laughed, bending over with her hands on her knees. 'You look like Scott of the Antarctic now,' she said.

He grinned, lifted himself onto his elbows and caught his breath.

'Do you need help getting up?' She walked over to him.

'No, I'll be fine. Just give me a moment.'

He started to pull me together in his hands until I was formed.

'I can see what you're doing,' she said.

'What? I'm just getting up.' He grinned as he pressed me into a ball. Then he forced himself up with a grunt, staggered to get his balance and threw me with his free hand. I was airborne.

'That wasn't even close,' she said as I sailed past her.

The man wheeled around with the impetus of the throw, over-balanced and fell again, laughing. I rolled in the snow and slabs of me broke away before I came to a stop.

She reached down, pulled snow together and made a ball of her own. She stood over the man, who was still laughing on his back as he swept his arms up and down to make the shape of an angel.

'You can't throw that at me, Kat. I'm a defenceless amputee,' he said, 'and it would be against the physio's code of conduct, not to mention the Geneva Convention.'

'You started it, Captain Scott,' she said and threw the snowball into his face.

They both laughed and he spluttered snow from his mouth.

He slowly stood again, she handed him the sticks and they walked off, now getting smaller. He was grunting with effort but still smiled as she followed behind him.

'Push through your glutes, squeeze that bum. That's better.'

Soon they left me. It was warmer the next day and I melted.

35

I was on my side among the low branches of a bush. An explosion had blown me there.

It was night and they were black against the rubble they clambered over. One of them turned on a torch and a cone of light illuminated fragments of wall and stone. The beam jumped across the jagged remains and was lowered into a gap and made the debris glow from within. It flicked off.

They didn't talk much but the sound of bricks and mud being pushed away and rolling off the pile continued all night. A few times they joined one another, working frantically, and then they dragged another dark shape from the rubble and carried it down onto the field. Once they stopped and sobbed together. But they kept going and dawn slowly saturated the landscape.

There were three bodies lined up at the edge of the wheat field. The man and woman still worked on the mound, her bright blue shawl hanging low and her hands grey with dust. He called her over and she stumbled across and hysterically pulled rocks away and reached in and wailed.

They pulled the final body out and laid it with the others. She knelt by its head and reared back and forth and then curled her face down into her hands and stayed bent over the body.

He stood over her and looked at the horizontal parade of bodies and then up across the field and saw me. He walked through the wheat that pulled at his long white shirt, now marked with chalky dirt. His arms were covered with scratches and blood smeared his hands. His face was hollow and eyes glassy above the wisps of grey that snaked from his cheeks into his beard. He pulled me from the bush and flipped me up onto my wheel. I was badly dented but I still worked.

The green shoots brushed against the frame that held my wheel as the man pushed me back across the field and I left a line where I flattened the crop. He dropped me on my leg supports and crouched down by one of the bodies. He put his arms under its shoulders and dragged it towards me. It was stiff and awkward and the corpse knocked into me and I fell over.

She looked up and asked him what he was doing and they argued. She tearfully pleaded with him not to go – it was too dangerous. He ignored her and tugged me back up. He tried to pull the body into me again but it flopped out. The man clamped his teeth in frustration as he pushed the front of my tray forward across the ground, trying to scrape the body up. But it sagged and folded and wetness filled the man's eyes at the indignity of it all.

The corpse was half in me, with my front end under it and my handles sticking up in the air. He managed to pull it farther into me and the distended head bounced off my metal side. Dried blood showed around its ears and nose and was red in its mouth. And then he pushed my handles down and I scooped it all up and the body squashed back into me and hissed air from its buttocks. Its limbs were bent unnaturally over my edge and a foot was turned back on itself.

She pleaded with him again but he said her husband should be here soon and would help her. He held my handles at the end of straight arms and walked me across the field. At the edge my tyre dropped into a hollow and was stuck and he couldn't push me forward. He rocked me back and forth, the body jolting inside me, until I finally bounced through it. He leant forward as he heaved me up the bank and onto the flat road.

The corpse's eyes had opened from the jolting and looked up at him. He looked down into them, at his son's face and the blue lips and purple blotching across his cheeks and he knew he had already accepted the loss. He lowered my handles and smoothed the eyelids shut again.

He pushed me down the road. The rising sun grew out of the horizon, bathing his face in orange. He was staring at the body in me, in front of him and his knees that brushed its hair with each step. His son was lifeless and inert now – was gone, was dead.

Death was familiar and simple for him. He had lost children and a wife before, but somehow this seemed more unjust. He felt the loss as a missing part of himself, wrenched from him. His arms ached from the weight of me. His son had become a man and was heavy, no longer a boy, but he'd hardly noticed the change and now he was gone. He kept walking and ignored the pain growing in his shoulders.

He wheeled me over a bridge. To his right down a short slope stood the deserted buildings ruined by the fighting. He knew the names of all the families who'd abandoned them, who'd come to him to ask what they should do about the fighting and explosions. He had no answer but continued to support the foreigners and told the families they must too. Up on the hill to his left and dark in the low sun was the cemetery; he didn't want to look at it yet.

He plodded on. He knew there might be bombs under the road, that my wheel might trigger one and he would be sent after his son, but he didn't care. Maybe it would be for the best. He knew it was his fault. He'd made his people support them. He'd let the foreigners into his house – given them tea – and now look what they'd done. No tears came but the anger seared through him.

Why had he sent his son to work near their base? His own pride, he thought, and his promise to the families who'd lived here that they could move back soon. And his arrogance, of course, that his people were bigger than this war and all the foreigners. He'd thought his son should share that belief, but he'd sent him to his death.

He looked down between my handles and the lolling head, at the ground passing beneath his sandals. Send me after him, he pleaded, explode around me and bear me away. But the packed mud was flat and hard and he walked on until he saw their base, its high perimeter wall a flat diamond in the landscape with aerials and a flag at its centre. The watchtowers were dark, thin eyes at each corner draped in camouflage nets.

He pushed on and I vibrated over the surface, the body trembling in my tray. The watchtower rose above us as we approached and he glanced up at the dark slit and knew a weapon would have pointed at him since he'd come into sight. He thought how different this was from the last time he'd been here, when they'd invited him in as an honoured guest and served him their disgusting foreign tea.

A voice called to him from the watchtower and he bent down to lower me onto my legs. He stared back up at the black slit and then the heavily accented voice said again that he should come no closer. He waited and gazed at his son. The first mirages of the day puddled on the road and he looked along the wall of their camp to the entrance. An unarmed figure walked out. It was one of their interpreters. A soldier appeared next to him.

They made him open his shirt. He lifted it up and anger flared through him at the lack of trust, the lack of respect, and suddenly his eyes weren't dry any more. But he controlled himself and explained with as much dignity as he could that one of their bombs had killed his son. His voice nearly faltered but he didn't want them to see any weakness. Instead, he pointed at the body in me and said it was his son, Faridun.

They made him leave me in the middle of the road with the body. He walked away towards them and they took him into the camp. Before he disappeared he pointed back at me but they ushered him through the gate.

I waited, holding the body of his son that had stiffened below the watchtower as flies weaved above me and then landed on its face.

36

I was printed and strapped to ninety-nine identical others in a bundle of a thousand. My bundle was one of four in the brick that was shrinkwrapped with many more onto a wooden pallet. Together, we were worth millions. On one side of me is printed the image of a man; he died in 1845. On the other a Palladian building with white columns and a country's name in a scroll above.

The pallet was forklifted onto an aircraft and I was flown to another place and unloaded. The plastic film was pulled away and all the bundles were removed and sent across a country where there were no Palladian buildings.

I was placed in a brown envelope and delivered to a small room in an isolated patrol base, where BA5799 unwrapped me and put me on a shelf next to a notebook labelled *Claims Record*.

BA5799 entered the room now, yawning, his greasy hair sticking up. 'Hi, Dan,' he said to one of the men sitting at the table.

'Hey, Tom.'

They were on a bench in front of stacked radios and headsets, an open logbook and empty mugs ringed with caffeine stains.

'Get much sleep?' the man said as he stood from the bench and pushed a headset away.

'A few hours.' BA5799 placed a book on the table. 'Anything happening?'

'Not much. We changed the encryption on the radios at midnight and they all seem to be working. It's been quiet at both checkpoints. The first patrol's due out at six from Mark's lot. Just a quick area defensive.'

'Great, thanks. And when are you back?'

'I'm due back on at eight.'

'See you then, sleep well,' BA5799 said.

They swapped positions in the room and BA5799 sat on the bench, looked at the log and entered his name and the time.

'Morning, Signaller Williams,' he said to the man sitting next to him.

'Morning, sir,' the signaller said. 'It's dead. Nothing doing.'

'What time did you get on?'

'Just after midnight. It was a bit of a nightmare changing the radios but it's all done now. Do you want a brew?'

'I'll make it,' BA5799 said.

'No need, I want a stretch. I'm getting the two-hour itch.' The signaller stood and took a couple of tea bags from a tin on the shelf I was on and left the room.

BA5799 opened a book and started to read.

'What have you got there?' the signaller said when he came back. He placed the mug in front of BA5799.

'Just some crap I found in my room. The last lot must've left it.'

'Looks pretty highbrow to me, sir.'

He put the book down and picked up the mug and studied the map in front of them with the flags pinned to it and callsign stickers lined up along one side. He located the building they had destroyed yesterday evening.

He looked over at the signaller. 'What are you up to?'

'I was writing home,' he said, pushing a blue envelope out of the way. 'But I don't know what to say, so I'm drawing a tattoo.' He slid a piece of paper over the desk.

'Hey, that's cool,' BA5799 said.

'If you think it's cool, boss, I might have to start again.'

'Probably not a good sign. Where would you have it?'

'On my back, I think. But I'll have to clear it with the missus. They're expensive but I've got a mate in my town.'

They talked for a while but fell silent and then one of the radios transmitted through a speaker. The signaller put on a headset and told them he could hear them. Other voices, heavy with the boredom of keeping watch, sounded through the speaker, testing their radios. He replied to them all and then told BA5799 that the three o'clock check was complete. BA5799 jotted this in the log and then asked if he'd like a coffee. He went out and the signaller doodled on his design with a black biro.

BA5799 came back, put the man's mug next to him and sat on the bench, blowing on his own mug. 'Do you know the service station near our barracks back home, Signaller Williams, on the motorway?' he asked.

'Know it well, boss.' The signaller put his pen down and pursed his lips to his coffee.

'If you could go in there now, what would you order?'

'Now you're talking. It's got everything, that one, hasn't it?'

'Yup, any fast food you could possibly wish for.'

'How much have I got to spend?'

'I'll give you a tenner,' BA5799 said, staring into space over the mug.

'Is that all?'

'How much do you need? Our bellies are so small.'

'I could eat for a week, sir,' the signaller said and started to doodle again.

'So what would you go for?'

'Well, I'd have a burger from the King.'

'Obviously.'

'And chips from Mr Mac.'

BA5799 smiled. 'Controversial. So you'd mix it up a bit?'

'Of course. Then I'd get a side of chicken from the Colonel.'

'It's making me hungry just thinking about it. Finishing with chicken's a great shout.'

'And I'd take it all back to the car park and sit in my car and listen to the football scores come in. Bliss. I hate sitting inside with all the horrid civis.' He slurped his coffee. 'I think I may have to make that trip on R and R now,' he said.

'You could take Mrs Williams.'

'God, don't. We're not married yet, boss.'

They opened a melted pack of biscuits and prised them apart with a knife, chatting and laughing. Then they were quiet again and the signaller continued to draw while BA5799 read. First light showed dull in the doorway and the camouflage netting outside sighed with the first wind of the day.

One of the radios hissed on and they both looked up at the square speaker.

'Zero, this is Sangar Five. Over,' it emitted.

The signaller picked up a headset, pressed the switch and spoke into the microphone. 'Zero, send. Over.'

'I've got an unknown male walking towards the base from the east. He's pushing a wheelbarrow. About five hundred metres away but looks like he's heading for us. Over.'

The signaller turned to BA5799. 'What do you reckon, boss?'

'Give it here,' he said and took the headset.

'Hello, Sangar Five, this is Zero. Normal procedure. Stop him short, send out the guard commander and make sure he's searched. Then take him to the holding area and see what he wants. Out to you. Front Gate, this is Zero. Over.'

'Front Gate, yup, we've seen him,' the microphone emitted a new voice. 'Corporal Carr and the terp will go and intercept if he comes towards the base. We'll wake the medic if needed. Over.'

'Great, thanks. Let me know if you need any help. Over,' BA5799 said and put the microphone down on the desk.

'Roger. Out.' The microphone clipped off.

BA5799 wrote in the log and then picked up his book again.

Moments later a man dressed in full combat kit stepped through the doorway. 'Boss, there's an old dude here. Says his name's Kushan Hhan—'

'Kushan Hhan? Great, what's he doing here?' BA5799 said and shut his book.

'Not so great, I'm afraid. You'd better come. And I'd bring the compensation pack if I were you.' The man ducked back out of the door and was gone.

'Oh shit,' BA5799 said and stood, walked over to me and took the pile I was in.

'You okay holding the fort, Signaller Williams? I won't be long. I'll be at the front gate if you need me.'

'Tickety-boo, boss.'

BA5799 carried me out of the ops room. He picked his armour up from beside the door and dropped it over his head. With his helmet at his side, he walked out under the netting and across the flat open vehicle park to the front gate.

Next to the gate was a temporary lean-to. Rock-filled protective walls surrounded it, wooden slats were pushed together as a roof and a hessian cloth hung over the entrance. He held me in his hand with the notebook and approached the building. A soldier standing by the concertina wire that covered the gap out onto the road looked around.

'Morning, sir,' he said. 'The man's in there, we've searched him. Nothing on him but he's not best pleased.'

'Okay, thanks, Rifleman Dean,' BA5799 said and pulled the hessian to one side and went into the small room. The old man was sitting in a white plastic garden chair, talking to the interpreter. He spoke quickly and the interpreter replied, his arms gesturing in the small space.

They ignored BA5799, who put me down on a little table with the notebook and his helmet and turned to the soldier. 'What's going on, Corporal Carr?'

'I have no idea. I can't get a word in edgeways. But neither seems to be very happy. The man brought a dead body in his wheelbarrow.'

'Where is it now?' BA5799 said.

'We made him leave it below Sangar Five, he wasn't too chuffed with that. We haven't searched it yet, I didn't want to get too close.'

BA5799 stepped forward and tried to interrupt. He rested a hand on the interpreter's shoulder but it was brushed away and they kept talking. The old man looked up and recognised BA5799. He stopped talking.

BA5799 stared down at the old man and he didn't know what to say. They'd last met across a rug and sipped tea in his house with its garden oasis. Now he looked like any other labourer from the fields. He was covered in dust and his hands were flaked with dried blood. He smelt of stale sweat. And seeing him now, BA5799 realised he wasn't that old. Hidden behind the beard and sun-damaged skin was a middle-aged father.

The interpreter explained that he had brought his dead son to the camp. BA5799 hoped it wasn't the young man he'd met on the bike and told the interpreter to offer the man water, then sat down in a plastic chair opposite him.

'He does not want your water,' the translator said.

BA5799 looked up at him and then back at the man.

'Tell him we are pleased that he has come to our base.' As his words were translated, BA5799 knew they were ridiculous. The man stared at him and there was confusion and bitterness in his eyes.

'He says that your bomb last night killed his son,' the interpreter said and fidgeted. 'He says he has tried to support you and now you have killed his son. He asks why you have done this?'

There was a leaflet that BA5799 had read tucked in the notebook next to me. It described how to deal with this. What to say, what not to say. But the man's eyes were full of mistrust. BA5799 thought of the leaflet; in front of this man, it meant nothing.

'Tell him that if this is true, I am sorry,' he said. He felt uncomfortable; the clear, glassy eyes wanted an explanation but he had none and the man started to speak again in the undulating language that was so alien.

'Why?' the interpreter said. 'That's what he wants to know.'

'Tell him we were attacked by insurgents yesterday and we used aircraft to stop the threat. If his son was caught up in that then I am sorry, but we were defending ourselves. The compounds around the base are generally empty.'

'He says his son has never held a weapon. He does not let him.

He was innocent and working to make the land better.'

The man shook his head, stood up and walked towards the door.

'Tell him to wait,' BA5799 said.

'He says he is going to his son. He does not like leaving him out there on the road.'

'Tell him I can help him.'

When the translator started to speak the man stopped and turned to look at BA5799. He shook his head and the bulge of tears grew in his eyes as he spoke.

'He says that he does not see how you can help now,' the interpreter translated.

'We can help him claim compensation for his loss.'

The man listened, said a few words, then turned and pushed through the hessian.

'What did he say?' BA5799 said.

'Well, he swore at you. It was not very nice, and then he told you to follow him.'

BA5799 put on his helmet, grabbed me and went after the man. He felt very young as he followed the old man under the hessian screen. He was dealing with death in an alien culture and he had no idea how to relate to this man or the death of his son. It was too foreign. It felt like some odd training exercise and he was getting it wrong.

One of the soldiers followed him. 'Boss, don't go out there, it might be a trap. Remember what happened up north.' He put his hand on BA5799's shoulder. 'We haven't searched the wheelbarrow.'

'It's all right, Corporal Carr. I know him. It'll be fine.'

'Sir, I'm not sure you should go out there.' He walked with him up to the concertina wire.

'Stay here, Corporal Carr,' he said to the soldier and stepped around the wire.

'Here, you're unarmed, sir. Take this,' he said and offered a pistol.

But BA5799 turned to follow the man down the road next to the wall of the camp. He held me and the notebook under his arm. He looked at the wheelbarrow and the dread that this might be a trap pulled through him, constricting his throat. If we can't trust then we have nothing, he thought and walked on.

BA5799 felt naked without his weapon but glanced up at the slit of the watchtower and knew they would be covering him. I was his weapon now and his palm was clammy against me. He could hear the interpreter behind, jogging to catch up. The man was by the wheelbarrow. A bent leg flopped over its lip and BA5799 could see the top of a head as he approached.

And then he was standing next to the man looking down at the twisted body. Through the swelling and frozen violence, which was somehow worse for not having ripped the body apart, it took him a moment to recognise the boy who had helped him. He tried to see if there was anything suspicious hidden beneath or inside the body and hated himself for thinking only of his own safety. He checked again and all he saw was the glint of the eyeballs through the nearly closed lids and trickles of dried blood from the nose and ears. BA5799 wanted to feel compassion for the man and his dead son but only felt discomfort and the man's eyes challenging him. And all he cared about was getting back into the base and the loss of a potential asset in securing the area.

'Tell him I am sorry,' he said. 'I know this is his son and I know they are good people.'

The interpreter turned to the man and then delivered his

response. 'He says he is not sure he will continue to be good any more. He thinks – how do you say it? – he thinks he can no longer command trust so he will not believe you again.'

'Tell him I understand. It isn't what any of us wanted to happen, but we still need help from good people like him. This will never be undone, I know, but if we let the insurgents win there will be even greater loss.' BA5799 felt the absurdity of what he said – he'd never experienced any loss. Suddenly he was thinking of a wedding he'd been to in a country church and the flowers and laughter, the falling pink confetti – he had no idea why and now felt like a child who couldn't take it seriously.

The man listened and then said he didn't think the soldiers understood anything – there is always loss, he said. But their lives had been much harder since the foreigners had come. He went to the handles of the wheelbarrow and lifted it.

'Ask him to wait,' BA5799 said and stepped towards the man. 'I can help.'

He pulled me out with four others. He rested his notebook awkwardly on his knee and scribbled on a piece of paper, then he held me out to the man along with the receipt.

'Here, please take this. I can only offer you one hundred dollars. It is all I'm allowed to give to one person, but if you take this receipt and go to the district centre you can claim more money. These dollars will more than pay for your journey.'

The interpreter translated and the man lowered the wheelbarrow back down.

'He asks how much he will get. How much is his son worth?' the interpreter said.

'I'm not sure,' BA5799 said. 'Probably two thousand dollars. It will be a life-changing amount.'

The man's face was rigid as he stepped forward and took me. He looked down at the foreign words and symbols printed on me, the face of the long-dead politician, then peered at the slip of paper. If he could have read it, he would have known that the foreigners did not accept liability for the death of his son but said he could be compensated.

The man spoke quietly while looking down at me.

'He says this is a sad thing. He says taking money from you in payment for the death of his son is the very worst thing he has ever done. You talk of life-changing money; his life is already changed. He wishes he could be strong and reject your offer but he says you are correct, he cannot resist this much money. He wishes he could, because he wants no debt and no link to you.'

The man looked up from me at BA5799 and spoke a final sentence.

The interpreter didn't translate.

BA5799 glanced from the old man to the interpreter.

'What did he say?' he asked.

'He wishes you no peace,' the translator said. 'Or words like that.'

Then the man picked up the wheelbarrow again, crushing me between his palm and the wooden handle, and started to wheel it down the road. BA5799 and the interpreter watched us go and then returned to the camp.

As he walked the old man became angry and tried to swipe the flies away from his son's face but they landed again and he couldn't keep stopping, so he watched them gather on the body as he pushed it back to the village. He knew he must bury his son today and the thought made it final.

When we got back to his home and his garden, which was

suddenly a deceit and arrogance and brought him no pleasure, he thrust me in his pocket and held his wife close.

When he next took me out he was standing in a long queue in the district centre. Men used to queue up to see him and he was ashamed. He finally got to the front but the man said it was too late, they were closing and he should come back again tomorrow. He tried to use me and the others he'd been given by BA5799 to bribe the man behind the counter but he was ignored. He waved the receipt for his son through the glass. The man at the desk looked up at it and said they no longer accepted that form and he would have to return to the issuing officer for the new paperwork.

He walked out into the busy street. He used me to buy his journey home and I entered circulation.

37

'It's good to see you, boss,' said the man who held the box I was in. He lifted me out and handed me to BA5799. 'How are you doing?'

'Not too bad, thanks, Sergeant Collins,' BA5799 said as he took hold of me. 'I'm just back from an admission at the rehab centre.'

'Well, it's good to see you on the mend, sir,' he said and moved to the next person and gave them one of me.

We were on the edge of a parade ground that had a white car-park grid painted on it. At the other side, on the grass, green tents were lined up and people gathered around rows of chairs. BA5799 looked down at me in his hand.

I glinted at him. I am an operational service medal, a thirty-six-millimetre-wide silver disk with a crowned effigy on my front. I have a clasp with the name of a country embossed on it and a three-coloured ribbon folded into a square that rested in his palm. He turned me over and studied the four-pointed star on my reverse and then my edge, which had his rank, name and service number engraved on it: *Captain T Barnes 565799.*

'I suppose this is it, then,' a man next to us said. He was in a wheelchair and flipped his one of me over in his hand. 'This is the silverware.'

'Looks like it, Carl,' BA5799 said, 'although we'll always have the metalwork strapped to our legs if we need reminding.'

The man glanced up from his chair. He had no legs and his combat trousers were tucked under his thighs. 'Wish I could've worn mine today,' he said.

'You'll get there, mate. Still early days for you.'

They were a group of five: two in wheelchairs, two on crutches, and BA5799 leaning back awkwardly on a bollard. They looked up at the man who'd handed me out.

'Right, has everyone got a medal?' he said.

They nodded. They all wore dark-green berets, with cap badges in the shape of a bugle above the left eye.

'Good. The lads will march on from over there and form up in front of the tents. Usual sketch. B Company, then C, then Support. The band will play them on. Once they're all settled I'll give you a nod.' He turned to BA5799. 'Sir, are you happy to lead out?'

'No problem.'

'Thanks. Line up at the end of B Company. It'll be a bit of a wait and then the general will come out. There'll be a salute, the usual rigmarole. And then he'll present the medals – you fellas are up first. All you do is hand him your medal and then he says how wonderful you've done and gives it back.'

'God, doesn't he even pin it on our chests?' one of them said and smiled.

'Too difficult for the tailors, I'm afraid, Rifleman Dean,' he said. 'Don't wait for everyone else to get their medals, just go to the side of the tents. There's some chairs laid out for you. You can watch the rest of the parade from there.'

'I've already got a chair,' said the man in a wheelchair.

'Well there's a space there for you too, Rifleman Spiers. Any questions?'

'What do we say to the general?'

'Say whatever you like, but try not to give him your life story. These things can drag on and it's too bloody cold today.'

He walked away and we waited. I was still in BA5799's hand and its warmth heated me. The others talked about when they were due back at the centre and complained about the wait and how freezing it was.

Finally the band marched on. The cheery tune filled the square and the crowd clapped. Then the rows of soldiers appeared and snaked forward, three close columns that rose and fell with every step, their arms rippling together and the sound of their boots dull on the tarmac as they swayed up onto the parade ground and pivoted before extending out in front of the tents.

BA5799 watched them come. He knew them all. He'd been part of them, one of their best; he didn't mind the arrogance of thinking that – it didn't matter now. He'd made a mistake that confined him to the small group that looked on. Even if he'd wanted to march with them he couldn't.

His hand tightened around me and I pushed a red mark into the folded creases of his palm. He was embarrassed that he was the one who'd made a mistake. He was supposed to be good at his job – some of them had even looked up to him, depended on him to make decisions – and it was never going to happen to him, he was meant to be lucky. But he wasn't, and it had, and he'd failed.

Suddenly he hated the thought of them seeing him like this, broken and maimed. He didn't want to walk out there in front of the watching crowd. He wanted to go back to the centre and its different rules and measures of achievement that none of them would understand. Where he could be the best.

Men shouted and the ranks shuffled straight. And then the nod came. BA5799 switched me into his other hand and took his stick. 'Make it look good, lads,' he said and walked out across the open ground to the lines of men. The wheelchairs followed and those on crutches swung behind. And the crowd started clapping. BA5799 wondered what they were clapping for. You shouldn't clap failure, he thought and he was ashamed and wished they'd stop.

He held me in his hand and I brushed beside his combat trousers. His legs looked odd and their sharp edges pointed through the camouflaged material with each step. He tried to march like the men had, but the jerking gait and stick made it ridiculous and the effort hurt. So he walked as normally as possible and the applause sounded full of pity and he hated it.

He lined up with the front row of men and waited, positioning the walking stick in front of him to support his weight. His stumps hurt and shook and he wanted it to be over. He looked at the crowd, wrapped against the cold, sitting in rows and he spotted his family but he kept his expression firm. He rocked back and forward as the pain built and he concentrated on staying upright.

His legs started to quiver beside me with the effort and he wished the parade would start. Then they walked over. One wore gold braid on his uniform and a peaked cap and another introduced him to each of the waiting men. He worked down the line of injured, bending over the wheelchairs to shake their hands and saying a few words before moving on.

He stood smiling in front of us and BA5799 handed me to him. He was older with grey hair and he held me there between them. He asked how BA5799 was, about rehabilitation and his family and told him how well everyone thought he was doing and what a great example he was.

In reply BA5799 only said, 'Thank you, sir.' He said it three times and then they shook hands and I was handed back to him. He had seen the man's lips moving but couldn't register what he'd said: the pain in his legs and the concentration required to stand was too much. Then the man continued down the line.

BA5799 had stood for so long his stumps were numb, and he wanted to move to the seats. He started to walk but his legs felt so stiff and heavy that he nearly fell. He thought of all the people watching and the man beside him stepped out to help but BA5799 managed to stop the stumble and steadied himself. He was embarrassed again with the crowd watching as he slowly limped to the chairs.

He sat down and rested me in his lap. His stumps were throbbing and he wanted to take his legs off but they were stuck in the trousers. The band played a tune from history and it was glory and country. He looked over at the lines of men and the general moving down the front rank and shaking hands and presenting more of me.

One of his friends stood alone in front of a platoon. That's where he should have been, if he'd survived. He caught his eye and the man winked and half smiled while standing to attention. He looked down at me and swept his thumb across my surface and felt the ridges and mounds of the head moulded on me. He was a maimed relic that everyone wanted to forget. None of the men in those ranks wanted to be reminded of the truth – of what might happen. I am that truth, he thought.

After each soldier had been given one of me and the band started playing again, the men on parade turned to their left in one movement and marched quickly away, the columns rocking from side to side as they stepped in unison. He watched them go and knew he would never feel part of them again. They were heading away to their R and R, convinced they were invincible and knowing it would never happen to them, while he was going back to the centre to adapt to what had happened to him. My fight goes on, he thought and slipped me into his pocket.

When he took me out again he was in a kitchen and he placed me on a lime-green tablecloth next to his wallet. He was sad and he dropped his trousers down so the carbon and silicone of his legs was revealed, then he pulled them off with a sigh of relief so the two legs stood absurdly against the table still in the trousers. His mother was there. She gave him a nice cup of tea.

He peeled away the socks from his stumps and saw the cost of being upright for so long and not showing weakness to those around him, for not accepting a chair when one was offered. And he was relieved to be back at home, where he was safe and she would do anything for him, where there was no one to impress and he could allow himself to be weak.

I was mounted next to another medal, like me but awarded for a different operation in another country. And then I was put in a drawer and forgotten.

38

We were pressed together in a row and light distorted through us in greys and blues and bright refractions. The room below me bulged around my surface as it was reflected through me.

It was quiet and the man behind the U-shaped bar was bent over a newspaper. He looked up as the door opened and they came in and the traffic hissed through the rain outside. Tom was wearing shorts and he rocked sideways and hitched a leg up to step into the room. The other man pulled out a chair in the corner near the window and Tom lowered himself into it.

The barman folded up the newspaper. 'What can I get you, mate?' he said.

'I'll have a pint of lager, please,' the man said, and rested an elbow on the bar. He turned back to Tom, who was adjusting his legs. 'What do you want, lager?'

'Thanks, mate.'

The barman reached up and took me off the shelf as he had a hundred times before. I was held below the nozzle, he flicked the handle and liquid poured down my side, curling up bubbles that collected in a foam.

I was placed on a mat and the liquid in me turned the room's light iodine-yellow. Another glass was filled and the man carried us over to the table and put me in front of Tom.

'There you go, mate,' he said, sitting down opposite and taking a sip from his glass.

'Thanks, James,' Tom said and looked down at me. 'It's good to see you. Cheers.' He lifted me up and they clinked us together in the middle of the table. And then Tom's lips were against me and he sipped through the foam.

'I'll have to be careful. This is the first full pint I've had in months,' he said and grinned over me. 'It'll be interesting to see how it mixes with the drugs.'

'Well, it's good to see you up in town, Tom,' the man said. 'Hey, listen, I'm sorry I didn't come and see you in hospital, mate. You know how it is, I just didn't want to be a nuisance and everyone—'

'It's all right, I wasn't much fun in hospital anyway. It's probably best you stayed away.' He dragged his fingers down me through the condensation and I reflected his blue jumper and the dark window and rain-flecked streetlight outside.

'And rehab's going well? You seem to be smashing it.'

'It's hard work but I'm into the swing of it now. I'm spending four weeks there and then a few at home.'

He nodded to below. 'The legs look good.'

'This leg's new,' Tom said and twisted a grey robotic knee from under the table.

'And that's helping?'

'It makes a massive difference. I haven't used a stick since I've been on it.'

'How does it work – and why's the other one different?' he said, staring at the two prosthetics under the table.

'Do you mind if we talk about something else, James?' Tom said. 'I'm just a bit sick of all the leg stuff. How are you? How's Vicky?'

'Of course, mate, I'm sorry.' He lifted his glass and drank and they talked.

Tom watched the bubbles grow and then pop off my sides as they discussed their friends and work and girls. He used his damaged left hand to lift me once and the man opposite glanced at it before looking away.

The room filled with people and the hymn of voices grew. His friend finished first and went for another pint after joking that Tom needed to work on his drinking strength.

While he was at the bar, a man walked towards us across the room. I reflected his jeans. He nudged the table as he sidestepped past and I tipped but Tom caught me.

'Sorry, mate,' Tom said.

'Oh, sorry,' the man said and looked down. 'Didn't see you there, fella. Hey, cool leg, mate.' He smiled. 'Blimey, you've been in the wars, haven't you?'

Tom smiled up at him.

'Bomb, was it?' the man said. 'Looks like it.'

'Afraid so,' Tom said. 'Explosively assisted high jump.' He picked me up and took a long gulp, staring out the window.

'My mate's friend has the same thing. Car crash, mind.' He peered under the table. 'Shit, you lost both. Sorry, mate.'

'Yup,' Tom said.

'Good bits of kit now though. Must be expensive?' the man said. 'You heroes deserve it. Can't think what it's like. I've got a sixteen-year-old. He wanted to join up. Wouldn't let him go near it. I'll tell him about you.'

The man perched on the next table and crossed his arms. He smiled at Tom and whistled and shook his head. 'Does it hurt?' he said. 'Must do.' He held out a hand. 'I'm Graham.'

'Tom.'

They shook.

'Let me buy you a pint, Tom,' the man said.

'No thanks, I'm fine.'

'Go on, it'd be my pleasure.'

'Honestly, I'm fine. Just catching up with a mate.' Tom pointed at his friend pushing back between the tables with his drink.

'Oh, sorry, I'll leave you to it then,' he said and stood out of the way. 'You lads are so brave.'

'Not brave,' Tom said. 'Just trod on the wrong piece of ground.'

'Well, good to meet you, Tom,' he said and walked off to the bar.

'What was that about?'

'Just another of my adoring public,' Tom said. 'Can't be too ungrateful – he meant well – but I hate that sort of thing.'

'Must be grim.' He looked over his pint at Tom. 'I'm not sure I could do it, mate. I'd probably have committed suicide if it happened to me.'

'What's that meant to mean?' Tom put me down sharply on the table.

'What? I just think it's amazing how you're dealing with it. I'm not sure I could, that's all, you know, running and stuff's so important to me.'

'Well, that's a bloody stupid thing to say, James. My life's not over and it's a bit insulting to be told it should be,' Tom said, watching the rain stream down the window. He tipped me up and drained the dregs through the last of the foam.

They were silent and then the man shook his head. 'Sorry, Tom. I didn't mean it like that.'

'I know, mate,' he said and smiled sadly. 'Just remember, I was quite into running too.'

'Want another?'

'In a second.' Tom rocked me on my base and watched the remainder of the foam slide around inside me.

'I suppose I'm just angry for you,' the man said and lifted his pint again.

'Don't be, mate. I'm not.'

'I mean, what would you do if the people who'd made the bomb walked into the pub? Fuck – I'd fill them in with that stool.'

Tom stared back at him. 'I don't think you get it, James,' he said and started to get up.

'Where are you going?'

Tom pushed himself up off the chair and levered forward over his legs to stand, slid the chair back under the table and looked down at his friend.

'If the men who did this to me walked in here right now,' he said, 'I'd offer them a drink.' He knocked me as he turned and I tipped over and rolled across the table. His friend caught me before I dropped and stood me upright.

Tom walked away, held each side of the doorway and lowered himself down the step out of the pub and into the rain.

'Wait up, mate, I'm sorry, Tom. Stop. I need to pay the tab,' he called after him, jogging over to the door.

39

It was dark. BA5799 knelt beside me and silently mouthed something he needed to remember. He switched knees and retied the other boot, wrapping the laces around three times. He pulled his faded combat trousers back down over the boots and sat on the camp bed.

His day-sack was next to him and he arranged equipment inside, pushing a black water bottle down the green canvas and switching on a radio. He pulled the drawstring and clipped the flap shut.

He felt my cover. It was still damp from the last time he'd worn me. He sighed, lifted me up, pulled apart my protective plates and dropped me over his head. I passed his face and he smelt the sharp odour he'd layered into me over the past two months. He liked my smell; it was experience and survival. He held my sides together and pressed my Velcro down with the palms of his hands so I drew tightly around his body.

BA5799 had already put me on once that night. We'd been ready and he'd walked to the front gate to meet his platoon. But someone had run out and said they had to delay: there was no air cover. The others had gone back to their tents and we had returned to the courtyard, where he had ripped open my Velcro and chucked me back down next to his bed.

He'd tried to read and then sleep but couldn't. The operation consumed him and the time was dead; all he could do was wait. And as he did, the will he'd summoned earlier ebbed out of him and he hoped the delay would become a cancellation. The hours passed as men finished cooking and eating and talking and went to sleep, until only those on guard duty moved across the still camp.

And when he finally thought there was no chance it would happen tonight and he'd let himself relax, a man ran in and told him they should go. He'd begun the ritual again, but rushed and incomplete this time, and he forced the resolve to return with each piece of equipment he secured to himself.

BA5799 now checked me again. He opened the pouches attached to the front of me, pulling out a magazine and rolling his thumb across the top round, making sure it was correctly seated. Grit crunched so he removed it and blew down into the magazine before pushing the copper cylinder back. He stood and felt the weight of me. I had become part of him, another layer of the courage that let him step out of the gate.

He lifted the day-sack over his back and it banged into my rear ceramic plate. He caught its strap and tightened it against me. All of our weight moved as one and he jumped up and down to make sure nothing rattled.

He took a map from a small pouch on my breastplate and thought the plan through, bending his head forward as he studied it so his chin rested against my sweat-stained neck opening. He looked at the small T he'd drawn to indicate where they would form up for the strike.

A soldier walked into the courtyard and waited silently as BA5799 marked the map's surface with a pen.

'Sir?' the man said quietly, not wanting to interrupt. 'Can I have a word, please?' He took a step forward.

BA5799 glanced up at him. 'Oh, hello, Rifleman Lewis,' he said and looked back down at the map. 'How can I help?'

'I just wondered if I could have a word.'

'Shoot. Make it quick, though, we need to be at the gate in five.'

BA5799 was still peering at his map and then sat back on the bed and took a GPS from his pocket. The soldier was in full combat kit. He wore his armour with pouches attached and glow-sticks and pens pushed down its front. His zap number and blood type were written on it in marker, *LE2482 – O NEG*.

On me was *BA5799 – O POS*.

He held a light machine gun at his side. His kneepad was pushed down to his ankle and a dump-pouch hung by his thigh. His helmet shadowed his eyes.

'I was chatting to Rachel last night and, well, she's not happy,' he said. 'And with the little one on the way—'

'Rachel?' BA5799 said as he entered a grid into the small hand-held machine.

'Yes, my wife, boss.'

'Yes, of course. Sorry.' BA5799 made another mark on the map.

'Well, she's having a few problems with the pregnancy and she hates me being out here. So I wondered if there was a chance, you know, I could sit this one out – she really wants me to call her. And maybe,' he looked down at his boots, 'maybe I could get home on compassionate soon? She had to go into hospital, I think.'

BA5799 pushed the map back into its slip and pulled his headset on. He pressed the radio switch and spoke into the microphone at his mouth. 'Hello, Zero. This is Three Zero Alpha, radio check. Over,' he said. Then he looked up at the soldier. 'I'm sorry, Rifleman Lewis, what's up?' He pressed the switch again and said, 'Okay. Out.'

The rifleman explained again but his voice tailed off.

BA5799 stood up and walked over to the soldier. He looked under the low rim of the man's helmet and saw the boy from a small town. 'So your girlfriend wants you home and you don't think you should go out tonight because you need to speak to her on the phone?'

'I'm just finding it tough, sir, and my slot on the phone's already booked for later,' he said and dropped his eyes. 'And with what happened to Davies a few weeks ago . . .' He glanced up at BA5799. 'She keeps bugging me on the phone, that's all, and I told her I'd ask. And well – I don't like going out any more.'

'You know you can't sit this one out, Rifleman Lewis. Your section needs you, and we'd be down a man.' BA5799 placed his hand on the man's arm. 'The platoon needs every man it has. I can't do this strike without you.'

The soldier hefted his weapon and they both stood in silence.

'Swap places with Rifleman Taylor,' BA5799 said abruptly.

'What?' The man looked up and his eyes glinted in the dark. 'I can't, boss. He's point man and I haven't done that job yet.'

'You'd better get to the front gate, Rifleman Lewis. We're leaving soon,' BA5799 said and checked his watch. He turned away from the man, back to the camp bed.

The young soldier watched him readjust my shoulder popper, attach his night-vision goggles and pull on his helmet, tilting his head to clip the chinstrap together.

'And Rifleman Lewis,' he said, his back still turned. 'You can, and you will. You've done the same training as everyone else in this platoon.'

'Yes, sir,' the soldier said quietly and walked out.

We were alone in the courtyard and BA5799's body heat

warmed me. He picked up his rifle and we strode out past the ops room. The antenna protruding from his day-sack brushed the camouflage netting above as we passed the model pit and its little wooden blocks in the dark.

We approached the front gate and he saw the single file of his platoon lined up and ready to leave. Some of the men stood when they saw him, dragging their kit up onto their shoulders. Others held ladders between them and someone forced a laugh at a nervous joke.

A man trudged over to him from the back of the line. 'On the bus, off the bus, sir,' he said. 'All good to go now though.'

'Thanks, Sergeant Dee.'

'You swapped Rifleman Lewis to point man. What's that about?' the man said, looking at the front of the line near the concertina wire.

'Is that okay with you?'

'Of course, boss. And Rifleman Taylor's over the moon.' His teeth flashed in the blackness. 'I moved him back into Corporal Monk's section.'

'Thanks.'

'I hope this works, boss. Our first chance to really get at them.'

'Let's go,' BA5799 said. He stepped towards the front of the line, passed the lead soldier and glanced back at his men. He gave a nod to the man guarding the gate, who pulled the wire aside. He made to step off but the man behind tapped my shoulder panel.

'Sir,' he whispered, 'I thought you said I was point man.'

'I'll go first, Rifleman Lewis,' BA5799 told him. 'I'll tell you when it's your turn.'

'But you said in orders you'd be second in the order-of-march. I should lead, we don't need you at the front.'

'Well, I changed my mind,' he said and smiled. 'Stay well spaced out and keep me covered, Lewie. You've got my back.'

BA5799 reached over his rifle and dragged the cocking handle back and the sound of other weapons being made ready rippled down the line. He stepped past the wire and out onto the road.

He led the platoon under the dark watchtower and out into the gloom. He turned off the road and they walked parallel to it through a field and towards the remains of houses. His head swivelled above me, his face fixed under the dark rim of his helmet.

The compounds were destroyed and he skirted around craters and past crumbled walls. The buildings were no more than fifty years old but now were ancient ruins in the night and he knew the weapons that had accelerated their return to dust. The compounds had been abandoned and he thought of the destruction required to create peace.

He twisted his head and looked out to his left at the black strip of trees bisecting a field and then walked backwards to check on the man behind him and the other soldiers snaking through the open country. He held his rifle across me in two hands and its telescopic sight bumped against my front plate. He passed around a corner, stopped and lowered himself down. He beckoned and the man behind handed him a detector.

And then we were moving again. He pushed his rifle back on its sling so it dangled off me and I pressed down on his collarbone as he swept the detector over the track ahead, its red lights indicating what was below the ground. He focused on the task: on the track, on his route – which he held as an image in his head – on the radio emitting in his ear, and the detector in front of us. All the time his jawbone protruded above me, his teeth clamped.

We moved on into the murky night and the still trees. Insects grated around us and the crops stroked his legs. He lowered the night-vision goggles on his helmet above me and they swivelled as he scanned the landscape. The tension built in his arm as it waved the detector beside me, his damp combat shirt rucking up so that his lower back was bare. He stopped and the bottom of my protective plate pushed into his thigh as he knelt. He let the men compress together and waited for a message that the callsign was complete. And then we moved on, deeper into the countryside.

He led them through tracks he knew well and down others that were less familiar and then on into a field he'd never crossed. He collapsed the detector and the man behind strapped it to the side of his day-sack. He walked on without it and tried to ignore the humid night air and the weight of me making his shoulders feel hollow.

Panic grew slowly as the depthless features around him didn't match the route he'd memorised and then he risked a path because it must be that way. It led to a wall that shouldn't have been there and he swore under his breath and didn't know where he was. He thought of the men behind, trusting him and following him blindly into the night.

He pulled a compass from my front pouch and watched the fluorescent needle floating in the dark. It settled in the wrong direction and he swore again. He slid it back and his head turned above me as he tried to orientate himself but the shadows bounced back distorted blind spots he couldn't decipher. He pumped his hand down and the following soldiers crouched.

BA5799 lay flat on the path and my breastplate rested in the fine dirt. He pulled out his map and flicked on a torch and bent over it.

The man behind moved up and whispered, 'Sir, wait. Let me get ahead and cover you.'

'Thanks, Rifleman Lewis,' BA5799 said quietly, knowing he shouldn't risk using the torch in the open but not wanting his men to suspect he was lost.

'You okay?' the rifleman said as he moved past and knelt down in front.

'Fine, just a quick nav check, Lewie.'

'There's no rush, boss.'

Another man made his way along the line. He squatted down beside BA5799 and rested his hand on my yoke. 'This is the wrong way, sir,' he said.

'Thanks, Sergeant Dee. Just getting back on track.'

'I reckon the FRV's about six hundred metres to our right,' the man said, squinting down the track.

'Yup, looks like it,' BA5799 said and turned the map to show him. 'We're here,' he said and dust floated through the thin torch beam. 'If we cross this irrigation ditch we should see the tree line.'

'We're going to be early anyway, sir. Take your time.'

And then the map was back in my pouch and BA5799's body rotated in me as he stood, pushing through the weight of his kit.

He used the detector again and led the men over the ditch and away from the wall. He waved it from side to side over the path and then it spiked, the lights rushing to fill the display. He took a step back and he waved at the men to go firm. They waited behind us.

BA5799 was lying flat again and I was against the ground. He reached out with straight arms and scraped down with a metal rod. He hated this, and he stretched his fingertips into the hole he'd created. His dog tags had worked up his shirt as he walked and they slipped out and now dangled on me, glinting matte in the darkness.

He twisted and I scuffed on a stone as he picked up the detector and awkwardly moved it over the hole and its lights flashed again. He put the detector back down and continued to dig, gritting his teeth at the awkward position and the day-sack pulling off me. His neck strained and his jugular throbbed against my collar as he worked.

He kept digging but found only bits of stone and debris. And then he held the detector over the hole again to make certain, the base of his helmet pressing into me as he peered forward. The red lights didn't jump and he stood, sweat glistening on his face. He held a thumb up to the man behind, stepped around the rubble and walked on.

We stopped in front of a wood and BA5799 pressed the radio switch. 'Zero, this is Three Zero Alpha,' he whispered. 'My callsign now fifty metres short of the FUP. We're going to clear it and then occupy, over.'

The metallic response sounded in his earpiece and then we were moving into the dark foliage. The branches scratched over me as we pressed through and he worried about the noise and stepped carefully in the dark below.

At the other side of the trees he peered through the night-vision that glowed green against his eye. He raised his hand and motioned a team of men forward and they slid out of the wood and down into a dry ditch. They unfolded detectors and started to sweep the sides of the hollow, fanning out to an old sluice gate. A dog barked in the distance and BA5799's stomach muscles contracted in me.

Once it was cleared, the other soldiers peeled into the ditch and BA5799 lay against the forward edge below an overhang, my side panel pressing into the baked mud and exposed roots. His men waited either side of us. He sent a message on the radio that they were in position with the target a hundred metres to his front. He confirmed he would wait until H-hour.

The dog stopped barking and the soldiers crouched together in silence. They looked at each other: dark shapes with dull eyes, housed in armour and bristling with weapons and antennas. BA5799 thought how exposed they were in the ditch, thousands of miles from home, and grinned at the absurdity of it all. Only their training and their trust in one another allowed them to be here.

He could hear his men breathing and stretching uncomfortable legs, sucking on drinking tubes and suppressing yawns. They were wrapped in the shadows and BA5799 should have felt alone, gripped by danger and cut off by fear, but crouching in the ditch he'd never felt so connected to others and he loved being among them.

He thought of the people in the compound. They'd have no idea his platoon was so close and he imagined them sleeping on the floor beside the flickering embers of the fire. He wondered if they had posted sentries, or if this was the wrong ditch and in the morning he would be disorientated. Or maybe they knew we were here and he had led his men into a trap.

I cooled and BA5799 shivered in his damp combat shirt. One of the soldiers' heads drooped under the weight of his helmet and the next man nudged him awake. Another scraped at the mud of the ditch with a twig. They waited and finally the greys of dawn evaporated from the ground, separating the solid mass of men into individuals, their faces ghostlike along the ditch.

BA5799 stretched in me, his muscles now stiff, then glanced at his glowing watch and held his hand up to the next man. He flashed it open twice. 'Ten minutes,' he mouthed.

The signal repeated along the line and the soldiers began to fidget. BA5799 raised himself up on his elbow and peered over the edge. He could see the compound's wall hovering in the dawn. There was no scale to it and nothing moved. A cockerel sang in the distance.

He slid back down into the line of men. They were helping each other stow their night-vision goggles. BA5799's were unclipped from his helmet by the man next to him and he reached over me to push them into his day-sack.

'Thanks, Lewie,' BA5799 whispered into his ear. He rested his rifle on the ground and handed the detector to him. 'Clear a path straight to the door. I'll be behind you and the two cut-offs will move up on each side, just as we did in rehearsals.'

The man nodded and grinned. They stared at each other and at the mud of the ditch, fiddling with the tops of their weapons and waiting as the light filled. And then BA5799 looked at his watch again and tapped the man's leg. He nodded and pulled himself up and over the edge.

He was ahead of us, staring down at the ground and sweeping the detector over the dry grass. BA5799 knelt behind him and lifted his weapon, the sling tugging around me. He bent his head to the sight and looked past the man at the walls of the compound.

The other soldiers clambered out of the ditch and followed. To the right and left, two teams pushed on and the platoon was now in three columns, walking towards the compound, led by men sweeping detectors.

We crossed to the building and BA5799 crouched up against

the wall, pressing me into its cracked surface. He gave a signal and the man continued to wave the detector along the wall
towards a door. He inspected it and then stepped aside to wait.

BA5799's neck swivelled in me and he looked at the men lined
up behind him. The team commander nodded and BA5799
pointed with a flat hand. The soldiers moved past us and stacked
up on both sides of the door. One leant a ladder against the wall
and held it firm while another gingerly climbed until he was near
the top. He swung his light machine gun up and ready.

BA5799 checked his other teams and saw one of them settle
into position. The other was in place to cut off down the side of
the compound. His heartbeat quickened and he looked at the men
around the door, their weapons held in their shoulders. He knew
each of them and excitement surged inside him. They waited as
he crept over, pulling his weapon's stock firmly into my panel and
pausing behind the last man, ready to follow the team in.

BA5799 nodded at the commander, who reached out a gloved
hand, twisted the handle and barged through the door. It banged
open. The next two men stepped into the courtyard, lifting their
weapons up, fingers poised on their triggers.

BA5799 followed them through the door and swung his rifle
across the internal openings of the empty courtyard and then
moved to one side. A soldier pulled out a detector and led the
team across and towards a room. They whispered to one another
as they approached and then surged in. There was a call of 'Room
clear,' and they were out and heading into the next alcove.

But BA5799 knew the compound was empty; there was rubbish
and debris everywhere and a water barrel lying on its side.

The team cleared the rooms and found nothing and BA5799

walked into the middle of the courtyard and placed his hand on the cold black remains of a fire.

One of the men walked over and stood by him. 'Looks like it's been used recently, boss. But not last night.'

'Damn,' BA5799 said, then unclipped his helmet and put it on the ground. He pulled the palm of his hand over his eyes, squashing his nose, and reached for the radio switch at his shoulder.

'Hello, Zero, this is Three Zero Alpha. Over,' he said, brushing the ash from his hand on me and listening to the earpiece. 'Roger, Compound Kilo Five Four cleared, nothing found. I'll collapse back to your location. Should be with you in about forty minutes. Over.'

He looked up at the soldier. 'Good work back there, Corporal Carr. Very slick. Let's fold back down the cleared route to the FUP.'

'Roger, boss,' the soldier said.

BA5799 hooked his thumbs under me, parting me from his body, and rotated his aching shoulders. He picked up his helmet and clipped it back on. The men were filing out of the compound and he walked after them.

Two shots suddenly cracked overhead, amplified sharply by the walls around. BA5799 ducked, hunched his shoulders in me and ran to the door.

'Contact,' one of his men shouted from outside the compound, 'in that fucking tree line. Two hundred metres.' And then the same voice screamed, 'Rapid fire!'

The air ripped apart above BA5799's platoon and their weapons clattered and banged in retaliation.

'Zero, Three Zero Alpha,' BA5799 said into his radio. 'Contact, small arms, Kilo Five Four, wait. Out.' He wanted to sound calm

[283]

but excitement snatched at his voice.

He pushed past two soldiers crouching in cover by the door. 'Out the way,' he said and then he was in the open and running along the wall. His day-sack rocked against me and the wall above burst in a cloud of dust, adrenaline and years of training making me feel weightless as I bounced around him. He was heading to the loose line of soldiers kneeling and sprawled at the edge of a corn field, their weapons bucking and spitting. He saw pink walls and bushes in the distance, the flashes from the dark shadows and the sparks of tracer that leapt across the field. He heard the bullets splitting the air and tearing out into the country behind him.

Then he was sliding on a knee and my hem caught in the dust as he came to a stop next to the team commander.

40

You sat on the treatment table and looked at me leaning against the wall and knew I was yours. You recognised my socket that only your odd-shaped stump, with its deep scarring, could fit. A man walked over and unplugged me from the wall.

'Hi Tom,' he said. 'Easy drive?'

'Not too bad, thanks, Mike,' you said and watched him bring me over and prop me against the bed.

'Here it is,' he said. 'I just need to get the laptop so we can set it up.' He walked out of the room.

Your hand caressed my grey surface and felt around the hydraulic piston under my knee joint. You studied my copper connections and wires that led to my microchip. You'd been waiting for me but were nervous about what I might do for you. Ever since they'd mentioned you were ready for me, I'd filled your dreams as a fetish of the possible, a high-tech solution to your problems. Together we would walk faster and farther and you'd be a step closer to yourself. And now I was in front of you and you wanted me to fix you.

My sensors can feel the angle of the floor, the speed you're walking and the slope we're on. I can prevent you from stumbling and stabilise you on stairs. I adapt to you.

The man sat on a stool with his laptop. He made it communicate with me and establish a wireless connection. He clicked an option, which sent to me, and my motor whirred into safe mode. 'Right then,' he said. 'Whack it on, Tom.'

You pulled my black carbon-fibre socket onto your stump. The air pushed out as I slid onto you and the seal gripped. You wiggled your stump and I waved in the air.

'Comfy?' the man asked.

'Feels fine,' you said, rocking the socket with your hands.

'It should be, I just copied your last leg.'

'No, it feels great.'

'Take a walk but be careful while I set it up,' he said. 'I'll send it instructions from the computer. You might feel it change under you.'

As you walked around the treatment room, I felt odd beneath you, flicking out and swinging in a way you weren't used to. The man continued sending me signals and I changed my parameters, dampening my cylinder and increasing my resistance. A burn developed in your thigh as you struggled to control me and you went up and down the bars, watching us in the mirror at the end of the room.

You leant over the parallel bars to rest, breathing heavily from the effort of controlling me.

'How does it feel?' the man asked.

'Fine thanks, Mike,' you lied. I felt odd and heavy at the end of your stump. You glanced over at your old leg, resting by the treatment bed. I was its replacement and meant to be an upgrade, but I was different and you weren't used to me yet. You wished I moved more like the one you knew.

'Great,' the man said. 'You're doing well, it'll just take a bit of time to get the hang of it.'

Slowly, with each adjustment, I improved: I didn't kick up

behind you or swing sluggishly and we started to walk more smoothly. You pushed through the socket to force me forward, creating energy that I bounced back off the floor to propel us on. We walked faster between the bars and then out in circuits of the room as your T-shirt grew wet with sweat.

The man suggested you should try some stairs, so you walked me out of the room and I oscillated on the socket below you. We went up and down a flight until you were exhausted. He changed my resistance, swing rate and extension so I was as good as he could get me. Then we were back on the treatment bed and you were sliding me away, pushing the valve to release the socket's vacuum, and we separated.

You peeled the rubber liner off and your bare stump was red and hot and sweat dripped onto the floor.

'Here, have this,' he said and brought over a roll of blue tissue. 'Weather's hotter again. Not sure the heating's been turned off yet.'

'I've sweated buckets,' you said.

'What do you think to the leg?'

'I need to get used to it,' you said. 'Still feels a bit odd, to be honest.'

'It will for a bit, mate. But it looks like a massive improvement already. You're walking well on it.' He handed you my charger. 'Try to plug it in every night, though the battery should last a few days.'

As you drove away from the rehabilitation centre, you looked down at me and felt disappointed. I wasn't everything your dreams had promised. Your stumps still hurt and sweated, your back ached and your arms were strained from pulling us up the stairs. You were still an amputee. I couldn't change that, couldn't spring forward into a run below you or skip around obstacles or quickly adjust when you tripped. I was inert and restricted you to a frustrating walking pace.

A few days after we first joined, we were back in your car. Your other leg moved beside me. Like me it was made of metal and composites and it worked the pedals as you spun the wheel above me. The indicator clicked and we turned and stopped. You switched the car off and pulled the key out.

We were in a car park. You shut the door, clicked the key fob and the car blinked behind us. We walked and I swung, my sensors calculating how fast your stump thrust on and where you placed my foot, smoothly adjusting to your gait as we went through the automatic doors and picked up a blue basket.

We walked down the aisles and you held the basket beside me, adding vegetables and then something from a fridge cabinet that hummed next to me. Your stump started to hurt in my socket but you concentrated on your shopping list while my microprocessor adjusted as the basket became heavier.

People pushed their trolleys by and some didn't notice; they reached for a tin or felt for unbruised apples, muttering to themselves. But others were transfixed by the grey-black rods of technology extending below your shorts instead of bare legs.

You saw them look and challenged them with a stare and they turned away embarrassed. You wished they wouldn't look at us; we weren't a freak show and you wanted to be ignored. But we were the strangest thing to walk down those aisles all day. As soon as we were past and they knew you couldn't see them, they stopped picking tomatoes and stared at us walking away. They couldn't resist watching and they wondered how we did it. We were science fiction, you and I, and they didn't see the pain in your socket or the sweat collecting in your liners or the effort you expended to swing me down the bread aisle. All they saw was the magic of me and a young, upright man who had overcome the unsurvivable.

When you queued up to pay your stumps had gone numb and you thought about slumping back in the car. In front of us a young boy held his mother's hand and pointed at the checkout display. 'Please, Mum,' he said.

'No, Gerard,' she told him. 'You can have one when we get home.'

The boy looked up at her and back at the rows of sweets. He begged again and then noticed you queuing behind. He saw both of us but we were so odd he didn't understand and he looked away in confusion. And then he was curious and turned back and stared at me. He couldn't take his eyes off me and then he looked up at you.

You smiled at him but he turned his face away and tugged at his mother's skirt.

'Look, Mum. Look at that man.' He was urgent.

'Shhh, Gerard. Not now,' she said, then glanced down at me, smiled at you and turned away.

'But, Mummy, that man's a robot. Look,' he said. His eyes pleaded with her and he tugged at her again and pointed at me.

She turned back to you and rested a hand on the boy's head. 'Sorry, love,' she said.

'Don't worry.' You smiled at the boy again. 'I'm actually only half robot.'

But he buried his head in her skirt away from you and then they funnelled down to the checkout. He kept glancing back at us as he held on to her and she filled shopping bags.

Back in the car, you lifted me into the footwell and closed the door. The remains of your femoral artery throbbed against my socket. You dropped your head back against the seat and your eyes were closed and your mouth hung open. You pushed the key in but then paused and saw the orange shopping bags you'd placed on the passenger seat and you looked down at me.

You remembered the bang, the pain and the loneliness on the helicopter. You remembered the men who'd pulled you off the battlefield and being broken in hospital with tubes and drugs invading you. You remembered wishing you'd never been saved. You remembered: 'We've just had to amputate your second leg.'

You remembered everyone who'd helped you: the nurses who'd gently washed you and the doctors who'd cut more of you away to save you, the physio and 'squeeze those glutes', the man who gave me to you.

You remembered the last time you'd carried shopping bags, before you'd been to that distant country, when you didn't need me, and it was a lifetime ago. You remembered your friends and your family and 'a nice cup of tea'. You smiled at the shopping bags and turned the key.

41

I was there as BA5799 ran along the wall. My overhanging rim cut his vision as a black horizontal blur and my chinstrap bounced up against his stubble as he pounded onto each stride. I was his window on soldiering: the straps that held me to him framed the action.

Above me the wall burst open and dust hovered as he ran towards the field. A shock slapped around me and in his ears and then another, closer. He held his rifle in one hand; the other was clenched in a fist that he drove forward as he skipped around a log and down a track and then he was on the hard mud and crawling through the field to his team commander.

Soldiers were kneeling in the corn and firing their weapons. My weight pulled his head forward but the muscles in his neck were trained so that he didn't feel me. I made him comfortable and safe in this environment and he raised his head above the leaves and tried to make sense of it. The fear that had flooded up at the first crack was now pushed away and converted by adrenaline. And he wanted to understand everything that happened and control it and exist in it.

Metal passed above me and he heard it, sharp and claustrophobic. It was a roof of sound that pressed down and crushed the world around BA5799 until it was only his forearm pushing him up, the rifle he lifted into his shoulder and the knee that he

stepped out; my rim bumping into his weapon sight and his finger curling around the trigger; the flash in the distance that he
aimed at; the cracking above and the thump and then the squeeze
and the clumping punch of the rifle in his shoulder as he fired
again and again.

Cones of sound churned the air and his left eye squinted shut
below me as he took aim and fired again, his forehead pressing
against the pad that held my dome of composite material on his
skull. I trapped heat and sweat started to pool among the hair I'd
matted flat and dripped over his brow into his eye.

One of the men in the field shouted as he rolled onto his side to
change magazine. Then he was up, back in the fight. The team
commander next to us shouted at him to fire at the base of a bush
at the end of a compound. A flashing pricked in the shadow and
then the crack of rounds sprayed above us and the world crushed
in even tighter. He ducked and I was hidden in the yellow stalks
again. The men around returned fire, escalating the violence.

I swivelled as he looked back. On my rear, above where his bare
neck extended from his body armour, he had written *BA5799 O
POS* in black marker. And now that writing pressed into his day-
sack as he looked at the compound where his other men waited
for him to decide. They needed him now and he knew he must
drag himself out of the tunnel of noise and heat that was the
small patch of leaves he'd flattened. He thought of the enemy and
where they might be, what they were trying to accomplish. The
fear that they might try and cut off his platoon flashed through
him – just do something before they do – and he cupped his hand
around his mouth.

'Move back to the FUP. Make sure three-two go with you,' he
shouted to the men in cover behind us and pointed over at a ditch.

A man acknowledged this with a wave before ducking back through a doorway in the compound as bullets cracked past and then peered out again.

BA5799 shouted again and his jaw pushed down against my chinstrap. 'We'll give you rapid fire in thirty seconds.' Then he turned back to the team commander. 'Rapid fire in thirty, Corporal Monk,' he said.

There was a lull as the men around him inserted fresh magazines and the combat became an exchange of single bangs and cracks. The team commander crawled up into the line. BA5799 lifted his head again and looked out across the field but couldn't see the enemy. He pressed the radio switch on his shoulder and updated the network, speaking into the microphone that jutted out from me and curved in front of his mouth.

'Hello, Zero, this is Three Zero Alpha, I'm going to withdraw from Compound Kilo Five Four back along the cleared route to the FUP,' he said. 'My intention is to break contact and return to your location. Request air cover. Over.'

A calm metallic voice sounded in the earpiece squashed between me and the side of his head. 'Zero, Roger, that's clear. Air cover already tasked. Should be with you any minute. Over.'

'Many thanks. Out.'

Then he glanced down at his watch and it was time. The team commander shouted at his men and they were up, their weapons kicking in their shoulders and brass spinning out into the green stalks.

He turned and saw the two teams spaced out and running across the open ground and sliding into the ditch. They were exposed and in danger. He clenched his teeth and we were up again, the rifle pulled back against his shoulder as he added his weight to the battle, knocking up into my rim with each pull of the trigger.

He looked at the ditch over to his left and saw the helmets appear near the sluice gate. Then they were firing and one of them called for rapid fire and their weapons burst and spat. The battle had a new geometry.

'Corporal Monk, go. You've got rapid from three-one,' he bellowed to the man kneeling to his right. 'Move now!'

They started to run, lifting their weapons up and peeling behind those who still fired, out of the field and back along the wall. The team commander waited and signalled to BA5799. 'Sir, move, I'll cover you,' he shouted, his face angry below his helmet.

'No, you go first. Go. Go. I'll be right behind you.'

The soldier turned and followed his men. Then it was only us standing in the corn. He fired wildly once more at the bushes and compound walls across the field, then he sprinted after them.

They were ahead of him in the unseen hail and running over the open ground. Noise told him everything: the men firing from the ditch and the metallic clang as the sluice gate was hit, a whining ricochet, and the machine gun pulled up out of the ditch, its bipod unfolded, filling the air with metal and trying to dominate the battle.

But there were cracks above us and BA5799 knew the enemy was still fighting. He crouched and ran and gripped and breathed and clenched his teeth in a grimace. He started to feel the weight of his kit as his legs burnt and I bounced on his head and he longed to be down in cover. The men in front were dropping into the ditch ahead until he was the only one left exposed and then a round cracked past me and he jumped down the slope into safety.

I knocked back as he jolted to the bottom and turned over,

gasping for breath. A soldier knelt in the middle of the ditch and counted him in.

'Good you could join us, boss,' he said and grinned. 'We're all here.'

'Thanks, Sarnt Dee,' he said, his chin pushing into the damp leather pad of my strap. He reached up and pulled me back down over his forehead.

'What's the plan, sir?' the man said.

I rotated as he looked over at the end of the ditch where his men were tucked over their weapons firing or swivelling down into cover to reload or change position. The symphony of battle changed as the cracks slowed and then stopped.

'Cease fire, Corporal Carr,' he called. There were more bangs as his men fired a few last rounds and finally it was quiet.

He turned back to the man. 'I think they may have had enough of us, Sergeant Dee?'

'Or it could be them,' he said and pointed up at the helicopter drifting in high above.

'True,' BA5799 said. I pulled back on my chinstrap as he looked up and another angular helicopter hovered into view, the landscape vibrating.

Still breathing hard, he pulled a map from a pouch on his armour and read a grid into his radio before discussing the helicopters and the platoon's route back. The men around him were lined up along the sides of the ditch, red-faced and hot and sucking on their drinking tubes as their chests heaved.

He pushed his hand up under my rim to itch his hairline. His ears whirred in the sudden silence and he puffed his cheeks out as adrenaline coursed through him. He called in three of the men and spoke to them.

'We'll keep one team static to cover the platoon until we're back in sight of Route Hammer. Stay on the cleared path. Just peel through each other. One foot on the ground at our rear.' He looked at two of them and they nodded that they understood. 'I'll control the withdrawal. Sarnt Dee, you lead us back. Use the route we agreed in orders. Go firm before we cross the road and then we'll roll back into camp.'

'Roger, boss,' he said.

He looked at the paths and walls that had seemed so different last night. He saw where he'd been lost and smiled: all the threatening shadows and looming shapes had disappeared. He checked back towards the tree line for the enemy but the landscape was empty. One of his teams huddled behind a mound dredged from a ditch and covered the platoon as they filed away. Above, the helicopters banked off to another task.

It was quiet and the sun baked the earth. He yawned. He had survived the morning and his adrenaline was gone. No one had been hurt and they'd all get back to camp. The combat had been brief and the energy slumped out of him as he sent a message for the next section to go firm.

The soldiers by the mound clipped up bipod legs, lifted their weapons and followed down the path as another section pushed out along a fence ahead to cover the next phase of the withdrawal. His men moved to his command and he studied the landscape and felt a rush of pride at the privilege of leading them in this place.

Farmers were in the fields and watched the men moving past them and BA5799 greeted them with the only words of their language he could speak. He knew another attack this morning was unlikely if the locals were out.

The sun had sharpened and beat down on me and his head was hot and sweated into my pads. His clothes smelt and chafed where his kit pressed in. His shoulders ached under the straps that pulled them back and he felt thin and spent under the weight of it all.

But he could do it; he could endure it, and more. He had wondered why people thought soldiering was romantic, and knew if they swapped places with any of his men most would crumple under the pressure and fear, the smell and heat. But he could feel the romance now as he watched the single file of men, with their day-sacks and helmets and antennas, bobbing up and down across this foreign land.

They moved back into the area of abandoned compounds near the base. The platoon had stopped along the track, waiting for the covering teams to catch up. He was the last man and before we pushed between two walls he turned to survey the flat fields and sparse lines of trees out to where the enemy had been. On a road in the distance, a man on a motorbike was watching us. I shook from side to side as he sighed and then walked on into the maze of walls.

He went through the platoon from the back and smiled and nodded at every man as he passed. They crouched by walls or sat on rocks to take the weight off their backs. Their faces were exhausted and grimy with dirt. He knew and trusted each of them. They were his: he could order them into danger and they would go, but he also belonged to them and would lead them there. Each grin and nod, every gesture was trust and the bond that had tightened again that morning.

They stood as he passed and followed him, peeling the platoon through itself so it reversed order. He stopped by the last man waiting beside a ruined building. 'All good, Sarnt Dee?'

'Good, boss. Home time, I think,' he said and glanced back. 'I'll count us through.'

'I'm starving,' BA5799 said. 'I cannot wait for breakfast. I'll lead us back in.' And he walked on out into the field.

He led his men towards the camp. The tops of the watchtowers showed above the road and he saw the flag and antennas. He thought about breakfast and the walls of the base rose up on the horizon as we approached. I had pressed into his skull for hours and he adjusted me and then looked back at the single file of men spaced out and moving from the ruins.

His boots were treading below me, pushing out over the dry, cracked mud and brushing through the yellow grass. We came to a dip in the ground and in a flash there was no longer any romance.

Later, after he'd been taken away in a helicopter and I was no longer with him, the platoon had collapsed back to the camp. One of the men carried me into a room and put me in a cardboard box. Someone was writing on it with a black marker: *Captain Tom Barnes BA5799 – WIA.*

He looked over as they tapped down the lid above me. 'Do you think he'll make it, Sergeant Dee?' he said.

'Not sure, mate. Looked pretty bad to me.'

42

I existed for a fraction of a moment. I was created by an explosive reaction from a device that functioned to form me. I passed through rock, through mud, through dust, through the air, through the sole of a boot.

Through a man.

I stamped through them all, folding them in shock and pressure and dragging them up with me.

I am also noise. Try bang, try boom, try dull thud-thump, try ker-krump, try piercing ping puncturing perforated drum.

I crushed him against gravity.

He couldn't stay whole and I disintegrated his foot, slamming through it and bursting it open: foot and boot fragmenting in my wake. I forced them up with the dirt I punched up. Up in my supersonic swell, tearing straight through skin.

Trashing all that should be sacred.

I was all around him and in him and through him: flaying a finger off, flashing flesh from a forearm, blasting a boot buckle deep inside him.

I ripped up his leg, flapping his calf off in my wind. I stripped his trousers away and his penis fluttered in my storm. I pulled open his testicle. I dragged bone deep into his thigh, pushing through pink flesh and vessels, bursting open grey globules of fat.

I went through him, shocking his nerves and muscles and

jarring his spine, crushing him in his armour. I beat through his diaphragm and collapsed his lung – and up – up his back, compressing his skull and banging it into his helmet. And over him with dust and dirt, into the sky in a pyre of bubbling, boiling brown.

He would have snapped if I had existed for any longer but he flexed in me and then flipped and clattered to the earth.

And then I was spent and wind dragged in to replace everything I'd blown out, all fleeting and invisible except for what I'd lifted, which now rained down around him, and my bang rolling out across the landscape.

43

It banged around us and lifted you with it. Rock, mud and bone thrashed past me as I swung out around your neck on my chain. Your face was stretched in shock next to me as we existed inside the shaft of violence. It flogged through us and you bent with it, flipping over so my chain was across your cheek and my metal discs floated up next to your helmet. All you felt was the flash, the dull thump, and being spun and airborne in an instant. All you knew was that something was wrong.

And then I clinked against the hard earth as you dropped back down from above. Sensation exploded from the bridge of your nose, overwhelming synapses and neurotransmitters and buzzing through you, too vast to be pain yet.

Your body bounced and slumped as debris and rocks pattered around us. There in the dust, my two metal discs hung from your neck and rested on the ground below your chin. You were face down and your forehead pressed against the inside of your helmet, holding your face away from dry grass.

Shock annihilated everything and you were gone.

And then you were back. You expanded from a scrap of consciousness to a head and nothing registered but disorientation and you knew with sudden certainty that you'd been decapitated. You couldn't feel your body. You opened your eyes to make it real. All you saw was the baked mud and the light pouring in from each side. Your eyes were massive with fear above me and then you shut them, crushing them together against it.

It was never going to happen to you and now you would stand up and dust yourself off. This happens to others, you managed to think, but the pain started to build and you couldn't move.

Anxiety overwhelmed you.

You wanted your body but it wasn't there. Your tongue licked across your teeth and you felt a chip and a blade of grass and grit at the back of your throat. You wanted to turn over and check how badly you were hurt but neither arm nor leg moved. But the pain did move. It built and obliterated any other feeling and dragged you farther away from yourself. It wasn't real yet but the potential of it shocked you and you feared it. It fought through the whirring fuzz that had replaced your body, coming with the anxiety and building with the fear. Your mouth creased above me. You whimpered.

The dust drifted away and behind you a man stood up. Another looked at you and didn't get any closer. He wanted to help but you looked odd and inhuman distorted on the ground and he'd frozen. You were bent and covered in rock and dirt with body parts twisted or missing, and he couldn't make sense of it.

Another soldier ran up from the rear and started shouting. You could hear him through the pain and recognised the voice telling them not to get any closer until they had cleared the area. And you wanted them now – to just get here now. And then your radio sounded in your ear and the initial confused reports were deadened by buzzing pain. It was about you this time – it was never meant to be about you. You heard them describe what was happening and wanted to be part of the conversation and tried to lift your hand to press the switch but there was no hand, no arm in time and space, just buzzing pain.

You heard them say your zap number: BA5799 had been in an IED strike.

And then that was all background and you realised it was hard to breathe and a weight seemed to press against your chest and you were drowning. You didn't have enough breath to get to the surface and your chest screamed silently as tension crushed it. And then you were gone.

The detectors swept alongside us and then past and they chucked them down and rolled you onto your back. Your head lolled in your body armour and your helmet fell off. They said, 'Sir, sir . . . Tom . . . sir?' but you didn't respond.

I had dropped back onto your chest. My discs rested there now and flashed in the sun. On each of my discs your information is stamped: *O POS, 565799 BARNES T, CE*. You were dying and when you did one of my discs would stay with your body, the other would go for notification. That would have been a certainty but now they were with you and trying to stop it happening.

They cut away your clothing and applied your tourniquet above the footless stump that was only sharp slivers of bones, dark red and filled with mud and dirt below your shredded trousers. They twisted its handle until it was tight and stopped you bleeding. They found open wounds on your other leg and pushed a tourniquet up into your groin and you had one on each leg. They realised you weren't breathing and they breathed into you.

You came back and it was dark and pain and you tried to open your eyes but you were sightless as you fought the pain and gritted your teeth. They held a clear bag of fluid above us and pulled you out of your body armour and cut away your combat shirt and you were lying naked on the cracked earth. I still rested on your chest and their hands left streaks of your blood on your white body where they handled you.

You started pleading with them. Save me, please, you said again and again and then you asked them to make it stop and you lifted your head and it waved around blindly. They hushed you and made you rest it back down and you couldn't see them wrapping dressings around you and strapping your leg while the pain increased until it was all of you.

You had imagined being brave if you were injured. It was always a wound from a bullet and you would have fought on, commanding your men in the battle, and afterwards you would have walked back into camp with a dressing over it and would have been a hero. But there was nothing brave about this, no dignity. You were broken and utterly pathetic lying in the dust as they crouched by you and tried to stop you bleeding out. Pain reared again and it was dark and you had never felt so utterly alone. You pleaded with them once more but it was too much and you were unconscious again.

They dragged us onto a stretcher and carried us across the field, a man at each corner and another jogging alongside holding up a bag of fluid. I had dropped around your neck and my discs rested on the green canvas stretcher staining with your blood. They left your helmet and armour and shredded day-sack on the blood-stained dirt next to the small crater. As they lifted us out of the field, one of the men behind picked up your things and brought them with him.

You came back and you were scared again and you bit something hard against the pain, it was the arm of one of the men who was carrying you. He swore at you.

You felt the stages of the journey to the helicopter. You knew from your training and watching it happen to others that you were in a vehicle and it was driving back to camp and then you were outside and could hear the whistle of the helicopter and it was all agony.

You didn't say any brave words and there were no thumbs up, you just whimpered and pleaded in the blindness. You were loaded onto the helicopter and you wanted it to take off immediately. Why wouldn't it take off? And then the whine escalated and we were airborne and out over the desert.

You were certain you were going to die. This is the end, you thought, and the pain pressed down on your chest and you were gone again. The men in the helicopter worked on you. They had to restart your heart when your body couldn't cope with the blood loss and trauma and it gave up on you.

Four times they shocked you and each time you came back and begged them to make it stop and then you pleaded with God to save you, it was your last option. I'll do whatever You ask, you thought, and gritted your whole body against the agony.

And you summoned anything you had left, any last hope and life you had to stay – to stay in the helicopter, to stay with the pain, to stay alive.

But you went again.

You came back once more. We were being carried from the helicopter and you knew you were outside but it was all darkness and pain and you tried to lift your head and then we were inside and it was over and you let yourself go. You had nothing left.

*

They didn't have to split me up and my tags stayed on my chain. I was taken off you by doctors before they operated and placed in a plastic wallet with your other records.

44

I fluttered off the stick they had pushed into the ground above the graves of the two young friends. Other flags were planted in the cemetery on the hill that overlooked the shimmering grid of irrigation and the patchwork of green fields, but I was the newest.

I flapped in the hot air blowing in off the desert.

Below me, where the land stretched away from the desert to the large river in the haze, stood the soldiers' camp. It was a solid rectangle built around old compounds with vehicles and towers and the mortars that sent bombs high into the air. The soldiers sometimes played, kicking up dust and celebrating when they scored a goal. And beyond the camp, in the village, specks of people moved around the market strip and out into the fields.

The soldiers left the camp in their armour and helmets and holding their weapons. They walked into the tree lines and blocks of houses. Most days the popping of gunfire hung over the landscape and sometimes it sprayed over me and tore out to dissolve in the desert behind.

One week after Kushan Hhan pushed my pole into the ground and led them away from the fresh piles of rock back to the village, after the sun had risen behind me and cast my long thin shadow over the graves, a dark line of soldiers were returning to the camp, crossing the fields and passing down the sides of buildings, tiny at first – a line of insects – moving over a crossroads and through the abandoned ruins below me.

They filed out over the last open field before their camp and the lead figure disappeared in a puff of brown and then a loud bang broke over the hill. When the small cloud had drifted away there was a horizontal shape on the ground and the other soldiers came up and crouched around it.

A heavy vehicle revved out of the camp on the road and waited by the field as the soldiers carried a stretcher and loaded it on. Soon after a helicopter flared into the camp and the downdraught curled up dust. The vehicle returned to the camp and then the helicopter lifted above the walls and ducked its nose away across the desert behind me.

For days it was quiet and then cracks clipped across the fields. Sometimes they were hidden in the haze and the world seemed peaceful apart from the noise clattering in the distance.

It happened again while I was planted there. A crossroads or field would erupt in a smudge out in the flat landscape and helicopters landed and there was fighting.

It rained and became cold and the battles were less frequent. The harvest came and the colourful crops were cut away and the fields were bare again. Fighting returned with the heat and I flogged on my pole and frayed while the soldiers patrolled the countryside. But slowly the fighting was pushed farther away into the haze.

During the next summer, people returned to the ruins below me and started rebuilding the walls. They planted the field by the road and it burst into colour before the following harvest.

After the soldiers had departed in long convoys of lorries and containers and the sound of the last helicopter had trembled in my pole, the sporadic fighting moved away.

Finally, in one violent storm, when the desert wind stripped through me and I slapped in the wind, I ripped free and tumbled down the hill across the sand and caught on a rock. I stayed there, weighed down by gathering sand, and I rotted to join the dust.

45

The thick green canopy rolled above me, reflecting on the rear window. You were in the front, driving and humming along with the radio. Then you stopped the car and opened the boot.

You sat on the tailgate next to me and drank from a bottle of water. In the park people were walking their dogs through the shafts of light and down to the pond that suspended a morning fog. Pulling down the silicone sleeves and removing your legs, you noticed the ring on your finger and smiled as you thought of her. Then you reached for me and my pair and pulled us on, tightening the Velcro straps before dropping the boot lid shut and locking the car.

You shuffled from side to side on me, trying to keep balanced on my spongy carbon-fibre blade as you stretched your arms across your chest and then up behind your back.

I only touch the ground at one point. I curve up in a sweep to a running knee that attaches to the socket your stump was in. You started bouncing up and down as you warmed up your muscles and remembered the feel of me. I flexed below you as you moved from one of us to the other and we sprang back and you felt our energy and lightness.

Then you flicked me out in front and tottered across the car park to the road beneath the avenue of trees that circled the park. You walked us up onto the smooth tarmac and started to run, pushing down through us, gaining height, and then you leant forward to turn the height into forward motion. And I compressed under you and sprang on, clicking with each step, whipping over the tarmac and down, bounce and on.

We were running and I felt light underneath you as I pounded into the hard surface. Your hands were open and pumping next to you as you concentrated on balancing. I flashed underneath as you passed the walkers and the bicycles and ran on through the park, free of the weight of your other legs.

Each impact hurt your stumps but you were used to it and worked your limbs back and forward through it. You could feel the wind around you and breathed deeply as your heart pumped in your chest and down through your stumps. I compressed and sprang on below you and you puffed in and out above. We overtook another runner.

We did this twice a week; we were part of the park now. Nobody cared any more or stopped you to tell you how amazing I was or ask how it felt. It felt normal and light and fast and free – and you were running.

You paused at the bandstand and shuffled around with your hands on your hips as your breath condensed in the morning air. You looked at your watch and then I was bouncing you forward again. A dog chased after a ball on the playing fields and then another barked alongside me at my strangeness but you ran on and told the owner not to worry.

The low sun shone solid through the trees into your eyes and you accelerated, lengthening your stride, and could feel the sweat in your liners and the pounding, clicking, flashing of me below you. We were in full flight, at the edge of balance and control, and you pushed yourself faster still: as fast as you could, as you did every time.

And the car was just there and your breathing was ragged and your heart pounded and I pounded, and there was the stitch in your shoulder blade.

The rubber pad at the end of me caught on the road. There was no way of controlling me and I was suddenly folding up under you and your hands were out in front, stopping us on the road. And I was pulling away from your stump with the liner that shifted in your sweat as you fell around me and I sheered to an unnatural angle.

They came running over, shocked at the speed of your sudden collapse and the cracking noise I made on the tarmac. They came with their dogs or the squeal of bike brakes. They asked if you were okay and you pushed yourself over and sat in the middle of the road, at the centre of the crowd of help bending over you. They were surprised when you smiled and told them not to worry. They said your leg was broken, pointing at me bent behind you. You adjusted me and said that luckily I wasn't real.

It did hurt but you didn't want them to know. When someone offered to call an ambulance you laughed and said there was no need. Another pointed at your hands and you noticed that the palms were bleeding. They asked if you needed to be carried anywhere but you nodded at the car and said you'd be fine.

They drifted away once you'd convinced them that you were all right. You removed me, adjusted me back on and then limped to the car and sat in the boot, catching your breath and thinking how unpleasant a sudden fall like that was.

You looked at the deep red grooves down your palms and the black grit pushed under your skin. It stung and hardened into pain as you stared at them, but then you smiled and started to laugh at the pain and the blood that dripped from your hands.

And tears came because you could, and it didn't matter any more. It was normal.

You replaced me with your other legs, shut the boot and drove to work.

ACKNOWLEDGEMENTS

Lee Brackstone for understanding this book, his sound advice and making the whole process a pleasure. Gary Fisketjon for his time, experience and keen eye. Thank you both for making this a better book. Gillon Aitken for taking me on and Matthew Hamilton, my agent, for guiding me through it all. Everyone involved at Faber for their enthusiasm and love of books: Ruth Atkins, Lisa Baker, Luke Bird, Lizzie Bishop, Angus Cargill, Catherine Daly, Walter Donohue, Hannah Griffiths, Katie Hall, Matt Haslum, Kate McQuaid, Anne Owen, Eleanor Rees, Alex Russell – there will be some I have missed. For encouragement, help and early reads: Nick Bridle, Catherine Goodman, Jamie Jackson, Graeme Lamb, David McLoughlin, Tom Mangnall, Andy Michael, Edna O'Brien, Ed Parker, Sam Parker, Orlando Roberts, Harry Whelan. And Caro, who has been there during all of it.